W9-AGB-889

SURVIVING DEMON ISLAND

When he stepped into the bedroom, he sucked in a breath of shock.

Gina was there, leaning casually against the partially open front door. Her hair was unbound, still damp from her own shower and hugging her shoulders and breasts. She wore a skimpy little orange-flowered sundress that clung to her curves.

"I didn't hear you knock."

"That's because I didn't." She shut the door behind her and advanced into the room.

"Unless you're here to throw me down on the bed and have your way with me, get out."

She paused for a second and looked at his bed. Was she considering it? And what would he do if she was?

"Believe me, that's the last thing I'd want to do with you."

"Too bad. And here I am all clean and almost naked."

She took a quick glance at his crotch before returning to his face. Okay, maybe not such a quick glance. More of a lingering one.

"Derek, I've worked my butt off since the day I got here, but for some reason you've made it a point to dismiss everything I've accomplished. Do you hate women in general, or is it just me? Never mind. I already know the answer. What I want to know is why."

She made him dizzy tromping back and forth so he stepped in front of her, halting her progress. "Would you mind getting the hell out of my room? I've had just about enough of your mouth for the day." And if she wasn't going to use it for something useful, he really wanted her gone.

"And I've had just about enough of your arrogant attitude. I don't know why I bothered coming here." She palmed his chest and shoved him, hard. He hadn't expected it and stumbled back. The towel came loose and fell to the floor and her gaze shot south, widening with distinct interest.

Ah, hell. Instinct roared to life and he grasped her wrists, but instead of dragging her to the door and throwing her out of his room like he should have, he jerked her against him, wrapped one arm around her back, and crushed his mouth against hers.

A DELL BOOK

SURVIVING DEMON ISLAND
A Dell Book / January 2007

Published by
Bantam Dell
A Division of Random House, Inc.
New York, New York

This is a work of fiction. Names, characters, places, and incidents either are the product of the author's imagination or are used fictitiously. Any resemblance to actual persons, living or dead, events, or locales is entirely coincidental.

All rights reserved
Copyright © 2007 by Jaci Burton
Cover art by Alan Ayers
Cover design by Yook Louie

If you purchased this book without a cover, you should be aware that this book is stolen property. It was reported as "unsold and destroyed" to the publisher, and neither the author nor the publisher has received any payment for this "stripped book."

Dell is a registered trademark of Random House, Inc., and the colophon is a trademark of Random House, Inc.

ISBN 978-0-440-24335-9

Printed in the United States of America
Published simultaneously in Canada

www.bantamdell.com

OPM 10 9 8 7 6 5 4 3 2 1

Dedication

To my agent, Deidre Knight. Thank you for believing in this story and in me, and for being a solid rock when I need one. I can't thank you enough for all you've done for me.

To my editor, Shauna Summers. Thank you for your patience and guidance through this process. I learned so much from you about what makes a good story, from characters to pacing to world building to romance. You made this a much better book and I'm so grateful.

An additional thank you to editor Micahlyn Whitt for your valuable insights during the revision process.

To the gang in Paradise—you've been there with me for years, and you're the first place I go to share triumphs and pitfalls. Thank you for your friendship, your kindness and generosity, and for being such an important part of my daily life.

To the BBs—Angie West, Melani Blazer, Shannon Stacey, and Mandy Roth—for putting up with the whining for so many months; for reading, editing, and offering insights, and for encouraging me with nudges and laughter. You symbolize the true meaning of friendship, and I couldn't make it through the day without you.

To Mom—for teaching me to believe in myself, and for standing by my side no matter what. You were my first and my best champion. I love you with all my heart.

To my other Mom—you've taught me about duty and sacrifice, about kindness and the beauty of love everlasting. What a true romance you have had throughout the years and one I hope to emulate.

To my sister—my first and forever best friend. Thank you for always being someone I could turn to.

To Kevin, Matt, and Ashley, for your love, your support, and your excitement. Thank you for hanging in there with me during these years of craziness. I love you all.

To Charlie—you are the reason I started this journey. Thank you for your faith and encouragement; for the time you take to read, edit, and discuss plot; for putting up with the stress, the dirty house, and the lousy cooking. And most of all, for the backrubs. Because you held my hand and took this walk with me, I believed anything was possible. I love you, babe.

Surviving Demon Island

Chapter One

Get into character, Gina. You're a fighter, a warrior, and this is your moment to save the world.

God, she loved these scenes. Deeply immersed in the role, her thoughts became the character's thoughts. She was now Melissa—archaeologist and adventurer, prepared for the battle to come, only needing the director's cue to spring into fight mode.

Funny how much of the real her was like this character, how closely her own thoughts mirrored those of this feisty adventuress. This was one of the easiest roles she'd ever played.

"And, action!"

She glanced around the stone keep, at the priceless artifacts on the walls. "You know, Rorg, I understand the allure of cashing in on all these treasures. But the difference between you and me is that I have scruples, and you have none. You take from the past and use it for gain in the future.

I can appreciate its beauty, its history, but I could never remove anything that doesn't belong in our time."

"And that's why you fail, my dear Melissa," he said, taking one step closer.

Lost in the fantasy, she backed up against the stone wall, realizing she had only two choices: Die or jump. One misstep and she would be impaled on her opponent's sword. But she hadn't come here to lose.

She hated to lose.

The tip of Rorg's sword was pointed at her heart. It was a life-or-death moment. Hers. The next step would decide. She had only a second to think because the time warp was unstable. If she didn't kill Rorg soon and get the hell out of there, she'd be forever lost in a century that wasn't hers.

"Make your choice, bitch. I don't have all day."

Her lips curled in a sneer. She refused to show fear to this barbarian, this monster who had killed without remorse. "Gee, and I thought I'd have time to get a manicure first."

Decision made, she leaped from the stairs and landed with a thud on the cold stone floor, then made a mad dash for the broadsword hanging on the wall. Lifting it off with both hands, she whipped around, swinging just as Rorg caught up with her. He sidestepped her attack, laughing at her.

"If that's the best you can do, this won't take long at all."

"Oh, but I was just warming up." *Arrogant asshole. Keep on thinking I'm just a weak woman and no match for you. Lots of now-dead men thought the same thing.*

Her breath blew white smoke in the early dawn, the chill still lingering despite the quickly rising sun. The torches flickered, trembling as she rushed past. She scrunched her shoulders then relaxed them again, hefting the sword up with one hand and leveling it in Rorg's direction. Excitement drove her. She loved being in battle again. She lived for these moments.

He nodded appreciatively, obviously having assumed she'd never be able to hoist the heavy broadsword with one arm.

"You have strength, I'll give you that. But it won't help. You're an amateur, a little girl playing a game reserved for grown men."

"If only I had a dollar for every time I heard that one," she said, grasping the sword with both hands and swinging it in a half-circle toward Rorg's middle. His sword met hers and the clash of steel against steel reverberated as the time warp sizzled, transporting them back and forth between ancient times and present day, between a fully functional castle and ruins. Momentarily distracted, their swords locked at the hilt, Rorg looked around at the constantly changing landscape. Gina used that moment to backhand him, then kick him in the stomach with the heel of her boot. He grunted and stumbled back, but managed to maintain his balance.

Too bad.

Rage turned his face a mottled red. He roared and dove toward her, his hands pulled in to his chest and his sword pointed dead-on. She stepped back, then lunged forward as he retreated. A game of thrust and parry ensued, a seemingly civilized match of fencing fought with medieval broadswords that had been used by highlanders to forge their freedoms. She fought for freedom, too, to free the past from a devil of the future before it was too late and all their lives were irrevocably altered.

"You won't win, bitch," Rorg spat, hatred sharing space with the madness glowing in his dark eyes. "The time portal was *my* secret, *my* wealth. Everything would have been mine if you'd just left it alone." He punctuated his sentences with each slice of his sword. "Why—didn't—you—die?"

"Because I enjoy tormenting you too much, Rorg," she replied, leaping from the ground to a long wooden table as he swung repeatedly at her knees. The loud whoosh of steel slicing air was the only sound in the quiet void between past and present.

She jumped over and over again, avoiding the blade. Her leg muscles burned, the heavy boots and sword taking their toll. But she refused to give up. She was the world's only hope. "You won't win. I won't let you destroy the people I love."

Sweat poured from her brow, the leather she wore growing warmer as the sun arched higher. The waves of the portal shimmered like silvery heat on blacktop road. There wasn't much time and she needed the element of surprise. Crouching as if in defeat, she waited for his attack. When he drew close enough, she twisted around and swung upward with all her might, slicing his sword arm. His eyes widened and he dropped the weapon. Without sparing a second's hesitation she went in for the kill, leaping from the table and slamming her boots into his chest.

He went down like a bull elephant, his body hitting the ground with a loud thud and sending up a cloud of dust from the floor. Before he could gather his wits she jammed the blade downward, rendering his fighting arm useless. He screamed in pain and reached for his sleeve, a crimson trail flooding his white shirt. With one booted heel she pinned his throat and pointed the sword at his black heart.

"Have I ever mentioned how much I *hate* to be called 'bitch'?" She affected a deep sigh and said, "I'm afraid you'll have to die for that, Rorg."

"Cut! Print! That's a wrap, folks. Great job, Gina, Bob."

Heaving rapid breaths to fuel her lungs, she was lost in this moment, in the action, the adventure, the pure thrill of besting an opponent. She barely registered the director's words.

"Gina. Wanna get your foot off my neck?"

She looked down at the strangled voice of her nemesis, remembering that this was a movie scene. Rorg was the character Bob played, not her real opponent. And she was crushing his larynx with her boot.

"Oh. Sorry, Bob." She blinked and forced reality to once again enter her mind, lifting her foot and holding out her hand. He grinned, grasped her palm, and leapt to his feet.

"You scare me sometimes, Gina," he said, kissing her on the cheek. "I think you enjoy this aspect of your work a little too much. But great job kicking ass."

"You know me, Bob. I live for the action scenes. And right back at ya on the ass-kicking."

Bob walked away and Gina rested her hands on her hips, breathing heavily. Exhilarated as always after a battle scene, she fought to keep from jumping up and down like a hyperactive child. The shot had gone better than she expected, the last retake they needed to wrap this picture. Josie, her assistant, hurried over with a bottle of water and a towel. Gina wiped the sweat from her face, dying to take a shower and wash off the thick glop of makeup they'd applied at the ungodly hour of three o'clock this morning.

"David, you need me for anything else?" She loved working for David Beasley. He knew how much she enjoyed doing action films and always called on her for the grueling ones.

"We're done here, babe," he shouted across the room. "I'll call you later for dailies."

Heaving a sigh and wishing he'd asked for another take, she headed to her trailer, grinning when she found her agent, Dee Hastings, waiting inside. "Hey, Dee! What's up?"

"My blood pressure," Dee replied with a grimace, shrugging out of her suit jacket. "It always goes up when I see swords swinging in your direction, or when I have to watch you poised to jump off a cliff, or when three beefy stuntmen are set to beat the shit out of you."

"Aww, come on, those are the parts I like," Gina teased, breezing by with a kiss to Dee's cheek.

"That's what scares me," Dee said, following her into the bedroom of the trailer. As Gina peeled off the now-sweaty leather and tossed it on a pile near the door, Dee flopped into a chair and smoothed the fine blond hairs away from her face. "You're going to give me gray hair. You're going to make me old before my time. My star, my moneymaker, taking risks like you do. You make me crazy, girl."

Laughing, Gina slipped on a robe, sat on the bed, and began to loosen the braid holding her hair. "I know what I'm doing, Dee. You know my background. You know what I'm capable of."

"I also know what you're worth. What if something happens to you during one of those crazy action scenes?"

"You afraid of losing your fifteen percent?"

Gina looked up at Dee's silence. Uh-oh. She'd hurt her feelings. She could tell by the furrows on Dee's forehead. Why did she always do that? Why didn't she think before she spoke? She'd known Dee for fifteen years. Dammit.

"I think you know better than that, Gina. I care about you."

Shit. That caring thing, that need for people to want to get close to her. "I'm sorry, Dee. Of course you do. I don't know why I said that."

"It's okay. You've had a long day."

Crisis resolved. Gina resumed unbraiding her hair, grateful she didn't need to do more groveling than necessary. She had to be careful what she said around Dee. Some people were so sensitive. Especially Dee, who'd taken it upon herself to act as Gina's mother figure. Whatever. She didn't need a mother, hadn't needed one since her own disappeared. Since she was eight years old she'd done just fine without one.

She shook her hair out and grabbed a brush to begin the untangling. Lord, she needed a shower. And a really big breakfast.

"You have to realize you are the number one female action movie star right now," Dee continued. "And there are plenty of stuntwomen out there who can do the risky stuff so you don't have to."

Gina paused and laid the brush in her lap, blinking innocently. "Then what would be the fun of doing movies, Dee?"

Dee rolled her eyes. "You could make a fortune doing a love story, you know. With your face, that mouth, that body . . . God, the roles I could get for you."

Gina scrunched her nose and stuck out her tongue. "Blech. I don't do romance."

"Don't I know it. The tabloids keep printing rumors that you're gay."

Gina snorted. "Like I care what they print."

"You could try dating once in a while. Or, God forbid, you could have an actual relationship."

Gina's eyes widened. "Now you *are* scaring me, Dee. I'd rather kick a guy's ass than kiss it, thanks." Men were so . . . complicated, so difficult to figure out. No, she didn't have time for those kinds of problems. As arm candy, fine. The occasional sex release? Definitely. As permanent relationships or, heaven forbid, husbands? Forget it. She'd rather lose a limb.

"It wouldn't hurt you to let someone get close," Dee grumbled.

Yeah. Because that had worked so well for her in the past. "I like my life the way it is. It works fine for me."

Dee looked like she wanted to argue the point further, but at Gina's warning glance, she shrugged and said, "Fine. And speaking of asses to kick, that's why I'm here. I have an offer for you. A reality show."

Gina scooted back against the headboard. "Are you insane? First off, I never do television. Second, I need a vacation. I've done back-to-back pictures over the past two years. I need a break."

Dee tilted her head and offered a secretive smile. "That's what I thought you'd say. And typically I wouldn't have even brought it up. But this is right up your alley. Tropical island, lots of weaponry. It's called *Surviving Demon Island*. Contestants try to 'kill' demons hiding on an island. Last one standing without being taken out by a demon wins. And not only do the winners get money, but there's also a contribution for charity, for that new worldwide relief fund for children."

"I like that charity. They've been doing great things. Okay, so you've sparked my interest. Who's doing it?"

"Some new start-up production company. Checked them out and they sound good."

Despite her utter exhaustion at the breakneck pace she'd led the past couple years, the thought of getting away from it all on a tropical island and playing with weapons at the same time held quite an appeal. She wasn't the type to sit back and sip mai tais on a beach. Vacation to her was a trek through the jungle or scaling a mountain or soaring down rapids. God forbid she should have some actual downtime. She liked to stay busy, and something like this might be fun. "Who else is going to be there?"

Dee reached into her briefcase and pulled out a manila envelope, drawing out papers. Scanning the top sheet, she said, "Actually, it looks like you're the Hollywood draw, but they've invited people with backgrounds in martial arts, weaponry, and extreme sports."

"No other Hollywood types? Really? Oh, hell. I thought you meant a bunch of spoiled actors who'd cry if they broke a nail or a sweat." She grabbed the sheet from Dee and scanned it, then handed it back to Dee. "Sounds like a blast. Sign me up."

Arching a brow, Dee said, "I thought you said you wanted a vacation."

Pointing to the contract, Gina said, "That *is* my vacation!"

A few weeks later, Gina peered out the porthole of the ship, bound for some undisclosed island where filming of the reality show would take place. The producers had shrouded everything under a veil of secrecy, requiring her to sign a confidentiality agreement. She couldn't bring anyone with her or tell a soul where she was headed. No cell phones and no contact with the outside world. As far as Gina knew the press wasn't aware of what was going on or where, and she hadn't seen anyone other than the production company's limo driver who picked her up at the airport and the lone crewman who'd escorted her onboard the ship. As soon as she arrived she'd been taken to a rather plain cabin and told to wait there until she was summoned.

All very dramatic, but then what did she expect? So typical for the industry. But her career fed her love of action and adventure and her chance to escape reality and become someone else. If she didn't have her career, life would be dull, dull, dull.

She took the opportunity to shower away the grunge from the long flight and change into a sundress, grateful not to have a makeup, hair, and clothing assistant trailing behind her. Staring into the mirror, she applied minimal makeup and brushed her hair until the sable strands shimmered, braiding and securing it with a single band at the bottom. Then she slipped on a pair of flat sandals and checked her reflection, hoping she projected a casual image, like an average person on vacation. She didn't want to look Hollywood, nor did she want to tip her hand and show up in full battle gear. Best to remain neutral until she had a chance to assess the competition.

Competition. Her blood damn near sizzled in her veins in anticipation of what was to come.

Finally satisfied, she pronounced herself ready, figuring if they were going to do actual filming today they would have given her a makeup and hair schedule. Or if she was really lucky and this was like some of the other reality shows, there'd be no beautifying of the contestants, which she'd much prefer over the glamour.

The funny thing was, she was actually nervous. Put her

in a room with her peers, and she was fine. But these people were different. They weren't actors or anyone else from the film industry. They were unknowns. Regular people. People who enjoyed the same things she did. Sports, weaponry, danger, and excitement. She couldn't wait to meet them. But she was still anxious as hell about it.

She turned at a knock on the door, opening it to the tall, thin crewman who'd escorted her there earlier. He stared at her with a bland expression on his gaunt face.

"Morning, miss. They've asked for everyone to come up on deck now."

Gina nodded and followed him up the stairs and onto the top deck. A group of about twenty people had already assembled at the other end of the wide stern, so she headed in their direction. Heads turned as she approached. She was used to being stared at, but their looks were more of curiosity rather than of fans who'd caught a glimpse of their favorite star. They were all probably wondering what an actress was doing on this adventure. Maybe they thought she was there to pull in ratings and nothing more. Most people didn't bother to look beyond the surface of her press bio.

Good. Let them wonder. Wouldn't be the first time people misjudged her.

An older gentleman approached her. Rather distinguished looking, he carried himself with an air of confidence. His thick, wavy, almost white hair was swept back off his well tanned face, his dark, penetrating eyes were almost black, and his gentle smile put her immediately at ease. "Gina, I'm Louis, your host."

Noting the slight British accent, she shook his hand, recognizing his name from the public relations packet. "Good morning, Louis. Thank you for inviting me."

"We're delighted you agreed to participate. Let me introduce you to a few of the others."

He tucked her hand in the crook of his arm and walked her over to a small group gathered near a table of coffee and breakfast foods. "Everyone, I'm sure Gina Bliss from Los Angeles needs no introduction, as her films are known worldwide. Gina, these are some of your competitors. Olivia is from San Francisco, Ryder hails from Texas, Jake is from New York, Shay is from Georgia, and Trace is our Australian. You'll have plenty of opportunity to get to know everyone more thoroughly on the two-day sail to the island. For starters, help yourself to something to eat and drink."

Gina smiled and greeted the group. There were others, too, so many names she knew she'd never remember them all. As Louis walked away, her gaze caught a man who stood back from the crowd. Someone Louis hadn't introduced her to.

Dressed in a black sleeveless shirt, black fatigue pants, and lace-up military-style boots, he leaned against the railing and surveyed the group, a lazy, bored expression on his face. A gray wisp of smoke from a fat cigar trailed circles into the pristine air above his dark head.

He was gorgeous. Not that Gina usually noticed that kind of thing. She was surrounded by men more beautiful than she on a daily basis. But this guy had a rugged, ugly beauty. Manly. A stubble of beard covered his square jaw and his nose looked a bit crooked. His eyes were a stormy gray, his brows a little too thick. If she had to cast him in a role in a movie he'd probably be the bad guy.

She always loved the bad guys.

It was his lack of absolute perfection that made him look so damn . . . perfect. Maybe she'd been surrounded by the pretty boys too long and craved a real man for a change.

"Hot, isn't he?"

Gina turned to the petite blonde who had moved next to her, her face all big blue eyes, full lips, and white teeth. When she spoke, it was pure southern accent.

"I'm Shay," the woman said, sliding her hand into Gina's.

Gina shook Shay's hand. "Great to meet you. And yes, he is." She turned away from Mr. Dark and Gorgeous and focused on Shay so she wouldn't look like she was obviously drooling over the man. "So who is he?"

Shay shrugged. "Don't know. He's been watching all of us but hasn't come by and introduced himself yet."

"Interesting."

"Very," another female voice said. A beautiful woman with golden eyes and raven hair spoke to them in a quiet, gravelly voice. "I'm Olivia."

Gina grinned. "Nice to meet you, Olivia. So, not much has changed in the world of women over the centuries, has it?"

"Hell, no," Shay said. "This ship is filled with some seriously good-looking men. We can't help it if we look."

"I'm just sizing up the competition," Olivia said with a shrug.

"Uh-huh," Gina replied with a smirk. She suddenly felt like a teenager ogling the cute boys at the school dance. Of course when she was a teenager she hadn't gone to the school dances, so she'd never had a chance to check out the boys. When other girls were busy primping for proms, she was already in front of the camera, her acting career taking off.

Never too late to make up for lost time, right? She slanted a glance at the man in black, then mentally cursed when his lips curled in a slight smile. He'd caught her looking.

She had the ridiculous urge to smooth back her hair, stick out her chest, and lick her lips. How old was she, anyway? Thirteen? Instead, she tried to affect a casual, noncommittal pose.

Honestly. She wasn't here to hunt down a guy. She was after a prize.

First place.

And that was *all* she was here for.

But then the man in black pushed off the railing and started toward them with all the predatory grace of a tiger on the prowl. Her heart lodged in her throat and her pulse kicked up a few more notches.

What was wrong with her, anyway?

"He's coming over here, and he's looking right at you," Shay said.

"He is not," she whispered.

"Shay's right," Olivia said. "He's zeroed in on you like radar, Gina."

Gina looked at Shay and Olivia and shook her head, suddenly speechless.

He chewed on the cigar like he had some kind of oral fixation. She would *not* keep looking at his mouth, even if he did have lips too full for a man. Lips made to do wicked things to a woman's body. Soft lips, despite the scratchy stubble surrounding them.

Shit.

"Let me introduce you to Derek Marks," Louis said, coming up behind them. "Derek works for me. He'll be helping me run the competition."

"Mornin', ladies," Derek said, pulling the cigar out of his mouth. "I'll be training you, running the competition, and making sure you follow the rules. Think of the island as boot camp and I'm your drill sergeant. I'll watch you sunrise to sundown, teach you how to defeat the demons, make sure you're in prime physical shape for battle, and kick your butts every time you fall. But the rewards if you succeed will be great. In short, I'll be both your heaven and your hell."

When his gaze shot to her, Gina felt a spark of heat sizzle from her belly and straight south. An achy, uncomfortable feeling of awareness.

A girly, feminine feeling.

And she didn't like it one damn bit.

Derek tilted his head and studied the dark-haired beauty, dying to tell her exactly how much fun he had in store for her—for all of them. But Lou would kick his ass if he revealed too much too soon.

"Heaven and hell, huh?" Gina replied. "I think we can handle it."

"You have no idea," Derek said, grudgingly impressed with the proud upward tilt of her chin. Her eyes sparkled with excitement, as if she fed off the challenge.

He liked a woman with some spunk, one who was unafraid to take a risk. Admittedly, when Lou told him Gina Bliss was one of the competitors, his first thought was smoke and mirrors—Hollywood style. All fluff and no action. Lou assured him he was wrong about her.

Maybe he was, and then again maybe he wasn't. Time would tell. One thing was certain, though. Just looking at her made his dick hard. Even flanked by two gorgeous women, she stood out like a sparkling diamond in the middle of a sea of coal. He'd thought the movie posters and big screen were makeup and airbrushing.

He was wrong. In person, devoid of makeup and glamour, she still took his breath away. Her eyes were an unusual turquoise blue, her lashes naturally black and long enough to almost touch her brows. The bridge of her nose was sprinkled with freckles, something the camera didn't show, but gave her a regular-girl look he found way too damn appealing.

Her body was a tight little package of curves, from her generous breasts to her narrow waist and full hips to her long legs and shapely calves. Her body was damn near perfect.

Wisps of warm sable hair had escaped her braid and blew in the gentle breeze, sweeping against her face. She ignored them. He wanted to grab the tendrils and see if they felt as soft as they looked.

"So, is this part of the game? Trying to scare the little women into quitting before the first day?" she challenged.

Her smoky voice drifted over him like a teasing caress, making him think of tangled sheets, sweaty bodies, and sex. And it had been too damn long since he'd thought about a woman that way. For far too many months his days and nights had been spent in other pursuits. He was long overdue for some action and his sex drive had just sat up and taken notice of one very prime, very attractive female.

"I'm not trying to scare anyone, darlin'. I'm just telling it like it is. It has nothing to do with your sex. The men will hear the same thing from me, so don't get your gender in a twist."

"What Derek lacks in social refinement he more than makes up for in battle skills," Lou said, shooting him a warning glance.

Derek shrugged. "Hey, I'm not here to make friends. This isn't a popularity contest and it isn't politics. It's survival. It's li—"

"Right," Lou interrupted. "It's a reality show where survival means winning."

Shit. He'd almost said life and death. Lou's timely interruption reminded him it wasn't yet time for revelations. Those would come soon enough.

"If you'll excuse us?" Lou said, motioning Derek away from the others.

Derek followed him down the stairs and into Lou's office.

"You've really got to be more careful," Lou said as soon as he shut the door.

"Sorry." Derek sat at the table and stabbed out his cigar. "Damn hard not to sit them all down and spell it out for them."

Lou took a seat across from him and folded his hands in front of him. "We've been over this. We have to take it slow. Let them get a feel for the setup, for each other, first. Let them hunt. See what they've got."

"From the looks of them, not much."

"I could have said much the same about you when you first arrived," Lou reminded him, leaning back in the chair and crossing his arms.

Derek laughed. "Okay, point taken. But I'm a fast learner and I had a good reason for hunting."

"So will they, once they're told."

"I don't know, Lou. I'm worried. We have a lot of ground to cover in a very short period of time. And while these new folks are all competent and athletic on paper, I'm not sure they can handle it."

"They can handle it. I know they can. Are they as good as you and the others at this moment? Of course not. Will they be at some point? Yes, I think they will. More importantly, we need them. You know as well as I do how much. And those who can't make it will be gone, without ever knowing why they were really brought here. The rest will find out the truth soon enough."

Lou was right. Didn't mean he enjoyed bringing them on or playing this moronic game, but then again he wasn't in charge here. Lou was.

And if this is how Lou wanted to test them, if this was how he put them through their paces, then this is the way they'd do it.

Better than tossing them out there in a trial by fire. Now *that* was reality.

People died doing it that way. Maybe Lou's way was better. It might keep some of them alive longer.

Chapter Two

"Derek sure made it sound all life-and-death, like, didn't he?"

Gina smirked at Jake, the pale skinny guy from New York. He sat under one of the umbrellas at a table, keeping his body shaded from the afternoon sun.

Jake was a chain-smoker, no sooner putting one cigarette out than he lit another. And his hands shook. A nervous kid in his early twenties, his gaze darted around as if he expected the bogeyman to jump out at him any second.

What the hell was this guy doing in a contest where strength, nerves of steel, and prime physical condition were the qualifications? He just seemed out of place.

"Obviously Derek's taking this reality show a little too seriously, Jake," Gina answered. "I wouldn't worry too much about him." She shifted sideways in the lounge chair, then flipped over onto her belly and reached for the iced tea on the table next to her.

"I'm excited about this." Shay had been lounging next

to her and sat up. "What an adventure. I couldn't believe they sent me an invitation."

"Neither could I," Jake said. "Though it's not like I'm really going to get the chance to slice anyone in half with a real laser."

Gina's eyes widened. "Laser?"

"Yeah. I'm working on handheld laser technology." Jake wandered away while lighting up another cigarette.

Gina looked to Shay, who shrugged. "Don't look at me. I figured they'd chosen people who were extreme sports enthusiasts."

"That's what I figured, too." And in Jake's current physical condition, he didn't look like he moved away from his computer desk much. "Interesting. Makes me curious what everyone else does. No one else around here looks like a pencil pusher."

Olivia sat down at the end of Gina's lounge chair. "Did he say lasers?"

"Yeah."

"That's strange. I assume the two of you aren't into anything quite that . . . dangerous?"

"Hardly," Gina said. "Weapons, martial arts, that's about it. You?"

"I run marathons, and I'm an expert at martial arts and the assorted weaponry that goes with it. Nothing else."

"I explore caves and collect daggers," Shay added. "Wonder what everyone else does?"

"I'm up for a little question-and-answer session with the rest of the team if you all are," Gina suggested.

"I'd say it's a really good idea," Shay said.

Gina rose and tossed on her sundress over her swimsuit. They wandered toward Trace and Ryder who were playing cards at the bar.

"So, it seems everyone involved in this competition has some kind of specialty," Shay said. "What's yours?"

"Specialty?" Ryder asked, surveying them with a steady dark gaze.

"Sports, weapons, that kind of thing," Gina explained, trying to appear nonchalant. "We're just curious."

"Uh-huh. Pistols, rifles, and knives," Ryder said, then bent his head and stared at his cards.

Such a conversationalist. Too bad. She liked his sexy drawl. "How about you, Trace?"

Trace grinned, showing off even teeth that appeared stark white against his deep tan. He leaned back in his chair and stretched out his long, lean legs, draping one arm over the back of the chair next to him. "You show me yours and I'll show you mine, gorgeous."

Gina laughed. "You see my movies?"

"A few."

"That's what I do."

He nodded. "I heard that you like to do your own stunts. Impressive. Me, I like guns and knives. Did some desert survival contests, too."

"Fascinating." Fortunately, the guys weren't in the mood to chitchat, so Gina motioned Shay and Olivia along and they headed toward the bow of the ship. "Okay, so that seems normal."

"Nothing like Jake and his lasers," Olivia said.

"No. And Trace and Ryder are clearly in prime shape for an outdoor adventure like this."

"I'll say," Shay said with a wink. "One with dark hair, one with light hair, both sexy as hell. What woman wouldn't want to be a sandwich between those two?"

Gina laughed. There were several other competitors so they split up to do some investigating. When they met up again, they compared notes. All the others were engaged in extreme sports or had experience in what Gina would consider normal weaponry. Nothing unusual.

Gina straddled her lounge chair and took a sip of her tea, puzzled by Jake's invitation to the reality show. "If we're going to be competing in a physical challenge, what the hell is someone like Jake doing here? He's a heavy smoker, thin as a rail, and totally out of shape, and he uses laser weaponry."

"Maybe he's in better form than we think," Shay suggested.

Gina rolled her eyes. "I find that hard to believe. I'd smoke him in a hundred-yard dash."

"I could, too," Olivia added. "Everyone else seems to fit just fine. Maybe he's a fluke, misrepresented himself or something. Or he's fooling all of us."

Gina shrugged. "Could be."

"I'm just going to look on him as one less competitor to worry about," Olivia said.

Or maybe Jake was the one to really watch.

After a nap, a shower, and a change of clothes, Gina went up on deck in search of Shay and Olivia. Something just didn't feel right about this whole reality show. While there were a handful of them like herself who seemed like fish out of water, anxious and excited and completely clueless about what was to come, the others seemed to keep to themselves and within a group on their own, almost as if they had banded together in secret. And those were the people who seemed to be spending a lot of time talking to Derek. Did they have some kind of "in" with him?

She didn't like alliances. The last thing she wanted was to start this game at a disadvantage. Maybe she'd hunt down Shay, Olivia, Trace, Jake, and Ryder and see if they noticed the same thing she had about the others.

But when she went upstairs, no one was topside. The sun was sinking fast into the water, and she took a moment to enjoy the few minutes alone and watch the glowing sunset.

The quiet was unnerving. Despite the gentle hum of the ship's motor and the waves crashing against the hull, she still felt alone with her thoughts.

And time to reflect was never a good thing.

Another adventure, another chance to escape. One movie after another, never a moment to go home and face herself in the mirror.

Who would she face if she did? Who was Gina Bliss? Wasn't even her real name. And where was home, anyway? It certainly wasn't the glass house on the beach in Malibu. The last real home she had was the one she and her mother had shared. The one she'd been wrenched from when she was eight years old. The ten years she'd spent in foster care after her mother disappeared had never been home.

She didn't have a home.

"Why are you all alone?"

Startled, she whirled around to find Derek standing behind her. Placing her hand over her heart to calm the skittering beat, she said, "You scared me."

"You need to develop nerves of steel and better sensing capabilities if you're going to survive this game. You never know who'll be sneaking up behind you."

Smart-ass. Was this some kind of test? "I'll keep that in mind, thanks."

"Everyone's downstairs and gathered for dinner."

"You aren't."

"Not hungry right now." He lifted his hands and lit one of the fat stogies, the smell of cherry and smoke filling the air.

"I see." She turned away and resumed watching the last quarter of the sun sink below the horizon. Derek stepped beside her.

"With all those starving men, you'd better hurry or you'll miss dinner."

"I'm not too worried about it." If he insisted on staying out here with her, this would be a good time to quiz him about Jake, about the competition.

"You need your strength for the competition."

She grinned. "I'll eat. You worried about me?"

He shrugged. "Just a friendly warning."

"So what do I have to look forward to?"

"You trying for some advance recon, Bliss?" He leaned his forearms against the railing and turned his head to look at her. The wind blew locks of dark hair against his forehead. Thick, dark hair. The kind a woman wanted to slide her fingers in. She curled her nails into her palms and bent forward against the railing, focusing her attention on the waves.

"I would never try to get you to divulge secrets, Derek. Besides, I already have an idea what's going to happen."

"Oh yeah? And what's that?"

She really had no clue, but he'd given her an opening and this was her chance to see if he'd reveal anything. "We're going to arrive on the island, then we're going to race around with paint-ball guns and chase after guys in demon makeup and shoot them and score points that way. Or maybe it'll be like flag football. First one to grab the flag from the demon wins."

He arched a brow. "Think so?"

Casting him a sideways glance, she asked, "Am I wrong?"

He took a long, slow puff of his cigar and blew it out, then grinned. "I think you'd better go eat your dinner. You're gonna need it." He slipped a hand in his pocket and strolled away.

Dammit! She'd gotten nothing from him. Nothing! Not even a hint. So much for charm and persuasion.

She might as well eat dinner, then huddle up with the others for a talk. Though she didn't have what she'd exactly call a psychic kind of sixth sense, Gina had keen powers of observation and the ability to read people. One wasn't successful in Hollywood for as long as she'd been without being able to cut through the bullshit.

And there was some definite bullshit going on with this competition.

She meant to find out what it was.

"Gina's suspicious," Derek said to Lou.

Lou raised a brow. "How do you know?"

"She was fishing for clues about the game earlier tonight. And some of our people said she and Shay and Olivia were asking about their specialties."

"Could be just sizing up the competition. Doesn't sound suspicious to me."

Derek stood at the wide window in Lou's office, watching the waves undulate under the cut of the ship's bow. "It was more than just trying to figure out what the game was about. Call it a gut feeling."

"You always have gut feelings."

"I'm usually right."

"Give it a rest, Derek, and quit worrying about these people. Even if Gina is suspicious about something, it won't do her any good. There's nothing to discover right now. All she'll find is the game and other competitors."

Derek paced the length of the all-too-small room. Tight places—he hated them. He couldn't wait to get off this ship and onto the island, stretch his muscles and get into some action.

Training. Who had time for this shit? Bringing on new

people was going to take up valuable time they didn't have.

Necessary? Maybe. Time-consuming? Definitely. And every day they spent playing this moronic game meant days he wasn't out there doing what he really should be doing.

"I know you hate this," Lou said, "but you know the reason for it. We need these people. And if we're lucky, they'll all pass the test and we can bring them onboard. We'll arrive at the island tomorrow and get started right away."

Couldn't happen soon enough for him. He felt like a caged animal lately. Something didn't feel right. Something inside him. He couldn't pinpoint what the difference was, but he felt a change—a churning, unsettling feeling.

Lou was the one with visions and premonitions, not him. He blew it off as cabin fever, of having to halt his normal routine for this test Lou had arranged for the newcomers.

What else could it be? He was just a normal guy, not special like Lou.

He just needed to get off this freakin' ship.

Disgruntled, Gina had gotten nowhere with the others last night. Neither Ryder nor Trace was suspicious about the competition, though they were more interested in playing cards than paying attention. But even Shay and Olivia felt they had been barking up the wrong tree, and maybe they'd been worried for nothing. They felt Jake was just an anomaly and nothing more.

Well, fine. But Gina still thought something was off.

At least they'd arrived at the island this morning. Maybe she was just annoyed at being cooped up—the reason she never took cruises. Ships were too limiting. There was a reason they called it cabin fever. And she was burning up with it right now.

Excited, she packed up her things and stood at the railing, watching the ship's approach. The sun was up and it was steamy warm already, hardly a breeze blowing. She wished she had a spare second to drink in the tropical feel to this place, to absorb the sounds and scents, but there was no time. They anchored off a tiny strip of island and took powerboats ashore. The island looked like nothing more than a sandbar with aqua waves lapping each side. How could they hide anything on this tiny patch of land, let alone big hulking demons?

Gina followed one of the silent crewmen to her cabana. She'd expected something barely more than a tent, but was surprised at the amenities inside the little log building. Of course, she reminded herself, this was reality TV. She seriously doubted the viewing public would ever catch a glimpse of where they slept at night. The focus would be on beating the competition. There was little she needed to do other than change clothes to be ready.

Adrenaline pumping, Gina donned green camo pants, boots, and a tank top. She was ready to rock and roll.

She arrived on the beach and met up with the others, all dressed in similar fashion. Some of these people looked tough, worldly, and experienced. Like they'd been through hell and back and had the scars to show for it. Mean-looking group, the ones who had a tendency to hang in their own little clique, unlike Gina and the others.

Derek was there, too, once again wearing all black. Her body reacted in that weird awareness way again when he glanced in her direction. Great time for her libido to spark up and take notice of a man. She so was not going to allow that to happen. Paying attention to him meant losing her focus on the game.

"So what do you think we're going to do first?" Olivia asked, rolling her shoulders and stretching her arms over her head.

"Your guess is as good as mine," Gina replied, deciding to ignore Derek and begin stretching, too. She bent from the waist and felt the sweet pull in her hamstrings.

"I've seen your movies." Olivia stared straight ahead. "You do all your own stunts."

"Yeah."

"I'd love to go one-on-one with you if we get a chance for some practice."

Gina stood and extended, glancing over at Olivia. "That sounds fun."

Olivia smiled, casting Gina a look of demure innocence as she bowed her head. Gina returned the bow, not fooled for a second. Olivia would be a formidable opponent. She looked forward to sparring with her. It would be a great exercise routine and keep her in shape during the competition.

"Ladies and gentlemen," Louis said, stepping onto the

beach as if he'd just appeared out of nowhere. "Gather around please."

They assembled in front of him, the sun already beating down on the hot sandy beach. The humidity clung to her body, any breeze felt on the ship long gone. Sweat pooled between Gina's breasts and she blew out a breath, wishing for a cold bottled water to quench her thirst.

"Before the game begins, we're going to place you into teams for pre-event training, a bit of physical conditioning to determine your level of fitness."

"What pre-event training? When do the games begin?" Trace asked.

"Soon. Just a little conditioning first."

"I didn't sign on for freakin' boot camp," Jake mumbled.

Gina turned to the quiet man, feeling sympathetic when she saw him pale. Not that he could really whiten any more than he already was.

"No, you didn't, Jake, but there's much more to this competition than just knowledge in your specialty," Louis explained. "You will have to hide out, you might have to engage in hand-to-hand combat."

"The contract states we would compete against each other in battling demons," Jake said, nervously biting his thumbnail. "Nothing about any preconditioning."

"Your contract also states that if you are not able to handle the physical aspects of the game you'll be dismissed."

Once again, Gina wondered about Jake. It was hot out here. Grueling hot. And Gina would bet they'd be hiking, running, putting up with punishing elements. If you weren't in shape you weren't going to make it. If the humidity didn't kill you, then hand-to-hand would. This was reality, not a video game.

"If you have any reservations, Jake, now is the time," Louis stated, making stern eye contact with the thin young man. Louis waited a few moments, but Jake finally shook his head.

"All right, then. Let's get started. Derek will be in charge of the exercises. He will see to it that you know how to adequately defend yourself."

"Defend ourselves from what?" Shay asked.

"We can't tell you that," Louis stated with a slight upward curve to his lips. "That would be violating the rules of the game and we're not ready to reveal those just yet."

"Bet you're disappointed, aren't you, darlin'?" Derek whispered behind her.

She felt the warmth of his breath against the nape of her neck, his deep voice like a caress to her skin. Despite the heat, she shivered, but she refused to turn around, forcing herself to shake off his hypnotic effect on her. "I can wait a little longer," she replied, but he was right. She was getting damned curious.

"Okay," Louis said, "I'm going to turn this over to Derek, who will assemble you into teams and get the ball rolling on a few simple skirmishes. Derek, try not to kill them on the first day?"

Oh, this should be fun.

Derek moved to the front of the group and took the

clipboard from Louis, surveying them like a gym teacher facing the scrawny freshman class.

"I don't care what you think your talents are. Consider yourselves underprepared, inept, and not even close to being ready for what you're about to face. As soon as you realize that, you might just survive this."

Oh, please. He was taking this way too seriously. It was just a game. How hard could it be?

"We'll start with a skirmish in teams of two. You'll be running the length of the island, and we'll do it in sets. Team One will consist of Gina, Trace, Ryder, Jake, Olivia, and Shay. Dalton, Linc, Mandy, Rafe, Punk, Rico, you'll be Team Two, so you can take a seat. We'll run you later."

Of course. Why didn't it surprise her that the group who hung with him wasn't running with them?

He then split them up into smaller groups, Gina paired with Trace.

"I'll be waiting here at the finish line, but there will be others running with you to check your progress throughout."

"Wait a minute," Gina said. "You're not running?"

"No."

"Why not?"

"Because I'm not participating in the games. You are."

"But you're supposed to be coaching us, drilling us. I'd think you'd run with us."

He rolled his eyes and stepped up to her. "I'd outrun you."

"Wanna bet?" She didn't know why she challenged him. Maybe to see what he had? For some reason she was disappointed he wasn't going to be joining them.

He stared her down for a few minutes, then said, "Olivia will race with Trace and Shay. Jake and Ryder on another team."

Oh, yeah. Now he was talking.

"Can you handle it?" he asked, challenge lacing his voice with sarcasm.

Her adrenaline levels shot up and she was primed and ready for a fight. Her nipples hardened, her panties moistened, and despite what her body thought it wanted, it was going to get something entirely different. A libido-crushing, ball-busting skirmish in the sand.

"I can handle anything you've got. Let's get it on."

Chapter Three

Derek could have winced at Gina's choice of words, his body reacting with a jolt of awareness that had nothing to do with brawling and everything to do with clothes-ripping, no-holds-barred sex.

"You gonna stand there all day with that shit-eating grin on your face, or are we going to dance?" she asked, an amused smile on her face.

Dance. Yeah, he'd like to dance with her, all right.

He turned to them and said, "First we run. The length of the island and back. Then after I wear you out, we'll see what you've got left. What I want everyone to do is run side by side with the team member I assigned you to. Don't run any faster than your partner. If they slow, then you slow. If your partner speeds up, then you'd better keep pace. The idea is to keep up with your partners, but don't exhaust them if you're a little faster. You don't want to run your team member into the ground, but you don't want to cut them too much slack, either. Play off each other's strengths but be mindful of weaknesses. Compensate for each other. You have ten minutes to warm up. Then line up at the starting point over there." He pointed.

He almost laughed at the way they scrambled to the ground to stretch. When he turned to look at Gina, she had a wide smile on her face as she assessed his body.

"What?" he asked.

"Well, I know I'm in shape. But judging from the cigars you like to suck on and the way you inhaled those beers on the boat, I'd say you'll have a pretty tough time keeping up. And you look like you carry about two-twenty, two-twenty-five on six foot three or so, which means I can't pick you up or drag you."

The woman was ballsy, he gave her that. "You think I can't keep up with you?"

"Yeah."

He laughed. "Try me."

"I intend to."

She was a smart-ass. He really liked smart-ass women. "Bet?"

"How much?"

"Baby, it's a guarantee I can't put up the money you can. I'm not a movie star. So it'll have to be something else."

She rested her hands on her hips and thrust her breasts out. She damn well did that on purpose! It worked, too. His dick twitched.

Down, boy.

"Name it," she said.

He couldn't help but think about exactly what he'd

want for a prize. Gina underneath him, naked, their bodies entwined, their mouths meeting and tongues meshing in a hot tangle. Instead, he said, "How about winner calls?"

"Fine," she said. "If I win, you toss those smelly cigars in the nearest trash." To emphasize her point, she jammed her finger in his chest and punctuated her statement. "Every single one of them."

Damn. Then again, he had no intention of losing. "You got it. And if I win, you start out the game fifty points behind."

She shrugged. "Since I don't intend to come in second, that's almost too easy. You've got yourself a bet. Prepare to kiss your stogies good-bye." She held out her hand and he slapped his hand in hers.

Good girl. She hadn't even flinched. But she was still going to lose. "Prepare to start the game with points in the hole, Miss Bliss." Easiest bet he ever made. He had stamina and plenty of it, enough to hold his own.

Her eyes sparkled like sunlit sapphires. "In an hour I'll be dragging your sorry ass across the finish line."

While she stretched, he made sure everyone else was ready, then they set up at the marker Louis had prepared. Lou shook his head. "Do you really have time for these childish games?"

"Just a way to stay in shape."

"If you say so."

They lined up into position and Lou fired the gun to set them off. Derek set the pace, though it seemed even in this Gina wanted to compete with him, running a bit ahead.

Let her exhaust herself. He'd already marked the length of the island and knew how long it was. No way was he going to blow his wad on the front end. Besides, she had to stay in line with him and it pissed her off they were running behind the others.

She needed to learn patience in this game.

Olivia, Shay, and Trace had the lead. Jake and Ryder were in second place, with him and Gina in last. And she was steaming mad. He grinned and slowed the pace even further, figuring he knew exactly what the other groups were capable of.

"Would you kindly move your ass before I get behind you and kick it?"

He could almost hear her grinding her teeth. "I'm moving said ass as fast as I can," he said, not even slightly winded yet. "But you know, those cigars make it kind of hard to breathe."

"I swear to God if we lose this race I will sneak into your cabana while you're sleeping and slice your balls off."

"A little competitive, are we?" He liked that about her. And she hated to lose—that would help with what they were going to face in the future. If she stayed around that long.

But he did have to start moving his ass. The others were pulling ahead, even Jake. And Olivia was a runner, so they had to start putting some spark into this, and now. He stepped it up a notch, hoping Gina would soon have a little trouble keeping up when he started pushing it.

She didn't.

Dammit.

In fact, she acted as if she'd like him to put a lot more effort into it.

Okay, he was getting winded when they reached the end of the island and made the turn. Not bad, but it was hot outside and he was really cranking it to keep this pace.

She was sweating as much as he was, her clothing completely drenched.

But she was smiling.

And didn't look one bit uncomfortable.

She probably did those aerobics classes every day, perspiring happily to music at the gym.

But he could keep up just fine. He'd handled much worse than this, and by God *he* was setting this pace, not her, so he slowed it down a little. They were far enough ahead of the others by now they could afford to relax a bit.

"Getting tired?" she asked, arching a brow as she jogged circles around him.

"No, I'm fine. Just don't want to demoralize the other teams on the first day so I'm cutting back a little."

"Uh-huh."

Okay, so she was in better shape than he gave her credit for. That didn't mean she could hold her own in the game. No comparison.

He sped up when they reached the halfway point on the way back.

"Ready to sprint?" she asked. "There is the bet."

He was so ready to subtract those points next to her name. "You're on."

Sucking in air, he forced his lungs to work, making his

feet pound the sand and dig for each step as they made their way down the path until each breath burned like fire in his chest, each step resulting in a knifelike stab of pain in his shins.

Concentrate. Almost there. Can't give up. He'd never let her win. As soon as he was sure he was ahead, he'd catch her out of the corner of his eye, her braid slapping against her breast as she pulled forward. Maybe just by inches, but still she'd get in front of him.

Sonofabitch, the woman was inhuman!

Finally, the finish line became visible. Sweat poured into his eyes like a waterfall over his head. He brushed it away with the back of his hand, the grit from the dirt on his hands blinding him. He pulled his shirt up to swipe it away which only made it worse. He blinked once, twice, and despite his blurry vision knew he had a clear shot at winning, but then he bumped something and his feet got tangled. What the hell? Was it a vine or was it Gina's foot?

Shit! The world suddenly spun as he lost his balance, skidded, tripped, and fell flat on his face, eating a mouthful of the island in the process.

"Get up, goddammit!"

His mouth full of sand and his eyes burning like hell, he felt hands at the back of his shirt, helping to pull him up with a sense of urgency and surprising strength. Blinded, he let her lead him as she literally dragged him by the scruff of the neck the last few feet and threw him over the finish line and back onto the ground. He landed like a beached whale, once again face first into sand and dirt.

He spit and choked his way into a half sitting position, feeling like half the island had settled in his lungs as he wheezed and coughed it out, trying to breathe.

"Well, that certainly wasn't one of your more stellar moments."

The sound of Lou's amused voice didn't help. "Bite me. I tripped."

Thank God he was still blinded by the sand in his eyes. He sat back and reached for the hem of his shirt, trying to wipe his face.

"See if this will help."

He sputtered as ice cold water fell onto his head, though it didn't feel all that bad considering his body was nearly melting. When he could see again, he wished for the nirvana of temporary blindness. He looked up to see Gina standing over him, looking smug and victorious with an empty pitcher in her hand. Surrounding her were the rest of the contestants and Lou, with an I-told-you-so look on his face.

Derek would never, ever live this down. Sonofabitch!

Gina squatted down to his level, her face even with his. "I think you owe me some cigars."

"You tripped me."

"Whiner."

"I'm not whining. You cheated." Okay, he did sound like a sore loser. But hell, he'd been blinded by sweat, otherwise he'd never have lost that race to her.

"Don't we have a competition to prepare for?"

He almost hated her right now. And at the same time

admired her guts and determination. She'd kicked his ass! Not many people could say that.

Score one for Gina.

Okay, maybe Gina had gotten in front of him a little during their race the first day while the sweat had been dripping down his face. Maybe their feet had gotten tangled and he'd fallen facedown in the sand, allowing her to drag him the last few inches across the finish line. Wasn't her fault he was so damn sweaty.

And he *had* promised to give up the cigars. Who knew he'd be so grumpy about it? Twenty-four hours later she was battered, bruised, and damn near bone-crushingly exhausted from the paces he'd put them all through. And the rest of the competitors looked at her like it was all her fault they'd been worked so hard, sweat dripping down their faces as they ended yet another skirmish, this time hand-to-hand combat with bamboo poles. Hell, she thought it had been fun, even though right now her biceps were screaming in agony.

How could it be her fault? She was just as tired as they were, had worked just as hard as they all had. And Derek was putting himself through the same grueling punishments. He worked them from sunup to sundown, abusing just about every conceivable one of their muscle groups until they crawled into their bungalows at night and collapsed. Then that infernal bell rang at daybreak, signaling another day of torture.

"If he pulls one more competition today, I'm going to

find a way to kill him while he sleeps," Shay growled, scrunching her shoulders and tilting her head from side to side. "My personal trainer never worked me this hard."

Gina nodded. "I always had punishing workouts before a shoot. But never this bad." Though she'd never admit that within earshot of Derek. And she really did enjoy this. Seemed like Derek did, too.

"You having fun?" Trace said, pushing wet blond hair out of his eyes.

"Yeah, I am, actually. How about you?"

He shrugged. "Just another day of sweat and work. I could be at home doing this."

She laughed. "Oh, but it's tropical. Think of it as a vacation."

He snorted and grabbed a bottle of water, unscrewing the lid and downing the contents in a few loud gulps before tossing the plastic carcass in a nearby trash can. "I could be on a lake fishing with a six-pack of beers and a couple sheilas to keep me company. Honey, this is no vacation."

She rolled her eyes at him and looked at Shay. "Okay, so maybe not everyone is having a good time."

Relocating to another island later that afternoon came as a huge surprise, but once they did, it all made sense. Where once they'd occupied a crackerbox, now they anchored offshore a gigantic spread of absolute paradise.

Gina had wondered how they were supposed to hide and flush out demons on the first island when they'd occupied such a narrow strip of land with sparse trees, barely any camouflage, and no hills to speak of. They might as well have painted a target sign on their chests and waited for the demons to come after them.

This new island was breathtaking, and she suddenly wanted a vacation. Time to hike the impossible hills peppered with tall, dense trees, explore the weathered mountain ranges they sailed by, and dive off the ship and delve into the secret sea caves located on the map Derek showed them.

Green valleys were carved along the sides of the mountains, thick emerald grass just waiting to be explored.

She'd never wanted to see the sights before, just take time to explore an island leisurely. Now she did.

And now she couldn't.

But damn, *this* was an island!

"You'll get your chance," Derek said in answer to her unspoken thoughts. "I can see you're itching to get off this boat and investigate."

"Maybe," she said, mentally drooling over the scenery.

"You don't strike me as the vacation sort."

She turned to him. "What does that mean?"

He shrugged. "Just that you're not the type to lay around and do nothing but soak up the sun. Bet you're an explorer. You crave adventure."

"You're right." She looked out over the island. "I'd love to backpack into those hills. Look how the clouds dip down over the peaks. The view from up there must be incredible."

"Maybe you'll get a chance to do some hiking."

"Really?" Excitement filled her. "Will the games take us that far out?"

"Can't say," he replied with a wink.

Dammit. He was good at keeping secrets.

As soon as they dropped anchor, they climbed aboard the Zodiac power boat and zoomed onto the white sand beach, where they were shown to their private bungalows, well within the depths of the island.

Even the cabanas here were more opulent than the ones on the first island. This place really was a paradise. A strange combination of rustic and lavish with a true tropical feel. The cabanas were luxurious, with crisp white sheets and bamboo walls, fans made out of palm-shaped wicker casting a balmy breeze over her flushed skin as she unpacked. She scanned the room, wishing she could strip naked and roll out on the sheets.

A flare of desire struck her at the thought of another body joining her on that bed. Not just any body, either, but Derek. His strong hands skimming her naked flesh, learning the secrets to her body, slipping between her legs and massaging the aching throb that had been present there since she'd met him.

How long had it been since a man had touched her, since she'd experienced the sweet release she so desperately craved? How long since she'd zeroed in on one specific man to cater to her desires?

Never, actually. No man had ever struck her so profoundly as Derek, had ever awakened her fantasies in such a fast and furious way. She shuddered at the visual of sweat-soaked sheets and writhing bodies undulating in this tropical paradise, sliding her hand between her breasts to feel the humidity moistening there. She closed her eyes, imagining Derek behind her, slowly stripping the clothes from her body, his lips touching every place her hands touched now. She palmed the back of her neck and lifted the heavy tendrils of her hair, shivering at the imagined feel of warm, masculine lips licking the back of her neck.

He hit her hot buttons, no doubt about it. Infuriated her, definitely. But did he ever light her up and turn her on.

The man would be an animal in bed. He'd be the kind to take what he wanted, not like some of the men she'd been with who'd been too afraid to even touch her.

Derek would touch her. He'd demand, ravage. She could already imagine what he'd be like. Hungry to get his hands on her breasts, to slide his cock between her legs and take possession of her.

She slid her hand down, desperate to quell the throbbing ache between her thighs.

"You ready? It's time to go."

Her eyes shot open and she jerked her hand away, turning to see Derek leaning against the open doorway. Her mind was drenched in thoughts of him, her body awash in the sensation of his imagined touch. It was as if he'd stepped right out of her fantasies, appearing there to make her dreams come true. Dressed all in black as usual, he wore a sleeveless shirt that showed off all his muscled areas. She fought to form words, her head still in a daze over this idiotic fantasy or vision or whatever the hell it was she couldn't seem to shake off.

"Gina."

"Huh?"

"I asked if you were ready."

"Uh, yeah." God, was she ever ready. But what she wanted wasn't going to happen. Sucking in a mind-clearing breath, she headed toward the door, but he blocked her.

"Something wrong?"

"No. Let's go."

Instead, she found herself staring into a brick wall of broad chest. She forced herself to keep her hands at her sides, but what she really wanted was to explore his body, to touch her lips to his neck and lick his skin. Would he be salty or sweet?

What the hell was the matter with her?

"Something's spooked you. Your face is flushed. What is it?"

"Nothing." *Everything. Go away.* She hated feeling.

"Look at me."

Though it was stupid, she didn't want to look at him. It was difficult enough grappling with her emotions and her libido right now, let alone having to make eye contact with her current sex fantasy.

Mind over matter, Gina. She tilted her head back and stared into curious gray eyes. God, she could get lost in smoky eyes like that. Such depth and mystery in them. His face was a never-ending source of interest to her. She wanted to trace his crooked nose and the chiseled planes of his cheeks and jaw, then slide her fingertips around his full mouth.

All while he rocked inside her and whispered wicked, naughty things to her.

Jeeeeesus! She shook her head and stepped back.

"Hello! Didn't you say we needed to go?" Maybe if she pushed him he'd want to argue and quit giving her that look like he was concerned. She liked him wanting to beat the crap out of her a lot more than looking concerned about her.

"You're acting strange."

"So are you. Now let's go." Before she really did jump him.

"You're a pain in the ass sometimes, Bliss."

"So are you, Marks."

"And what's up with that name?"

"What's wrong with it?"

"Is it your real name?"

She wasn't about to tell him her real name. "So what if it is?"

"Bliss?" He moved aside and let her pass, then stepped beside her as they moved out onto the path and headed into the jungle. "It sounds like a porn star's name."

"Bite me." The spell was broken and she felt normal again, that weird heated moment gone. Thank God. For a second there she might have actually considered acting on her fantasies.

They finally arrived at a clearing where Louis awaited them. Derek added his torch to the others that outlined the circle in which they stood.

Once everyone was assembled and seated, Louis stepped in the center of their circle, the camera crew hit the lights, and film began to roll. Gina watched the competitors squint and turn away, but to her, lights and cameras were second nature. She ignored them and focused on Louis.

"It's time for the game to begin. I know you think this is going to be fun, but there is danger about. There are demons on this island, hiding, lurking, and prepared to attack. If you are 'killed,' you will be asked to leave this island and you will forfeit your prize. For every skirmish you win, you will be given points. Points will be amassed on the board over there."

Derek stepped up. "Game rules. Pay attention."

Mercifully, they had all passed the torturous conditioning tests and it was finally time to get to the rules of the game. Gina would have whooped for joy if she had any strength left. She'd worked with some of the best trainers Hollywood had to offer, had even done a conditioning stint with the Army Rangers to prep for one of her movies. And she had to admit, she'd never gone through a more punishing workout than what she'd endured under Derek.

He was good. Damn good. Her body ached in places she didn't even know she had. Poor Jake was limping, Shay and Olivia weren't in much better shape than she was, and Trace and Ryder had spent most of the day groaning. The others were mostly mute but they had continuously shot Derek some evil glares. It's almost as if they took his conditioning drills like a personal affront.

Behind Derek was a covered tabletop. He yanked off the canvas covering, revealing some interesting-looking rifles and pistols.

"These are laser tag weapons, only a lot more sophisticated. The demons you're going to be hunting will wear targets, which will react when hit with the laser beam at various designated kill points on their bodies."

Gina's gaze shot to Jake, who was grinning like a little kid let loose at Toys "R" Us. Lasers. Figured. So much for her theory he didn't belong. Hell, he was going to kick their butts.

"Kill zones are their heads and upper torso. Hit a kill zone and you score a hundred points. A hit to the lower torso will score fifty points. Hitting arms or legs will score twenty-five points. Ten points for a hit on any other part of the body.

"High-scoring individual of the day gets double ammo the next day. Low score will have one more chance, but with only one-half ammo."

Okay, this sounded like fun. She felt the adrenaline rush pumping through her system.

"You'll start off in two teams of six. You'll be given headsets and you'll hunt and kill with your team. However, elimination and scoring will still be individual.

"Keep in mind you will also be scored on whether or not the demons can touch you. You will be given white shirts to wear, and all demons will be equipped with red markers. If a demon gets close enough to mark you, you're automatically eliminated from the game. One of the prime objectives is to stay alert, your eyes and ears open at all times. You don't ever want a demon to get close enough to touch you."

Yikes! The game had just gotten tougher. "So not only do we have to hunt and track the demons in order to make a kill, we also have to be on the lookout for them springing up on us?"

"Yeah," Derek said, a gleam in his eyes that she didn't like one bit.

"Dayum," Shay said. "This is going to be hard."

"Of course it's hard. If it was easy, what would be the point?" Derek challenged. "Lou and I will track your progress on a computer here at base camp. Each of your guns will be registered to your name and will record your weapons fire and your kills. We'll also be in communication with you at all times via your headsets, so listen for instructions. The demons will be equipped with headsets and will call out the numbers written on your shirts if they get close enough to mark you for a kill. If you're killed you're to report back to base camp immediately."

"That's not gonna happen," Ryder said, leaning back in his chair. "Not to me, anyway."

"Me, either," Trace said.

Of course then everyone said the same thing. Gina grinned. She imagined a lot of them felt that way right now. But someone was going to be eliminated. And it wasn't going to be her.

"We'll see, won't we?" Derek said. "Anyone have any questions?"

One of the men, Gina thought it might be Dalton, spoke up. "We all going to be hunting in the same place?"

"No," Derek replied. "Team A will hunt on the west side of the island, Team B on the east side. Your designated hunting zone will be well marked so you don't get lost. It's a pretty big jungle out there, so we've roped it off and marked it clearly to limit your hunting area. The demons must stay within the same bounds so there won't be any surprises."

What was the fun in that? "Why don't you just give us GPS systems and let us find our way around?" Gina asked.

Derek arched a brow. "I don't think you're ready for that quite yet."

"Try me."

"Later. Let's just stick to our game plan for the time being."

Whatever. Roped-off area. How limiting.

"Anything else?" When no one came up with a question, he said, "Everyone get your gear on. First day is a practice run. No points will be scored and no one will be eliminated. You have thirty minutes to get ready."

"Now?" Shay asked. "It's getting dark."

"We'll run all the skirmishes in the dark," Derek said. "Everyone will be given night-vision goggles. You'll be able to see just fine once you adjust to them, but you'll still have to learn to hunt in the dark. Got a problem with that?"

She held up her hands. "Not me. You're the boss." She walked away and whispered to Shay, "Is it just me, or does he seem unusually tense tonight?"

"It's not you." Gina had noticed it, too, and wondered why. Maybe it was just getting the game organized that ratcheted up his stress level. Couldn't be easy coordinating all this, and in front of cameras, too. While it was second nature for her to be filmed, some people got jittery. She didn't really know Derek's background, but she'd bet it wasn't in filmmaking. Maybe he was shy.

Right. The man didn't have a shy bone in his body. He was brash, forward, in your face, and not at all hesitant. She'd just bet he was the kind of man to take charge everywhere and in everything he did.

Like in bed.

Her body heated up at the thought.

Stop that. Now was not the time. It would never be the right time, actually. She was here to do her job, and she made it a point to never get involved with fellow actors.

Not that Derek was a costar or anything, but he might as well be as far as this game was concerned. And that made him off-limits.

Face it, Gina. Every man is off-limits to you. Any man who makes you feel anything is off-limits. And God knows, in a couple days Derek Marks has sure as hell made you feel something.

She got in line for her gear, ignoring her body and her argumentative mind. So what if he was hot and she was horny? So what if she wanted him? There was no time for sex and relationships on this island or during this adventure, so she might as well get those thoughts out of her head.

She was safe from entanglements, from having to think.

From having to feel.

Derek stood by the table and handed out gear while Lou entered gun numbers of the participants in the computer.

It was damn hard to stand by and just watch when what he really wanted to do was participate. Even if this was just a game, it was at least practice, a way to keep his skills sharp.

Ah, hell, what he really wanted to do was burn off some excess energy, douse the fire Gina stoked inside him. When he'd come to her bungalow earlier, she'd been seemingly lost in thought, her hand absently trailing over her body. Watching a woman touch herself was the hottest goddamn thing he'd ever seen. And even though he shouldn't have been watching, the hounds of Hell themselves couldn't have torn him from that spot.

Her eyes closed, her lips parted, she'd been lost in some kind of fantasy, her fingertips trailing between her breasts on their way down her ribs and belly.

What had she been thinking about? He really wanted to know what she'd been thinking at that moment. And like an idiot, he'd had to stop her, just when her hand had been about to hit the sweet spot.

Dumbass.

But when he'd caught her attention and she'd cast her gaze his way, the look she'd given him had rocked him back on his heels.

Her eyes had been filled with heat, lust, and longing. He knew that feeling of hunger, and in that moment he'd felt it zing across the room like a strike of lightning between them. He wanted to grab her and pull her into his arms.

Somehow he doubted she would have objected.

So what had stopped him? The game? That he knew he

shouldn't mingle with the participants? Maybe it was the fear that he really didn't know if he took that step exactly what he'd be stepping into.

Or quite possibly, if he touched her he wouldn't be able to stop with just a touch. If he kissed her, he wouldn't be satisfied with just one kiss.

He wanted inside her in the worst way.

She was beautiful, no doubt. Gorgeous, in fact. Spunky and challenging and strong and capable. But there was also a vulnerability about her that intrigued him, that made him want to sit down and talk with her, find out more than what was in her bio. Dig beyond the surface of Gina Bliss and find out how what happened to her all those years ago had shaped her.

And Derek wasn't the kind of guy who wanted to spend time talking to women he was attracted to. But dammit, they all had demons in their past. He did, she did, they all did. Would be nice to just once sit down with someone and talk about it. Though there were other people around him who'd been through it. Why not talk to them? What made Gina so special?

Right. *Like you're a big fucking talker. You want to strip her naked and lick her all over, not talk to her.*

"I want a big one."

And suddenly, there she was, the last one in line and standing in front of him at the table. Yeah, he had a big one for her. A big one that was twitching in discomfort right now. He handed her a rifle. She arched a brow.

"I said a big one."

At her dubious stare, he added, "Every weapon is alike

as far as number of rounds and max distance, Gina. No one will start this game at a disadvantage. Trust me."

"Why should I?"

She tilted her head, making him want to dive across the table and bury his lips against the smooth column of her throat. "Because I haven't given you a reason not to."

"I've heard that one before." She took the weapon and the rest of her gear and strolled away without a word, joining the other competitors.

He wondered what she meant by that comment. Another Gina mystery. He didn't want mysterious people on his team, which meant he was going to have to dig in and find out more about her—beyond just the file Lou had on her.

Oh, sure, he knew her background. He knew all their backgrounds. Hell, he knew more about these people than they knew about themselves. But it wasn't his job to psychoanalyze what happened to them in the past and how they ended up at this place. It wasn't his job to give them the "big revelation." That was Lou's deal.

His job was to make fighters out of them.

Of course Gina was right—he was lying to her, to all of them. So she really did have a good reason not to trust him, at least on the surface.

In fact, he'd bet some of these people were going to be pissed as hell when they discovered what this game was really about.

Chapter Four

Gina, Trace, Jake, Shay, Ryder, and Olivia were designated Team A and ready to head into the jungle. The other competitors made up Team B. And just like in conditioning drills, the other group who didn't mingle with the rest of them had all been placed on one team, while Gina and her pals had been placed on another.

Not that Gina was suspicious or anything. Much.

But it didn't matter. She had competent teammates and she was tired of standing around hearing rules. Headset on, gun in hand, night-vision goggles placed on top of her head and ready, she was primed for some action, even if this was just a practice run.

"All right, teams," Derek said. "Pay attention to each other, to your surroundings. And don't forget to look out for demons at all times. You never know when one will spring up on you. Listen to my commands and when this exercise is over, report back immediately."

Gina looked over at the other team who was poised at

the line ready to head into their part of the jungle. Her team was going to smoke their asses.

"Ready and go!"

They charged off into the dark jungle with Trace at the lead. Since he was an experienced survivalist and tracker, they'd voted him group leader for tonight's event. The path was marked with a series of torches and fluorescent, glow-in-the-dark tape to guide their way and indicate boundaries, but the further they trekked into the jungle, the harder it was to see. The torches grew more sparse, until she could see only one single light off in the far distance. As it was she could barely make out the other competitors, and in order to do so they had to stay right next to each other.

"I'd say it's time for goggles," Ryder suggested, bringing up the rear of their group.

"I agree," Gina said. "I don't know about the rest of you, but I can't see a damn thing. We can't hunt if we're standing on top of each other."

"I've played this game before, or at least something similar. We gotta spread out or we're sitting ducks," Jake said.

"Okay, then we all agree," Trace said. "Goggles on."

Gina slipped the night-vision goggles in place. Much better. Green, but better. At least she could see something besides complete darkness now. Everything was three dimensional, so she could make out people from trees.

"Let's spread out a bit," Ryder suggested. "Keep your focus and your ears sharp for sounds of approaching demons. There are twigs and branches and fallen palms all over the jungle floor here, so we should be able to hear anyone approach."

Gina couldn't wait to head out on her own. They all shifted and spread outward. She kept her gun at chest level, primed and ready to fire the instant she came upon a moving target.

It didn't take long. A shape moved out in front of a thick tree trunk in front of her. She aimed and fired a laser shot.

"Only ten points for that one, Gina, which means you didn't hit a decent spot on that demon. Calm down, sharpen your focus, and aim higher."

Derek's voice piping in her ear. The laser must send the data to their computers instantly. "Got it."

Pretty cool stuff, actually. Excited now, she headed out after the demon she'd shot at, tracking him east of their location. Her headset was filled with chatter from the other participants, Derek's feedback on whether they'd hit or missed, and location information. Gina tuned it all out, focusing only on the demon she was tracking.

"Shit, he marked me. Sonofabitch came out of nowhere."

Trace's voice. Gina winced, knowing it could have easily been her. She started moving in circles, looking from side to side and turning around to make sure no one was behind her. The white shirts the competitors wore were easy to spot with the night-vision goggles, so she didn't confuse them with demons.

Damn, these guys playing demons were good. But not that good, because there he was! She took off on a fast run and fired at his back, hitting him square on. He kept running, but she wasn't about to let him get away this time. Despite the night and the goggles, she could see just fine, leaping over the obstacles in her path. She circled around a copse of trees directly ahead, figuring he was going to have to go either right or left around them, and hoping he'd go left.

He did, and ran straight into her. She hit him square in the chest.

"Kill points, Gina," Derek said.

Resisting the urge to whoop for joy, she took off and headed back, on the hunt for more. She found one on Olivia's tail, snuck up on him, and got him, too.

By the time the event was over and Derek called them back to camp, Gina had killed four demons. She was ecstatic and ready to burst with energy.

"How'd you do?" she asked Shay.

"One kill. One damn near got me, too, but I skirted away just in time."

"I had two kills," Olivia said. "And then one marked me after that, dammit. Didn't even see him coming."

"Two kills," Ryder said, tossing his gun on the table.

"None," Jake said, frowning.

So Gina had scored high points on the practice run. She resisted the urge to grin, but damn, it had felt good out there.

Derek clapped Ryder on the back as he walked by, and told Jake he'd do better tomorrow. He nodded to Olivia and Shay who were huddled together and said, "Nice job."

Not a damn word to her. Nothing. What the hell? She'd

scored the highest points out there and he hadn't even looked in her direction.

"Okay, everyone," Louis said. "Some of you did well, some of you need a little more practice. Get ready, because the real game begins tomorrow night. Think about your mistakes and make any adjustments necessary, because tomorrow they could result in your elimination. Have a good night."

Gina turned in her gear and started to head to her bungalow, but this thing with Derek bothered her. She walked over to Derek, who stood alone repacking the gear.

"Well?" she asked.

Derek looked up, knowing exactly why Gina was there. The last thing he wanted was for her to get cocky and overconfident.

She was good. Damn good, in fact. But was it beginner's luck, or did she really have the natural skills? Pushing her a little harder would tell. Rewarding her with lots of attagirls wouldn't.

Firelight danced in the highlights of her hair, making it look alive, like golden snakes shimmered through it. Not that he noticed stuff like that or anything. "Well what?"

"What do you think?"

"About?"

She rolled her eyes. "I want your opinion about tonight."

He knew what she was fishing for. "It was okay."

"I scored high points."

"Uh-huh. You got in some lucky shots. You still have a

lot to work on." He stepped around her and headed for his bungalow. He was tired, needed a shower and a drink.

After spending some time reviewing the schedule for tomorrow, he stripped and turned on the shower, groaning as the warm spray hit his sore muscles. The years were starting to take a toll on his body. He never used to ache like this, but after several days of pounding the sand and skirmishing with Gina and the rest of them, he felt every muscle and creaky joint screaming at him. He'd been pushing them, and himself, harder than he'd ever pushed before.

Despite the desire to linger for about an hour under the hot water, he washed, rinsed, and with a reluctant sigh, turned off the shower. Grabbing a towel, he wrapped it around his waist and decided a glass of whiskey was in order. Nothing like a good, old-fashioned painkiller.

When he stepped into the bedroom, he sucked in a breath of shock.

Gina was there, leaning casually against the partially open front door. Now *this* he didn't need. He was wet, naked under his towel, and his cock lurched to life at the sight of her. Obviously *that* part of his body wasn't aging as rapidly as the rest of him.

Her hair was unbound, still damp from her own shower and hugging her shoulders and breasts. She wore a skimpy little orange-flowered sundress that clung to her curves and did achy things to his balls. Not good. He really could use that drink about now.

"I didn't hear you knock."

"That's because I didn't." She shut the door behind her and advanced into the room.

"Unless you're here to throw me down on the bed and have your way with me, get out."

She paused for a second and looked at his bed. Was she considering it? And what would he do if she was?

"Believe me, that's the last thing I'd want to do with you."

"Too bad. And here I am all clean and almost naked."

She took a quick glance at his crotch before returning to his face. Okay, maybe not such a quick glance. More of a lingering one. One that made his dick notice how she was noticing.

"Derek, I've worked my butt off since the day I got here, but for some reason you've made it a point to dismiss everything I've accomplished. I'm sensing some lurking animosity here. Do you hate women in general or is it just me? Never mind. I already know the answer. What I want to know is why."

If she had any idea what was going on under his towel she wouldn't be asking that question. Thinking complex math calculations, he crossed to the nightstand and poured himself a half glass of whiskey, determined to ignore her. Downing the contents in one gulp, he turned and said, "I don't hate women and I don't hate you. Conversation over. Good night."

Ignoring his dismissal, she pressed on. "I've decided you have some kind of Gina-hating chip on your shoulder that prevents you from telling me I did a good job, because you sure as hell don't seem to have that problem with anyone else around here."

What part of his good night didn't she hear? He perched on the edge of the bed and poured another half glass. Anger dissipated erections, right? "You're one of those feminists, aren't you?"

"What?"

"One of those 'all men hate women' kind of women."

"That's ridiculous. And thanks. I'd love a drink. How kind of you to offer." She walked over, took the glass from his hand, and downed it in one gulp, handing it back to him and resuming her pacing. "It's clear that a capable woman threatens your masculinity."

He set the glass on the table and stood. She made him dizzy tromping back and forth so he stepped in front of her, halting her progress. "You're just used to having flunkies surrounding you and kissing your ass."

Her eyes widened. "What?"

"You heard me. And it isn't going to happen here, so you'd better get used to it. Out here you don't have twenty assistants fawning behind you and drooling over every word you say."

"That has nothing to do with what I'm talking about and you know it. And I never have anyone fawning over me, you idiot."

"Bullshit. You're a pampered princess and you just can't handle not having a 'Yes, Gina, whatever you say, Gina' adoring puppy following you around telling you how wonderful you are."

Her eyes glittered with anger. "You are such an asshole. You know nothing about me!"

"And you're a prima donna. Would you mind getting

the fuck out of my room? I've had just about enough of your mouth for the day." And if she wasn't going to use it for something useful, like wrapping it around the thick, hard part of him that ached like a sonofabitch, he really wanted her gone.

"And I've had just about enough of your arrogant attitude. I don't know why I bothered coming here." She palmed his chest and shoved him, hard. He hadn't expected it and stumbled back. The towel came loose and fell to the floor and her gaze shot south, widening with distinct interest.

Ah, hell. Instinct roared to life and he grasped her wrists, but instead of dragging her to the door and throwing her out of his room like he should have, he jerked her against him, wrapped one arm around her back, and crushed his mouth against hers.

He knew she'd taste hot and spicy, like carnal pleasures he wanted and shouldn't have. But he had no idea just how hot she'd be.

God, he burned. He should have never touched her, never tasted her. His cock lurched between them now that he didn't have the towel to hold it back. She whimpered and tensed, almost as if she was trying to decide between shoving him again or melting into his arms. He didn't know which way he wanted her to decide.

She melted. He drew her closer, deepening the kiss, sliding his tongue inside to taste the whiskey that lingered there while he moved one hand over her back, jerking her dress up to her waist and balling the material in his fist.

The other hand glided over her ass, roaming casually over her soft skin.

Goddammit, she didn't have any panties on. He groaned. She whimpered.

He was in deep, deep trouble here. He wanted this woman. Wanted her bad.

A roaring inferno reared up inside him. His blood churned and boiled, threatening to burst through his pores.

Her ass was firm and hot, and he couldn't resist grasping one globe in his hand and pulling her closer. She raised her leg, wrapping it around his hip, positioning her sex against his raging hard-on and rocking against him. He could imagine the heat of her smooth, moist skin surrounding him. One thrust and he'd be inside her. One damn plunge and he could be buried deep in the fires of sweet heaven.

The scent of her drove him mad. Musky, aroused, coupled with a clean, citrus scent that was probably her shampoo or soap. He withdrew his mouth and dragged his tongue across her jawline and down her neck. Her pulse pounded erratically against his tongue, mimicking the crazy jackhammering of his heartbeat. He kissed his way down her collarbone and she shuddered when he dipped his tongue in the hollow there. He liked that, making her shudder.

And she didn't say a word. Not a damn word. Thank God.

He traveled further, enjoying the exploration, listening to her rapid breathing, the way her body signaled response without her saying anything. He drew the strap of her sundress down to taste the swell of her breast.

Her heartbeat pounded against his lips. She panted as if she fought for breath, tangling her fingers in his hair, her nails digging in his scalp, not to pull him away, but to push him toward her breast.

Then she did speak. One word.

"Yes."

Spoken in a harsh, desperate whisper.

Oh, yeah. He wanted her naked, spread-eagled, anticipating that first touch of his mouth. He wanted it all and he wanted it now.

"Please."

The deep, throaty sound of her voice penetrated the haze of his lust. He felt the stroke of her hands at his shoulders and growled. This was going to happen. Right here, right now. He reached for the strap of her dress, drawing it further down.

"Derek, I knocked but you didn't answer. If you have a minute . . ."

Sonofabitch! Lou!

He pushed away from Gina and snatched the towel, wrapping it around his waist.

"Oh, I'm so sorry," Lou said, his face turning a deep crimson. "I've obviously interrupted."

Gina jerked the strap of her dress back over her shoulder, shooting Derek a look of panic and regret before turning to Lou. "No, no, it's all right. I was just . . . leaving."

"That's not necessary," Lou said. "I can go."

"No. I should. *Really,* I should."

Without a backward glance toward Derek she dashed out the door and closed it firmly behind her.

His erection now sufficiently dead and buried, he grabbed a clean pair of pants from the floor, jerking the zipper up and turning around.

"I'm terribly sorry, Derek. I had no idea you and Gina were—"

"We aren't. It just . . . happened."

"Should I come back later?"

He wished Lou hadn't shown up at all. "No. Now is fine. What do you need?"

"I just wanted you to look at the results from today. I really can leave if you'd like to—"

"Lou, it's over, don't worry about it. Now is fine." He took the paper Lou handed him and sat at the desk, motioning Lou to the chair across from him. He stared at the sheet of paper, but the stats on there were a blur. His mind was still fully focused on Gina and it was going to take a few minutes to wipe the remnants of her from his mind.

Whatever had been about to happen between him and Gina was lost now. Whether that was a good thing or a bad thing he wasn't sure and didn't have time to think about.

Blowing out a frustrated breath, Derek stood and grabbed the whiskey, pouring himself another half glass, and sat down again. He stared at the amber contents, knowing it wouldn't help one damn bit.

Talk about a massive clusterfuck. He had to get back on track and focus. Having sex with Gina would have been a colossal mistake. Shit was going to happen soon, and he had to remember he was here for one thing and one thing only.

Sex wasn't that thing.

He still tasted her, smelled her, his balls were still throbbing with need; no amount of whiskey was going to make that go away.

"Okay, Lou, let's talk about these numbers."

Chapter Five

Gina sat in the middle of her bed and watched the sun rise, taking its sweet time cruising between the waving branches of the bushes outside her window. She cursed its appearance even as she was awed by its fiery beauty. The window was open, bringing with it the salty tang of ocean, a hint of balmy air that slipped through her unbound hair and swirled around her. Sadly, a short-lived relief from the heat that had clung to her throughout the night.

Not that she'd have slept if there had been an arctic blizzard in the room. And she really needed to sleep, to rest and recharge her batteries. No, that wasn't entirely true because she was still plenty charged from last night's encounter with Derek, her body still tingling and feverish from his touch. She drew her knees to her chest and rested her chin on them. Raising her fingers to trace her lips, she felt stupid but nevertheless awed that she could still sense the pressure of Derek's mouth against hers, could still taste his unique flavor on her tongue. She licked her lips and closed her eyes, remembering every caress, every second, replaying it over and over in her mind like she'd done all through the long, sweaty night.

Shit. She was like a lovesick teen, but good lord, she hadn't expected . . . what? To respond in the way she had? To feel the earth move? God, it had been incredible. A bomb had exploded inside her when he'd jerked her against him and kissed her. Anger had melted into a fiery passion and she'd been instantly swept away.

And Gina was never the type to be swept away.

She'd been kissed by plenty of men. Hot, virile men with more going for them than Derek. Movie stars and producers, successful men with ample experience in the sex department. But she'd never gotten so wet so fast from one kiss. Like an implosion that burst heat throughout her and she simply couldn't handle it. All she could do was hold onto him and whimper.

"You're an idiot, Gina." She dropped her forehead to her knees and wished she could take back last night. Why hadn't she said what she wanted to say to him and just walked out? Why did she have to melt like that? All girly and moaning and all over him like a groupie with her favorite movie star. If they hadn't been interrupted by Lou, they would have fallen on his bed and had sex.

Wild, wanton, no-holds-barred, scream-the-rafters-down sex.

Sweet mercy, it would have been good, too. And now every nerve in her body stood on end and she either had to come or kill something. They probably wouldn't let her kill anything. Okay, so she'd at least hurt it really bad.

Heaving a disgusted sigh, she pushed off the edge of the bed, stood, and stretched. Her body ached, dammit. God, she wanted an orgasm. How easy it would be to satisfy herself right now. She walked to the bathroom and stood in front of the mirror, grimacing at the way her nipples stood out, begging for his mouth, his touch. She reached up and touched them, sucking in her bottom lip at their tenderness, at the way the barest touch shot south and made her quiver.

But dammit, she didn't want to do this herself, didn't want release to spring from her own hand. That, in essence, was the problem. He'd started this fire inside her and she wanted him to douse it.

She jerked on her khaki shorts, wincing as she pulled the sports bra over her sensitive breasts. Her pebbled nipples still cried out for attention.

"Tough," she grumbled. She threw a white tank top over the bra, slipped on socks, and jammed her feet into her boots, cursing when she couldn't quite get the laces to work. What was wrong with her fingers this morning, anyway? She stormed into the bathroom and punished her teeth with the toothbrush, hoping to scour the taste of him from her mouth. Then she yanked out a few thousand hairs with her hairbrush and glared at herself in the mirror while she braided her hair, attempting to remove every remnant of the feel of his hands running through the tendrils last night.

Right. Like anything would erase his touch, his scent,

his taste, from her memory banks. He was burned there and he was staying and there wasn't a damn thing she could do about it.

She was so screwed. Or she hadn't been screwed, and that was the problem.

Gah! This was why she buried herself in her work and didn't do men and relationships and feelings.

She stormed out of her bungalow and flew smack into the chest of the one man she wasn't ready to face yet.

"In a hurry?" he asked, both dark brows lifting over inquisitive gray eyes.

"Hungry," she mumbled, trying to push past him. He moved in front of her, halting her progress, then looked around them as if he were gauging whether they were alone.

"Hey, Gina. About last night."

"I'd rather not talk about last night. It was a mistake." Oh, hell. Why had she just said that? Why didn't she just drag him inside her bungalow and make him finish what they'd started?

Because it would be so damn easy to get close to him, that's why. And because she was a total coward.

"You sure about that?"

"About what? About whether it was a mistake or whether I want to talk about it?"

His lips curled upward, and her mind registered that she'd had her mouth on those lips. Tangy with the taste of whiskey, full, with just a hint of roughness around the edges where his beard stubble was. He'd be like that inside her, too. Tangy, rough, and oh so perfect. Damn, damn, damn.

"About both, I guess. Either way, I'm sorry we were interrupted."

So was she. Very sorry. So why couldn't she say that to him? Instead, she shrugged and wrapped her arms around her middle, trying not to focus on the way he was studying her. "Wasn't your fault. We just got carried away. Shouldn't have happened."

"I don't think you believe that."

"I don't think I want to have this conversation." Now she did look up at him. "Look, Derek, things could get way too complicated between us, with the game and all. I really don't think we should start this, no matter how good it—"

She really had to learn to keep her mouth shut.

"No matter how good it could be," he finished for her. "And you're probably right. We shouldn't. But it would have been good. Damn good. Enjoy your breakfast."

He walked away, leaving her more achy and miserable than before, all because she was too damned afraid to let him in.

By the time she made it to the breakfast tent, they were all gathered inside, leaving only one spot available—directly across from Derek, who cast her a hungry look as if he'd like to eat her for breakfast instead. Tormented and frustrated, she barely tasted the food she forced herself to eat.

"So, Derek, how did you get involved in all this?" Trace asked.

Derek's gaze shot to Lou, who shrugged.

Interesting looks they exchanged, as if Derek had no idea how to respond to that question. Gina sat back and sipped her coffee, grateful to have something else to think about besides sex.

"Not sure what you mean by that."

Trace shrugged. "Just curious. You have reality show experience?"

"No."

"Didn't think you looked familiar. Maybe extreme sports or something?"

"No."

Okay, so Derek clammed up in a hurry. And that meant he had something to hide. Or he really didn't know how to answer the question.

"I follow the extreme sports circuit pretty closely," Gina offered. "I've never seen you around."

Derek shot her a scathing look. Gina smiled and refilled her coffee.

"I was military for a while, then met up with Lou after I got out. It's a really long, boring story how it all came to be, but we ended up forming this . . . organization. Lou's a philanthropist and enjoys sports, martial arts, weaponry, and the like. He asked me to join him and help with the game. Lou is really into the reality show thing and came up with the *Surviving Demon Island* idea. He wanted to bring it to television, so I agreed to assist."

That was vague as hell. And didn't tell them anything about him or Louis, actually. "A philanthropist?" she asked, looking to Louis.

"Old money," Louis replied with a benign smile. "Nothing like old men with old money and nothing better to do with their time than to spend it. If you'll excuse Derek and me, we must make preparations for the start of tonight's games."

Oh, sure. She had a million questions and they ran.

Military, huh? What kind of military? And for how long? And exactly what kind of helping did Derek do with Louis? What kind of organization did Louis run?

Gina knew Dee had thoroughly checked out the production company running this game, so she wasn't worried at all, but it sure as hell was mysterious.

More damn mysteries.

After breakfast, a long walk, and some alone time in her bungalow, she was still ready to climb the walls. Deciding she'd better figure out a way to eliminate her frustration, she spent the rest of the day working out her tension with Olivia, who was more than happy to oblige her with a little sparring.

Such an unassuming, petite woman, Olivia would be the type of person to surprise the hell out of someone who didn't know better. No more than five foot two and a hundred or so pounds, Olivia looked like she couldn't even lift a grocery bag. At five foot six and with a lot more muscle, one would think Gina could kick Olivia's ass.

Gina knew better than to ever underestimate an opponent.

They started on the sand by the beach, bowing as they faced each other. Every muscle in Gina's body screamed with taut tension and she needed a release. Sexual release would have been better, but this was a pretty good second.

Olivia launched first, but Gina was ready, warding off Olivia's high kick with her forearm. She pivoted and kicked Olivia soundly in the stomach, sending her to the ground, but Olivia twisted and scissored Gina's legs between hers, and Gina went down.

They both leaped up and the battle was on again, a mix of chops and kicks that Gina knew would leave her bruised and sore.

It was fabulous. Gina had to struggle mightily to fend off Olivia's every move. The woman was relentless, coming at her with everything she had. If they had weapons in their hands they could both do some serious damage.

Olivia was good. Very good. More than a match for Gina, a black belt. By the time they'd sparred for about an hour, Gina was wringing wet and ready for a cool swim.

"You're not quitting on me, are you?" Olivia asked as Gina stepped out of the unofficial battle ring.

"Are you kidding? You kicked my butt. I'm wiped out."

Trace, Jake, Ryder, and Shay had taken a seat on a small hill above the sand and watched them. "Yeah," Trace said. "Don't quit now, Gina. This was just getting interesting."

"Feel free to take her on if you're so inclined," Gina said, bending over and resting her hands above her knees, trying to catch her breath.

"Hell, no," Trace said. "I'm not dumb enough to let Olivia kick my ass."

Gina laughed. Guess that meant she *was* dumb enough. That's okay. She'd enjoyed the hell out of the sparring match. When she looked up to shoot a smart retort in Trace's direction, Derek stood above them, leaning against a tree, his arms crossed over his chest.

And she once again found herself at a loss for words. How long had he been up there watching?

Furthermore, what difference did it make if he was?

Maybe he should get down here and let her take out her frustrations on him instead. Except the thought of jumping on him had nothing to do with martial arts and everything to do with straddling him and rubbing the ache between her legs against his shaft until she burst with a mind-numbing climax.

Dammit. He was slowly killing her and he didn't even know it, because she was too stupid to just tell him how she felt.

Deciding to ignore him, she turned back to Olivia and bowed her head. "You are one hell of a formidable opponent. I don't know where you got your training, but I'd love to visit your dojo sometime."

Olivia bowed in return. "You held your own quite well. I'm impressed. And you're more than welcome to visit anytime."

"I'm going to change and go for a swim," Gina said. "Anyone want to join me?" When she looked up to the hill, Derek was gone.

"Some of them are very good."

The Master inhaled the darkness, breathing in the cool, fresh scent of earth and dank moisture. "You worry too much."

The other shot him a look. "With good reason. Louis recruits only the best."

"Bah. Louis thinks he is so smart bringing these people here."

"I'm worried."

He looked to the other, shaking his head. "Why are you worrying about this? They are of no threat to us. Our numbers grow every day. We hold the power. It is Louis's and the Realm's fear that makes them do this."

"You know who these people are, don't you?"

"Yes, I know perfectly well who they are, what their connection is to us."

"Yet you don't fear them."

"No, I don't fear them. They are tiny pests and we are the great beasts who will crush them under our feet."

The other shook his head. "I hope you're right. I will leave you in charge of this."

"You go about your business. I can handle this. There is much at stake here and I have plans to make."

"A reunion for you."

"Yes." The Master's teeth gleamed in the darkness. "It has been a very long time. I am anxious for this meeting to take place. But first there is the business of eliminating these humans."

He walked through the darkness with a smile on his face, confident of his supremacy, assured of the final outcome. "They don't even know we're here. Even Louis, the great and powerful Louis, doesn't know we're here.

"The killing will be so easy."

Chapter Six

Once darkness descended, the torches were lit and everyone geared up for the start of the game.

Despite the hokiness and the camera lights shining in her face and the whole Hollywood-like atmosphere of this shindig, Gina was still excited. After last night's practice, she knew she could do well at this. All she had to do was stay focused, keep her eyes sharp, and stay on the lookout for demons.

"Remember," Derek said, giving all of them a last-minute reminder of the rules, "anyone who's marked by a demon is out of the game for the night and must report back to base immediately. Listen up for commands. We'll track your shots and kills. Good luck, and stay alert."

Each team once again prepared to enter the jungle on opposite sides. Derek stood on the sand in between them, and when he signaled them to go, they moved out in a hurry. This time, cameras followed them, filming everything.

Gina and her team stayed together for the initial trek into the jungle. God, it was humid tonight. Her clothes clung to her skin and she was sopping wet already. There was no breeze, and the only sound was their footsteps as they crunched over leaves and twigs.

Trace took the lead again, stepping slowly through the dense part of the jungle. Thick palm bushes flanked either side of the marked path. Gina expected a demon to pounce out at them any second. Her muscles tensed, finger at the ready on the trigger of her weapon.

When they entered the part of the jungle where the torches grew more sparse, it was time to split up and go hunting.

"Everyone ready?" Trace asked.

"Ready as we'll ever be," Gina answered.

"Good luck, everyone."

The moon was a little brighter tonight, which helped some, but the lack of torchlight and the tree cover overhead nearly obliterated any glow the moonlight might have cast on the ground. Gina slipped on her night-vision goggles, a cameraman staying in step with her as she hunted. She ignored him, hoping he'd eventually go film someone else.

A sharp crack to her left had her swiveling around and taking aim, letting out the breath she'd been holding when she realized it was just Jake. Dammit. She moved further into the jungle, skirting south to avoid the others. The damn demons had to be out here somewhere, just waiting for them.

She got the idea the people playing demon had gone

easy on them last night, and tonight it was going to be tougher. This was the real game.

"Anyone see anything yet?" she commed.

"Nothing," Shay replied.

Trace and Ryder came back with the same reply.

"I thought I saw a shadow, but if they're out here I can't find them," Olivia said.

"All I've seen so far is you," Jake retorted with a laugh. "Scared the shit out of me, too."

Gina grinned. At least she wasn't alone in this. Those damn demons were hiding well.

"Wait. I've got something."

Ryder's voice.

"It's too far ahead of me, heading southeast."

She was the furthest out. Had to be heading in her direction. She scanned the area, then caught a glimpse of movement. "I'm on it."

This time, he wasn't getting away. She tore off in a dead run, hating these night-vision goggles that bumped the bridge of her nose every time she jumped over something on the ground. Damn heavy things. Too bulky. But she was blind without them, and right now she needed them to track the demon.

Oh, he was trying to be so smart, hiding from her. She stepped back, realizing what he was doing. He was going to pounce. She played lost, circling around like she was looking in the wrong place for him. But she ended up sneaking up behind him, keeping her footsteps purposefully light. While he was busy watching for her, she was busy aiming, crawling on the ground around the tree.

Almost there. When she sprang, he jumped back. She shot and hit him in the chest.

"Gotcha," she whispered.

"Shit," the demon said.

"One kill, Gina," Derek announced.

Yes! The demon turned and left. Adrenaline soaring, Gina went off in search of another.

"Got one in my sights," Trace said.

"Ditto," Ryder piped up.

Now they were cooking. Suddenly, she spotted four or five of them, slipping in and out behind trees and thick foliage. She sprinted in the hopes of making another kill, grinning the whole way.

She hoped the cameraman could keep up, because she was ready for a wild night and she was determined to come out the winner.

"How are they doing?" Derek sat on the edge of the table, watching Lou enter points into his laptop while he listened in to the sounds of the team engaging the "demons."

"Good so far. Gina, Ryder, and Olivia each have one kill. Shay and Trace have points. Jake, nothing so far."

Not too bad. Not great, but they'd just gotten started. Derek purposely withheld the demons for a while, making the team hunt them out.

And Team B, of course, wasn't really on the other side of the island. They were lying in wait just outside the base camp, so they wouldn't be spotted in case someone from Team A was killed and had to report back in.

No, the only ones being tested were on the east side of the island tonight. Six newbies. Untrained and mistakenly thinking they were playing a game.

"Time elapsed?"

Lou scanned the clock on the laptop. "Twenty-five minutes."

"Thirty-five minutes left, Team A," Derek said over his mic, then switched it off. "How many of these do you intend to run?"

Lou looked up at him. "The game is set for two weeks. We'll see how it goes. Have to play it out with the other team, too, then combine some of these new folks with our trained hunters and see how they react. We'll see who gets eliminated early and who stays around past the first few days, then we'll—"

Derek waited. "We'll what?"

But Lou didn't say anything. He stared down into the computer, frowning, then he looked up and cast a strange, faraway look into the jungle. Derek was about to ask Lou what was wrong when it hit him.

His blood went cold and he shuddered. Shit. He shot off the table. "Lou."

Lou stood and turned to Derek. "I know."

Derek didn't know exactly what was up, but a feeling of deep dread overcame him, like he'd just gotten news a close relative had died or something. Damn. He'd never had the senses that Lou had, but he sure as hell felt something off-kilter right now.

"They're here," Lou said.

"What do you mean, 'they'? Who . . . oh, shit."

Lou nodded. "Call the others. Grab the weapons and get out there. I mean they're here and right now, and they're after our new team."

Derek was already on the mic to the others before Lou finished talking. The other hunters charged out of the opposite end of the jungle and Derek went to the storage bin to retrieve weapons.

The real weapons.

"I don't want to call them back in. I don't want them to move," Lou said. "Don't even alert them. They start heading back to base, the demons will attack. I know it."

Derek knew better than to second-guess anything Lou said. "Got it." He turned to his team. "Grab gear and run like hell," he commanded.

"I'll stay here and talk to the new people, try to keep them calm."

"Nance, stay here with Lou as guard," Derek said to one of his men, then turned back to Lou as he buckled on his ammo belt and grabbed his eyeshades. "Lou, you gotta tell them. You can't let them go on thinking this is a game."

"I'll handle it," Lou said, studying the laptop. "I've already closed the signal to the new people and alerted our hunters out there."

"Shit, our hunters have no weapons." What a goddamn disaster. Derek glanced over Lou's shoulder. Imagery was showing the locations of the team and their own demons. So far no sign of anything else. "Where are they? Nothing's showing up on imagery."

"I don't know. But I'll signal you. Get going."

"I'm already gone." Six others followed as he hightailed it into the jungle, his heart racing madly.

What the hell were they doing here? How had they found this location, and more importantly, how had they gotten here without Lou knowing?

"Okay, hunters. We've gotta move our asses and get to these people before the demons do."

Now they were talking actual life and death, and if Derek and his team didn't get to the others in a hurry . . .

Game over.

Something wasn't right. Gina had gotten in two more kills, and after that the demons had just . . . disappeared. No matter how deep in the assigned area she searched, she couldn't find them.

"Anyone see anything?"

"No," Shay replied. "It's gone dead quiet. Are we out of time or something?"

"I didn't hear Derek call time," Jake answered.

Gina looked at her watch. No, they still had twenty minutes left. "We're not done yet. Wonder what's going on? Derek, can you hear me?"

No answer.

"Derek, this is Gina. We've got nothing going on out here."

Again, no reply.

"I don't like this," Ryder said.

"Ditto," Trace shot back.

An eerie sense of foreboding crawled over Gina's skin,

making goose bumps pop out despite the overwhelming heat of the night. "I think we all need to meet up and head back to base," she suggested.

"Good idea," Ryder said.

"This is Lou. I need you all to remain calm."

Finally! "Lou, what's going on?"

"We have a problem. A big one. I need you all to stay quiet, meet up with the men assigned as demons, and follow them back to camp as quickly as you can."

Gina frowned and kept walking, following the lighted torches and marked tape. "What kind of problem?"

Suddenly, there was a demon in front of her. She gasped and raised her gun, which he grabbed away from her. She was about to object when he lifted his finger to his mouth. "Shhh, this isn't a game anymore and you're talking way too loud."

Okay, what the hell was going on? He lifted his sensor mask off, his hair spiked out all over and his expression ominous. He stepped closer and whispered, "We need to get back to camp ASAP. So just shut up, stay close, and follow me. Lou will explain when we get back."

Now she was really feeling wonky. Was this part of the game?

"I've got Bliss, Derek," he said into his mic. "Heading toward base now."

Why wasn't she getting this conversation in her headset? "Can you please tell me what's going on?"

"We'll fill you in when we get back. Goddammit, I wish I had a weapon." He cast a worried look to the camera guy standing next to Gina.

A weapon? What did he need a weapon for? Just then a flash of light blinded her as the camera turned directly in her face. She pulled off her night-vision goggles. "What is that camera doing in my face?"

As soon as she said it, the camera dropped to the ground. She heard it shatter and everything went black. A high-pitched scream rent the air next to her. Something warm splattered across the right side of her face and arm, but in the darkness she couldn't make it out.

"Shit," the demon guy said. "Get down, Gina, now!"

He shoved her, hard, and she went flying several feet, her goggles and weapon flinging from her hands. When she hit the ground, instinct drove her to her belly and she put her hands over her head, expecting gunshots or explosions.

Instead, she heard noises. A grunt, a thud, scuffling around her, leaves and twigs snapping as if something was being dragged.

Then, nothing.

"Hello?" she whispered, almost afraid to speak.

No response.

"Anyone there?"

Again, nothing.

Dammit, where did her goggles go? It was pitch-black and she couldn't see a damn thing. Where was everybody? Her headset was gone, too. Great. No way to even contact anyone.

Dead silence. Okay, this was *not* good. And she was almost afraid to move. Something had just happened around her, there was wet stuff on her face and she didn't know what it was, and the two guys who'd been with her a few seconds ago were now gone.

But the quiet maybe meant whatever bad thing was around had now left. Or at least wasn't standing right next to her. Goddammit, where was Derek? She couldn't very well lie there on the ground frozen with fear all night, and she wasn't about to hope someone was going to come out there and find her. Especially if it was the wrong someone.

Rising up on her haunches, she felt around the ground near her feet in search of her goggles or headset. No such luck, considering the guy had pushed her so hard. Now she was alone and blind as a bat. She couldn't even see the torches or the glow-in-the-dark tape marking the playing field.

She was lost. Alone and lost. With something really bad happening. She stood and looked around, hoping for a sign, a light, something that would give her a direction.

Nothing.

Pushing fear and frustration to the back of her mind, she focused on what she needed to do. If she chose a direction and started walking, she could end up heading miles in the wrong direction, or walk right into whatever mess she was trying to avoid.

No. Common sense told her to stay put before she ended up hopelessly lost. She couldn't be that far from the main path. Eventually someone would come along and find her, or she'd see lights or hear noises from Derek or one of the others.

She'd just stand here. In this spot. And not move at all.

She wrapped her arms around herself, chilled despite the oppressive heat.

Dammit, she was scared. And Gina was never, ever scared. Even the normal jungle sounds of bugs chirping and birds squawking had gone quiet. It was as if she was suspended in some kind of time warp, and she was isolated.

Maybe she was the only person left alive. Maybe something horrible had happened and she'd been the only one to escape.

And maybe you watch too many movies, Gina.

God, the things her mind could conjure.

She stared out into the darkness, turning herself around in a circle over and over again until she got dizzy and made herself stop. But dammit, she was afraid of something coming up behind her and grabbing her.

Wonderful. She'd just given herself a wicked case of the heebie-jeebies.

How long had she been out here?

Her watch! She scrambled to push the button, illuminating the numbers on her watch. It wasn't enough light to guide her, but at least she had something to look at besides utter blackness. It was ten minutes past the time the game would have ended, so she'd been standing out there roughly a half hour. It seemed a lot longer.

Where was everyone?

Somebody please come get me. Memories washed over her of another night spent alone in the dark. Years ago, the night her mother disappeared. She tried to block them out, to forget, but there they were, as fresh and as painful as they'd been twenty years ago.

She'd been only eight years old at the time, and when she woke up thirsty in the middle of the night and went in search of her mother, she was gone. Not in her bed, or in the bathroom or kitchen. Nowhere. She'd panicked, not knowing what to do, with no one to call, and had ended up huddled in her mother's bed with the covers tucked to her chin. Every creak in the old house was a monster coming to get her. She waited all through the night, shaking and crying, hoping and praying her mother had just run to the store or something. She'd be back. She wouldn't just up and leave like that. Not without taking Gina with her.

She'd never seen her mother again.

Now the darkness closed in on her, that same clawing fear surrounding her. But this time she wasn't eight years old, and she refused to give in to the terror. She straightened her shoulders and reminded herself she was a grown woman now. A strong woman. Not an abandoned child.

They would come for her. Someone would come for her this time.

Then she heard it. Footsteps crunching on leaves. To her left. Hope warred with abject terror. Was it a good guy or a bad guy? She didn't know whether to call out or hold a deathly silence.

"I thought I'd never find you out here."

She didn't recognize the voice. God, she could hear her own heart pounding in her ears. Could he hear it, too?

"Are you okay? Louis sent me."

Exhaling, she said, "Yes! Oh my God, I thought you'd

never find me." She stepped toward the voice in the darkness.

"It's okay. I'm here now. You're safe. Come with me."

"Where's your light? Your weapon? How can you see out here?"

"Great night vision," he said, moving in close enough now that she could make out his features. Tall, well built, with a nearly shaved head and pale blue eyes, he smiled at her, but his smile didn't reach his eyes. They were almost vacant. Weird as hell. Maybe it was just the shock.

"Take my hand and I'll get you out of here," he said.

She slipped her hand in his, then jerked it back. Goddamn. His hand was ice cold. She shivered, her entire body freezing.

No. Something wasn't right. She backed up a few steps.

"Come with me," he said again.

She shook her head. Her gut instinct told her this wasn't one of the good guys.

His smile died and he frowned. "You're supposed to come with me. Now. I won't hurt you if you cooperate."

Oh, shit. He definitely wasn't one of the good guys.

"Get away from her, you sonofabitch."

She whirled around at the sound of a familiar voice. Derek's. He hit her with a flashlight, illuminating the area around him. Tears filled her eyes and she choked back a sob. Without even thinking of the man behind her, she sprinted over to Derek. As dark as it was, he was wearing wraparound sunglasses. And sporting one hell of a futuristic-looking kick-ass weapon in his hand. She'd never been happier to see anyone in her entire life. She wanted to throw her arms around him and hug him, but he hadn't yet taken his eyes off the guy.

"Do you know how many of us are here?" the blue-eyed man asked. "The Realm doesn't have a chance."

"Neither do you, asshole." Derek glanced at Gina. "Get behind me, turn around, and cover your eyes. Don't ask questions."

She wasn't going to. Not now, anyway. She hurried behind him, crouched down, and covered her eyes. In an instant a flash of intense light surrounded her and she heard a loud wailing groan, then a horrible sizzling sound, followed by the acrid smell of burning flesh.

Oh, God, what the hell was going on?

"You can open your eyes now, Gina."

Almost afraid to look but too curious not to, she removed her hands and stood, peering around Derek's shoulder.

There, in front of him, where the blue-eyed man had once stood, was a melted pile of flesh and bone.

She moved to Derek's side and saw a white trail of smoke coming from that strange-looking weapon in Derek's arms.

Holy hell, Derek had incinerated him!

Chapter Seven

Derek knew the expression of shock. Gina's eyes went huge, and even with his night-vision shades he could see her face whiten and realized she was going to drop. She was no sissy, but the scene before her was hard for even the strongest stomach to take.

"Oh, shit," she whispered, her gaze riveted on the melted remains of the demon. "Oh, shit." She turned to him and grabbed his arm. "One of your demon dudes—he was with me, along with the camera guy. Then everything went black. I heard scuffling, and it went quiet. I couldn't find either of them after that."

That explained the dark spots on her face: blood. Which didn't bode well for either of his men, dammit.

When she started weaving, he tossed the laser over his right shoulder and slid his arm around her waist. "Hang in there, baby, it's okay."

"It's not okay," she said, her voice shaky as she stared at the blob on the ground. "Is that the guy . . . ?"

"Yeah. Only it's not a guy. Or it wasn't a guy. Not a human guy, anyway."

She tilted her head up and shot him a look of utter confusion. "What? Of course he was human."

"No. He wasn't."

"I don't understand."

At least she wasn't fainting on him. Bewildered, definitely. But not about to pass out. They were making headway. Now he just had to get her back to base camp without having to answer a lot of questions.

"Derek?"

"Yeah."

"What the hell is that mess over there? Really."

Christ. Explanations were Lou's area. And they didn't have time for this anyway. "A demon."

Her brows lifted. "You mean one of the guys portraying demons in the game?"

"No. A demon."

She moved away from him then, though he noticed she didn't move toward the smoking pile of liquid demon garbage, but rather away from it. "Seriously. Did you just kill someone?"

"No. I killed some*thing*." He scratched his brow. "Look. It's complicated. I mean *really* fucking complicated. And there are probably more of these things out here. Our prime objective right now is to get back to base before we run into any more of them. I suggest you save the questions until we get back. Lou will tell you everything. I promise."

Her eyes were wide and searching as if she expected another one to jump out of the bushes. But she hadn't screamed or fainted or puked. He gave her big points for that.

"Okay. I really would like to get out of here now."

"I'm with you there. Let's go."

They trekked back to camp in virtual silence, Gina walking close enough to brush shoulder to shoulder with him. Okay, she was still spooked. He reached for her hand. She clasped onto his like it was a lifeline in a squall, damn near cutting off his circulation. When he glanced over at her, she offered up a tentative, apologetic smile.

Even if it was terror on her part that made her reach out to him, it made good sense to hold her hand. He had to lead the way through the path.

Oh, screw it. He just damn well liked feeling her hand in his. He didn't get to play the protective sort very often and he found himself enjoying it.

Especially protecting Gina.

They arrived back at base camp in about ten minutes without incident. Whatever attack had occurred was apparently over, at least for now, because they didn't run into any more demons along the way. Though he kept his weapon up and ready for any potential encounter.

Now it was time to count heads and figure out who was missing.

The new people were all there, looking shell-shocked and confused as hell. After a quick count, he noted two of his hunters were missing, no doubt the two Gina had spoken of being attacked.

Goddammit. They couldn't afford to lose any.

"We're two down, Lou. Griffith and James. They were with Gina," he reported, keeping his weapon close as they entered the tent where everyone was gathered. He assigned four of the hunters to stand guard at the perimeter.

They had until sunup. Once dawn hit, they were safe.

Lou cast his gaze downward, his shoulders slumped as he sighed. "That is deeply unfortunate." When he looked up again, his eyes were filled with sorrow. "I didn't know they were here."

"I know." Which was unusual. Lou always knew.

Derek almost asked Lou if he was slipping, but withheld his question.

"I had feelings, but I brushed them aside. I just didn't think they'd show up here," Lou said. "I should have been ready for anything."

"You're not infallible, Lou. None of us are."

"I should be."

Derek shook his head. Lou was harder on himself than anyone he knew. Sometimes it made Derek feel better just to know Lou was human and able to make mistakes like the rest of them.

Gina slumped into one of the chairs around the table, looking just as exhausted as the rest of the new people. Even the other hunters were wiped out, confused by all this. Derek jammed his fingers through his hair and looked at Lou. "Game's over. We have a real problem here. We were ambushed, hit unarmed. This shouldn't have happened."

"Someone going to tell us what the hell is going on?" Ryder asked.

He knew that one was coming.

"Give us a minute here, Ryder. We'll explain it all." He looked to Lou. "We've got to get these new folks up to speed, and now. The time for deciding whether or not they're in the game is over. They're in the game or they're not. And if they're not, you need to do your thing and get them off this island so we can go after the demons."

"Demons? What demons? Aren't the guys playing demon standing right here?" Shay looked around at the hunters in designated demon attire.

"No. They're hunters."

"Hunters. Okay, I don't understand any of this," Shay said, looking around at the others. "Did I miss something?"

Lou stood and held his hands up. "Please, everyone, hold your questions for now. I promise to explain everything about what happened tonight."

Gina braced herself for what was to come, though she already knew she wasn't going to like it.

"You were brought here under false pretenses," Lou started.

Two of the men on the other team, Rafe and Dalton, fired up the lanterns, the flickering lights not helping one bit. Instead, shadows loomed as giant specters over the tent, hovering like creatures about to pounce. Despite the humidity that refused to dissipate, Gina shivered.

Louis's lips formed a thin line. He lifted his chin, circling the main table to stand in front of the group. "The show was a setup. The cameras and filming were brought in to fool you into thinking you were doing a reality show.

We didn't expect to find actual demons here. They weren't supposed to be here. It was just supposed to be training, testing to see if you could handle the real thing." Louis skimmed his hand through his thick white hair and stared at the tabletop. "It wasn't supposed to happen yet."

Gina frowned, this whole nightmare of the unknown making her skin crawl. She could barely sit still. "You mean demons?"

"Yes."

Jake snorted. "Get serious. There's no such thing."

"You didn't see what I saw tonight," Gina shot back.

"Then why don't you tell us what you saw?" Jake challenged, his voice rising with a nervous tremble.

"He looked just like a regular guy. It was dark. At first I thought he was one of Lou's men who'd come out to find me and bring me back. But when he took my hand it was . . . ice cold. And though he looked human, there was something in his eyes . . ." She shuddered at the memory. "When I pulled my hand away, he tried to force me to go with him. Derek came then. The guy said we were all going to die. He charged at us and Derek killed him."

"You killed a man?" Shay's eyes widened as she looked to Derek.

"Not a man," Derek corrected, his voice low. "A demon."

"Let me explain," Louis said. "Everyone here, with the exception of Gina, Ryder, Jake, Shay, Olivia, and Trace, works for me."

"Even the other team?" Gina glanced at the others, who she had thought of as their competitors.

"Yes. Even the other team. Dalton, Mandy, Punk, Rafe,

Rico, and Linc are all hunters. Just like the men posing as the camera crew and those who posed as the demons you were hunting. They all work for me."

"Who are you people?" Jake asked in a near whisper.

"I'm going to tell you a story that you'll probably think unbelievable. I am what we call a Keeper, part of a secret organization known as the Realm of Light. Our kind have been in existence for centuries, since the time of Christ.

"We were given great power to guard the gates between Heaven and Hell, to maintain the balance between good and evil. Our goal, in essence, is to keep evil from entering our world. Demons, like the kind who showed up on the island tonight. We fight them, we kill them, and we send them back where they came from."

Gina's jaw dropped and she looked around at the others. They, too, were shocked.

"There were a select dozen chosen, our bloodlines gifted with a special sight to recognize demons. This gift was passed down generation upon generation for centuries, our children taught in the same ways, given the secrets of the Realm to pass down to their children, to hunt demons and become Keepers."

"This is preposterous!" Jake cut in, wide-eyed as he looked around at the rest of them. "Come on, this isn't real, don't you see that?"

Louis continued, ignoring Jake's outburst. "Each generation is trained by the elders of the Realm of Light, brought into the secret society and sworn by oath to always protect the gates between our world and the demon world."

Gina couldn't believe this. Demons couldn't exist, yet what she had seen out there tonight was real. What she felt when that thing had touched her hand hadn't been human.

"This is too far-fetched to be believable," Jake said. "If there were demons out there, wouldn't the world's governments know about it?"

Louis sighed and gripped the back of the chair. "The Realm of Light is unknown to any government or world military organization. It has always been that way, run without government or military influence or interference. We must operate under the radar, if you will. Governments change power too frequently, and are too slow to be of any help to us. We could not ever afford to involve politics and bureaucracy in what we do. It is simply too risky. They don't understand it, they can't fight it like we do."

"But their knowledge, their firepower," Trace suggested.

"Are useless," Derek answered. "Trust me. Trust Lou. This organization has remained secret for good reason. We have to fight the demons on their own ground and without interference. Only we can do this."

Louis nodded. "We know how to fight them, and we have the resources to respond more quickly. As it is, even we're too slow sometimes in modifying our tactics and weaponry as quickly as they do. In the meantime, demons are increasing their numbers. Killings are becoming more frequent and the demons are spiriting away humans at a rather alarming rate. Something needs to be done, and needs to be done now.

"My intent in inviting all of you here was to recruit you to join the organization and help us in our battle. To train and prepare you for what is to come."

"Why us?" Trace asked.

"Because you all have the physical capability of becoming hunters."

"Wait a minute," Gina said, shaking her head. "You said that the Keepers, the demon hunters, were of this pure bloodline. If that's the case, why us? Are all these people here of your untainted bloodline? Are we part of the same lineage?"

"Uh, no." Lou cast a look at Derek.

"Tell them, Lou," Derek said, crossing his arms and leaning his hip against the table. "They have a right to know the reason they were chosen."

Gina so did not like the sound of this.

Chapter Eight

Derek braced himself for the reaction to Lou's revelation, feeling shitty for all these people, knowing what they were about to hear was going to shatter them. His gaze shot to Gina. He wished he could hold her hand, do something to comfort her, but he knew she was just going to have to ride it out like the rest of them. There was nothing he could do to make it easier for her.

"Your paths have all crossed with the Sons of Darkness," Lou explained.

"Who are the Sons of Darkness?" Olivia asked.

"The demons," Lou said. "They are who we have spent centuries battling. They are, quite literally, descendants of the great evil."

"So what you're saying is the Sons of Darkness are the sons of the devil?" Trace asked, his voice indicating utter disbelief.

"No, though they are descendants. The great evil has

sired many over the centuries. The branches are too complex to follow."

"Holy Mother of God," Shay said, crossing herself. "This cannot be happening."

"I'm afraid it is," Lou said. "The Sons of Darkness are real."

"How have our paths crossed with them?" Gina asked, almost afraid to ask the question, but needing to know the answer.

"Through some unknown genetic anomaly or heavenly curse, we don't really know which, for the past few centuries, female demons have been born sterile. This resulted in a fast regression of their numbers. As a result, the Sons of Darkness began capturing human females and using them to breed demon children."

"Human females?" Trace asked. "You mean running off with young human women and using them to breed with demons?"

"Yes."

"Holy shit," Gina said, feeling a chill skitter up her spine.

"I don't think I want to hear any more," Jake muttered.

"I know you don't. But you must, because this is how the demons tie into all of you." Lou inhaled deeply, then exhaled, his shoulders slumping as if a great weight sat on them. "You all have mothers who went missing when you were very young."

"What does that have to do with—oh God," Gina said, her hand flying to her throat as she made the connection. "Oh, God, no. That's not true."

Derek winced as he watched Gina pale and tears glitter in her eyes over the realization of what Lou said.

"No. Not my mother. That's a lie," she said.

"I'm afraid it's very true," Lou said. "All of our hunters here, with the exception of Derek, experienced the loss of their mothers through kidnapping by demons."

"How do you know this?" Olivia asked.

"My connection to the Sons of Darkness is strong, but it took us a while to figure out what they were up to. When reports of so many unexplained disappearances of young women started coming in, we investigated on our own and confirmed the presence of demons in each of your cases."

Ryder stood and pushed back from his chair. "This is bullshit."

"No," Shay said, shaking her head and whispering. "No."

Olivia didn't say a word. Neither did Trace.

"See what I mean?" Jake said, his voice rising as he stood and lit a cigarette. "I told you this was all a lie! My mother's dead!"

Lou shook his head. "No, Jake. Your mother didn't die. She was captured by demons and she—"

"No! She was not captured! Don't say it!"

"Are you trying to tell us our mothers were kidnapped from our homes and used as breeding machines for some kind of evil creatures from hell?" Gina asked.

Derek saw the horror and disbelief on Gina's face, on all their faces, could well imagine what was going through their minds. He knew their pain, knew what they were going through, because he'd been there. Only it wasn't his mother who'd been taken by the demons.

"All your mothers disappeared?" Olivia finally asked, looking around at the others.

Gina nodded. So did Trace, Ryder, Shay, and finally Jake.

"Christ," Ryder said, shaking his head and staring at the ground. "Unfuckingbelievable."

"So some of these demons running around could be our little brothers," Trace said with a sarcastic smile.

"Oh, that's so not funny," Shay said, swiping away tears. "That's not funny at all."

"I know this is hard for all of you to take in, and believe me, this is not the way I wanted to break it to you. But I had no choice, given that the demons showed up so unexpectedly."

"Just what exactly was your plan, Lou?" Ryder asked. "What was this fucking game all about anyway?"

Derek stood. "I can tell you that. Our plan was to test you, see if you could handle the physical aspects of becoming a hunter."

"And if we couldn't?" Gina asked.

"You'd be eliminated from the game and sent off the island without ever knowing what was really up."

"And if we managed to pass your test? Then what?"

"Then we'd have told you about the Realm of Light and the Sons of Darkness, and invited you to become a demon hunter."

"What if we refused?" Jake challenged.

"Then I'd have erased your memory of what you'd

been told, and the only thing you'd remember is your time playing the game and that you'd lost," Lou said quietly.

Gina sat up in her chair, not sure she'd heard that right. "What?"

Lou hinted at a smile. "I have the power to give a psychic hypnotic suggestion. Those who leave the Realm of Light or who decide not to join us will have their memories selectively erased. It's perfectly harmless, I assure you."

"Who the fuck are you people?" Jake asked, tossing his cigarette on the ground and stabbing it out with the toe of his shoe. He backed away from the table and crossed his arms over himself.

"Dear God," Gina said. "This is unreal. This whole thing is out of this world." She wanted to run away, to hide, go home and curl up into a ball and pretend none of this had happened. It was all a bad dream. Her mother hadn't been taken away from her by demons. She wasn't being used as a breeding machine for some evil creatures. She wasn't. Gina refused to think of her mother that way. Fresh tears pooled in her eyes, but she blinked them back, unwilling to open the floodgate of memories to the only person she'd allowed herself to love.

"You are all insane," Jake said, his hands shaking as he reached for another cigarette. "I'm not staying here. I want out and I want out now."

"That is, of course, your choice, Jake, as it is all of yours," Lou said. "Your memories of what happened tonight will be erased and the ship will return you to the mainland,"

"I don't want my memories erased," Jake said, his mouth set in a firm line.

"I'm afraid you won't have a choice in the matter," Lou said.

Jake looked to Lou, then to Derek. "You'll force me?"

"It's not like that. We just can't afford to let anyone leave the Realm of Light armed with knowledge about us. You won't be harmed, I assure you," Lou said.

Gina closed her eyes for a second. How easy it would be to forget this, to go back to her life the way it was, to pretend this had all been nothing more than a game. She wouldn't even remember any of it, would never know what had really happened to her mother.

She could forget again.

But when had she ever turned her back on a challenge? How many years had she wondered what had happened to her mother, had she wondered who had taken her—because she knew in her heart her mother had been kidnapped—she'd never have abandoned Gina of her own accord. How many years had she wished for vengeance against those who had ripped her mother away from her, and her own childhood along with it, her sense of security and belonging?

"And what if we decide to stay?" she found herself asking.

"Then we'll train you, arm you, and you'll become a demon hunter," Derek replied with an upward curve of his lips.

"What about our lives back home?" Shay asked.

"You won't have one any longer," Lou said. "The life of

a demon hunter is a full-time one. But you will be fully supported here. I have the funding to take care of all of you. We travel wherever the demons are, and we're on the road a lot. It's not easy, and it's damned dangerous. I won't lie to you. You have to make the choice yourself to do this. No one will make it for you."

"Demon killers. Fucking unbelievable," Ryder said. "I know, I've said that already." He shook his head and stood. "I'm in. Fucking asshole demons. I don't even need to think about it. I need some goddamn air. I'll be back." He stood and left the tent.

Olivia stood next. "I'd be honored." She bent her head toward Lou. "If you'll excuse me, I could also use a few minutes before we hear anymore."

After she left, Trace stood. "Better than rock climbing, and I'd like some goddamn revenge myself. I'm in, too." He shook Lou's hand first, then Derek's. "Looking forward to kicking some demon ass. Now I need a beer."

Gina cracked a smile as she watched him leave, then looked at Shay, who was probably the most shell-shocked of all of them.

"I don't know what to think of all of this," Shay admitted. "For twenty years I thought my mom left on a business trip and just decided not to come back, that she didn't want to come home. She was always so busy. Too busy for a family, really. I watched my dad shrivel up and die over losing her." Her lower lip trembled and tears pooled in her eyes.

Gina's heart wrenched for Shay, because she knew that anguish. Dammit, she didn't want to feel that pain again, wanted to tune out the empathy, pretend her own heart wasn't breaking all over again.

"And now I find out that some . . . demons took her away from me and my dad? That she didn't have a choice? That I could have had a chance at growing up with a mother and she was taken away from me? I don't like it. It pisses me off, dammit." Shay sniffed and stood. "I've spent my whole life wondering what I wanted to be when I grew up. Well, now I know. I want to be a demon hunter. I want to kill them all. I don't have anything to go back to. Count me in. And I need a freakin' tissue." She turned and left.

Gina only wished she could make an emotional admission like that. Instead, she was frozen inside, still unable to come to grips with the turmoil within. What did she want to do?

"You still want to leave, Jake? Are you going to turn your back on what they did to your mother? Or are you going to stand with us and fight?" Lou asked.

Jake opened his mouth to speak, but then Derek asked, "Have you seen the weapons we kill these fuckers with?"

"Uh, no. What weapons?"

"There's another reason we brought you here, Jake. We're quite impressed with your mastery of lasers."

Gina watched the play of emotions cross Jake's face. Shrugging disinterest at first, then curiosity. "Are you shitting me? You use lasers?"

Derek grinned. "We use weapons our own government doesn't even use. Join us, and we'll knock your socks off. No shit."

"I don't believe you."

"Gina, tell Jake what happened to the demon I killed out there."

Gina shrugged. "Some kind of weapon I've never seen before. He told me to cover my eyes. There was a flash of light. After that, all that was left of the demon was a quivering, smoking blob on the ground."

"Holy shit!" Jake said, an excited grin sprouting on his face. "Tell me more."

"It's pointless to inform you further if we must erase your memory," Lou said. "The more knowledge you have, the more difficult it becomes to eradicate."

Jake chewed his lip and took out another cigarette, looking first to Lou, then to Derek. "They really took my mom?"

"They really did," Lou said.

"Join us, Jake," Derek said. "We need you."

Jake nodded. "I really wanna see those weapons. I'll stay."

"Excellent!" Lou said, taking Jake's hand. "You won't regret it."

Crushing out his last cigarette, Jake said, "I need another pack. I'll be back."

Gina realized she hadn't yet committed, that she was the only one left.

"I'll be back in a little while," Lou said, slipping out of the tent.

"Gina," Derek said to her, "you have some scratches on your neck and the back of your shoulder. Did that demon hurt you?"

"I do?" She touched her neck. "Oh. No. He only held my

hand and then I pulled away. Those probably happened when I was pushed away by one of your hunters. I hit the ground pretty hard. The demon never touched me."

Derek blew out a breath. "Good. But still, some of those look pretty deep. Come with me to the first-aid shack. You need a walk and some fresh air anyway."

He was probably right. She stood and followed him across the beach, grateful for the beacon of his flashlight. Suddenly, the darkness didn't offer the peace it once had. Monsters lurked there now, just as they had all those years ago, the night her mother disappeared.

Oh, God. Demons were in her house that night.

She shook her head, cleared her mind, refusing to think about it anymore.

The shack was a short distance from the beach, a small, boxy room containing all the medical supplies, one small examination table, and a chair.

"Hop up," he said, grabbing the kit and setting his weapon nearby.

She slid onto the table and waited, drumming her fingers on the tabletop, feeling every inch of how small this room was with just her and Derek inside. He tore open an antiseptic towel and wiped her face and neck, using slow, tender strokes along her cheek and throat.

"Shook you up pretty bad tonight, didn't it?" he asked as he worked closely.

"Me? No, I'm okay."

"You don't have to play tough girl with me. I've seen stuff that left me puking in alleys, Gina. And I'm the toughest person I know," he said with a slight curve of his lips as he straightened and faced her. "This is some scary shit, and most of it damned unbelievable."

"Yeah." She couldn't bring herself to look at him, instead deciding to study her boots.

"I saw my first demon when I was ten years old."

Her gaze shot to his. "You did?"

"Yeah. I woke up when I heard a sound in my bedroom, and there it was. Ugly motherfucker. Big and nasty and goddamn did it stink."

Eyes wide, she asked, "What was it doing in your bedroom?"

"Kidnapping my little brother."

Chapter Nine

Now what in hell possessed Derek to tell Gina that story? He'd never told anyone about Dominic's kidnapping. The only one who knew was Lou. Maybe it was the lost, lonely-little-girl expression on her face that just tore his guts out.

He felt something for her, something way more than he felt for the others, and he damn well knew it.

"Demons kidnapped your brother?"

"Yeah." He opened the antibiotic ointment and spread some on the scratches on Gina's neck.

"Why?"

"Hell if I know." Circling around to her left, he adjusted the light to the back of her shoulder and opened a cleansing wipe.

Gina craned her neck to look at him. "Derek, what happened to your brother?"

"Don't know. Never saw him again." He swiped away

the blood and grit from her wound. It was fairly deep and would need further cleansing.

"Your mom and dad?"

"Dad wasn't around by then. He'd . . . taken off. Don't know what really happened to him. My mom said my brother died suddenly. She kept telling me I had a bad dream."

Gina pulled away from him. "She lied to you?"

"Gina, I can't work on you if you keep moving."

"Dammit, Derek, talk to me. What happened?"

He sighed, knowing he should never have brought this up. Instead, he reached for the hydrogen peroxide and another cleansing wipe. "I still don't know why she lied. I know what I saw, though. And my mother was never the same after. We moved right away. She said Nic was dead, but it was obvious she was scared shitless about something. Changed our names and we left town in a hurry. She said it was to keep my dad from finding us, that he was a bad person who would hurt us if he found us. I figured he was on the run from the law or something. She was pretty much mentally unstable from that time onward, could barely hold a job. By the time I was sixteen I was working to support us while trying to finish up school."

Gina sucked in her lower lip and shook her head. "Oh, Derek, I'm so sorry."

He shrugged. "Don't be. I survived. It made me tough. She was sick, mentally and physically; died when I was eighteen. I joined the Navy and straightened myself out."

"My God, what you went through, though. What you saw as a child."

She reached for his face, cupping his cheek and rubbing the palm of her hand across the rough beard stubble.

The last goddamn thing he needed right now was her pity. And her touch made him hard, dammit. He took her wrist and pulled her hand away. "Don't do that."

"Why not?"

Because you look gorgeous and vulnerable right now. And because fucking you in the first-aid tent when we're in the midst of demon hell isn't a really smart idea. "Because I need to fix up this wound on your shoulder. Turn around."

"Oh."

She pivoted and he finished cleaning the wound. Okay, maybe she was a tough girl. She didn't even flinch when he poured hydrogen peroxide into the deep cut, though she did wince.

"This could probably stand a stitch or two."

"I'll live. Maybe I'll get a tattoo to cover the scar. Make me look like a warrior."

He smiled at that. "You *are* a warrior. You've already survived your first battle with a demon."

"I didn't do anything."

"You lived through it. That's a lot. Your instincts were right on and you pulled away from it."

"His hand was ice cold."

"Good instinct. See?"

"Thanks."

"Though you would look sexy with a tattoo right here," he said, circling the area around the cut with his finger.

She shivered and shot him a look over her shoulder that

made his cock take notice. Damn, even in the midst of chaos and demons, she made him hot.

Their gazes locked and before he knew what was happening, he was bending down to press his lips to hers. Maybe it was just a need to offer comfort, maybe it was just the pain shadowing her eyes that got to him. And maybe he just wanted her and there wasn't any other reason.

She came off the table and damn near threw herself in his arms. He tightened his hold around her, drawing her close as if he needed to shelter her, protect her from the demons around them.

Because the demons *were* still around. On the island, within the island, somewhere close. Instinctively, Gina had to know that. Maybe she was kissing him with such wild abandon because of fear, because of stress, because she wanted to shut out what she'd seen and heard tonight. Maybe she was molding her body against his and digging her nails into his back because she was trying to crawl inside him for comfort and safety.

Honestly, he didn't really care, he was just damn grateful that she was. He slanted his mouth across hers and deepened the kiss, gladly taking whatever she was willing to give. And when he came down over her she didn't protest, just wrapped her legs around him and lifted her hips, whimpering into his mouth.

He realized then what she needed, and why, and how important it was that this be for Gina right now. What he needed could wait.

Only three words rolled through Gina's mind as

Derek's firm cock pressed insistently against her soft, aching center.

Please. Don't. Stop. Not this time. She wanted no talk, no interruption, nothing to keep them apart.

God, she needed this between them, this joining. Maybe it was just to forget they were in the middle of some kind of unbelievable madness. She needed human contact, an act of complete normalcy between a man and a woman. When he reached up and cupped her cheeks, sliding his tongue so tenderly against hers, she ached so badly she wanted to cry.

She never let anyone get close. The emotional scars left from her mother's departure had left holes deep inside that she'd long ago sealed up. And those were places she never let anyone touch. No, what she craved right now was the sensation of a man's hands on her body. Like the way Derek caressed her now, dragging the straps of her tank top down her arms. Pure, normal, and wholly without any history between them. No past hurts or remembrances. For a while, she could block out everything else tonight had dredged up.

She shuddered as his lips moved from her mouth to her neck, licking with insistent strokes that made her crave those same sensations much, much lower. Dear God, he could make her come in an instant.

The air inside the small shack was thick with heat. So hot she could barely breathe. Moisture beaded between her breasts, and when Derek pulled down her bra and a shot of air wafted over them, she almost sighed in relief.

But that relief soon turned to steamy torment as he covered the tip of one nipple with his mouth.

She whimpered and arched, filling his mouth with the aching crest, burying her fingers in his thick, dark hair. The harsh light above the table glared at her. She wished for moonlight and cooling ocean breezes, but no way in hell was she moving. Emotions and physical sensation at fevered pitch, she wanted this right here, right now.

She'd take the tiny, heat-filled shack, the cruel overhead light. She'd take any inconvenience as long as he didn't stop sucking at her nipple. Pleasure shot between her legs. Instinct drove her own hand there to massage the ache, but he grabbed her wrist, intercepting her. She looked up to find him staring at her, his eyes gleaming dark gray.

"Uh-uh," he whispered, his voice tight. "That's mine."

He skimmed her belly, lifting her shirt out of the way so he could get to her shorts. With deft fingers and in only seconds he had unbuttoned and unzipped her shorts, sliding one hand under her butt to lift her up while jerking the material over her hips with the other.

Her shirt and sports bra were gathered around her ribs and her shorts and panties pooled on the floor. And he still had his damn clothes on.

"Derek," she whispered, reaching for the hard bulge straining the zipper of his dark pants.

"Later," he said, pushing her back down and leaning over to capture her mouth again. With relentless strokes he coaxed a moan from her with his teasing lips. His mouth was soft, his lips full, his tongue like wicked velvet as he licked against hers. Hot moisture trickled between her legs as desire coiled tight and hot within her.

Then Derek was palming her, his hand cool against her flaming heat.

The sensation was so unexpected, so erotic, she lifted her hips off the table and met his hand as he stroked her, whimpering into his mouth as he rubbed the swollen nub against the heel of his hand.

She was panting. Panting! When his fingers slipped inside her, his hand still making contact with the tight bud of nerve endings, she tore her mouth from his and cried out, knowing she shouldn't, realizing someone could be walking by the shack and hear them. But God, it was so good, and she couldn't help herself.

"Do you scream when you fuck, Gina?"

Her eyes shot open. He was leaning over her, watching her as his fingers moved rhythmically inside her. It was too intimate like this. She looked away.

"Look at me."

His voice was soft, yet insistent, his fingers coaxing, gentle, his palm rubbing her back and forth and making her insane. How could she not respond? She turned her head and looked at him.

His face was harsh, the lines on the outside of his eyes more pronounced as he watched her with an expression akin to pain. She glanced down his rock-hard body, wondering why he wasn't inside her yet.

"I want you to come for me, Gina. I want to feel you squeeze my fingers, want to watch your face when you let go."

And still, he moved his fingers inside her, making her wetter, making her lift to meet his hand as he drove more insistently against her.

"That's it, baby. Show me how much you want it."

She bit down on her bottom lip, feeling the tension coiled tight within her. She'd never done this before, given this much of herself to a man. Yet Derek inspired this level of trust, this intimacy she craved to share. And goddamn, she needed this.

"Let go, Gina."

She did, reaching down with both hands to grasp his wrist as she tightened, then flew. And she never once took her eyes off him as she came. He bent down and took her scream into his mouth, allowing her to let loose and cry out as her climax poured over her and she shuddered on the table. He held her close, sheltering her with his body while she trembled through an almost unbearable orgasm.

And even after, when the quakes subsided, when she felt raw and naked, he still stroked her, held her, lifted her and helped her right herself and find her clothes.

"Wait," she whispered. "What about you?" She looked down at him. So hard, a rigid outline against the zipper of his pants.

"No time." He smiled, but there was no regret, no irritation in his smile.

She'd never expected anything like this from a man like Derek. But somehow he'd known exactly what she needed.

She wasn't about to question how or why he knew.

"The attack went well," the Master said to them, walking along the dark cavern. "They were unprepared for us."

It couldn't have gone better, actually. If he'd wanted to, he could have wiped them all out tonight. Oh, it would have been too, too easy. They had been unarmed, running through the jungle playing with weapons that had no power to harm. If Louis had not sent his hunters out in such a hurry, they could have at least taken the women. Sadly, they had lost one of their own. A small price to pay.

But it was his desire to toy with them a bit, play the game. That was why they were all on this island, wasn't it? To play a game?

He had taken a couple of their hunters, and that satisfied him.

"Master, why did you pull us back?"

Whipping around, he growled at the demon. "Do not *ever* question me!" In an instant a human hand turned to a claw and a face became a bloody pulp of shredded skin. The demon crawled over to the corner, whimpering. The others backed away, cowering in fear.

Just as they should.

Addressing the others, he said, "None of you may question me. There is a plan, and it is my plan. And it will be executed on my orders in the time frame I desire. Does anyone else wish to second-guess me?"

Of course, there was silence. He nodded and walked away, breathing in the fear and dismay from above.

Turmoil, terror, shock. Ah, yes, being soaked in those emotions strengthened him.

He knew exactly what he was doing. Tonight was merely giving notice to Louis and the others that they had arrived.

It was a declaration of war.

A war he intended to win.

Chapter Ten

Derek downed his second cup of coffee and waited for the rest of the hunters to show up so they could get started. The sun was straight overhead and hot and humid as hell.

Brand-new day. Brand-new battle plan.

Lou never did let them reconvene last night. After Derek and Gina left the first-aid shack and found him, Lou decided everyone had been through enough and they all should go back to their bungalows and process the information they'd learned. They'd meet again in the afternoon.

Derek and the other hunters had buried the two they'd lost and departed without a word to each other. This wasn't new territory for them—they'd done it before. There really was nothing to say. They all knew it could have been any of them. This was what they did. There was no time for tears or wallowing in sympathy.

You fight demons, sometimes you don't come out on the winning end. They all knew it, accepted it, and moved on.

So Derek had said his quiet good-byes to two men he had called friends, and had gone to his bungalow. Which was probably a good idea, but it left him with a lot of time alone to think. He supposed he could have invited Gina to his room and picked up where they left off, but the faint shadows under her eyes told him she'd had enough, too. What she'd seen in the past twenty-four hours would have any normal woman curled up in the fetal position crying her eyes out and refusing to deal.

Then again, Gina wasn't a normal woman. That was one of the things he admired most about her.

She was tough. A fighter. A survivor. Her past told him that. She'd make a great hunter.

And last night he'd been the one who wanted to crawl into his room and curl up into the fetal position. His balls were wound up tight and aching after watching the way she came apart for him. Her body writhing underneath him, bathed in the overhead light, glistening with beads of sweat as she worked for her orgasm.

She'd felt like heated silk inside. He wanted desperately to finish what he'd started, to linger and taste her, to spend all night learning the secrets of her body, but he couldn't. Not then. But instinctively, he knew they would find that time somewhere during all this chaos.

If they lived through it.

Now he needed to focus, to get his head screwed on straight and his game plan in action.

He picked up Gina's unique scent before she even

entered the tent. How strange that he could recognize her smell. Of course, why wouldn't he? He had absorbed it by now, since it clung to him as he lay in his bed, still hard and unsatisfied, kicking himself over his act of self-sacrifice. He'd thought about jacking off, but knew it wouldn't begin to relieve the ache. He didn't want to do it himself. He wanted to be inside her, releasing the tension, feeling her surround him, bathing him with her moisture until he couldn't hold back anymore.

"Afternoon," she said as she entered the tent and grabbed a cup of coffee, then slipped into a chair across the table. Her cheeks were a cute shade of pink as she made eye contact.

"Afternoon. Sleep well?"

"I got a little," she said, then realized what she said and her cheeks darkened even further. She bent her head and dove into the coffee.

He laughed. "I'm glad one of us did."

When her gaze met his, she arched a brow and offered up a saucy smile, clearly recovered from her moment of embarrassment. "You'll get yours eventually."

"Oh, I know." Just the thought of it had him hardening and wishing they had more time alone together. He downed his cup and rose for another, adjusting his tightening pants along the way. Damned unruly dick. He had to get it under control, and fast, because everyone else was up and heading in their direction.

Most didn't look like they'd slept much, but at least they didn't appear as shell-shocked as they had the night before. Their faces fixed in determination, staring straight ahead, they ate in near silence, and when they were finished, Lou led them outside to a shaded area near the beach. Derek had already sent the other hunters to grab the weaponry and lay it out on the tables behind Lou.

"Okay, let's pick up where we left off. We have a lot to do before dark."

"I guess they only come out at night?" Ryder asked with a half quirk of his lips.

"You guess right. Demons can't tolerate heat and light, one of our advantages over them."

"Any other weaknesses we need to know about?" Gina asked.

"Let me give you some basics first," Lou started. "There's more than one kind of demon."

"Are you serious?" Shay's eyes widened as she looked to the others.

Yeah, Derek figured that would throw them. Now they had the shocked looks again. This was going to take some time to assimilate. God, he wished they had weeks, months, to train them, fill them in on what they needed to know. Instead, they had hours. Talk about trial by fire.

"When the Sons of Darkness realized their females were sterile, they quickly also realized they were at a fighting disadvantage. The more demons we killed, the fewer their numbers. So they went about evening the odds in two ways. One, to try and decrease our numbers, and two, to increase their own."

"How could they kill more of you if there were fewer of them?" Trace asked.

"By destroying our lineage," Lou said.

Derek hated when Lou had to tell this story, but knew it was necessary. It was like a light went out in Lou's eyes whenever he had to reveal what had happened to the Keepers and their families.

"For centuries, the bloodline of the Realm of Light has been slowly dying out. Only a handful of pure descendants of the Realm now exist."

"Why?" Gina asked. "What happened?"

"The Sons of Darkness began killing the wives and children of all the Keepers."

Gina gasped, knowing without asking that that included Lou's wife and children. She looked to the others, saw the shock and pain on their faces, too. So they weren't the only ones to have suffered a great loss at the hands of these demons. "My God. I'm so sorry."

Lou shrugged. "It's in the past and we deal with what we must."

Gina fought back tears, angry at herself for being so damned emotional. For someone who hadn't cried in years, she sure had gotten close in the past several hours. The misery, the torment, it was all too much. The pure evil wreaked by these creatures was unbearable. They had to be stopped.

"I hate to ask this, Lou, but why haven't the Keepers remarried and had more children?" Olivia asked.

"Some did," Lou said with a slight smile. "The Sons of Darkness managed to get to many of them and kill them, too. Several of the Keepers were too fearful of trying again, of putting women and children at risk. Quite a few of us have remained single after losing our wives and children. As a result, the Realm is aging. Which is why we have been forced to recruit hunters outside our bloodline. Though we aren't able to pass on our psychic gifts, there are other ways to battle demons. The fight must continue. If not, the Sons of Darkness will win, and we will all be lost."

For a few moments, everyone went silent.

Until Lou cleared his throat. "Let me continue. In order to increase their numbers and ensure the survival of their species long enough for them to cure their own females from whatever has caused their sterility, demons have begun capturing humans and turning them into demons."

"They're genetically altering humans?" Gina asked.

"Yes."

"Christ," Ryder said.

Derek stepped up beside Lou. "Pure demons as we know them look very much like us. Basically human in appearance, except for having exceptionally pale blue eyes and unnaturally icy cold skin. They're very fast, cunning, can communicate with humans, but they're also more vulnerable to our weaponry, which I'll show you in a little while. However, they also have fangs and claws that excrete a toxic, paralyzing substance which will freeze you on the spot. If they get a bite or gouge in your skin, you're screwed."

"Oh, nice. Like a freakin' vampire," Trace said.

"Sort of," Derek said with a shrug. "That's why you need fast reflexes. Just don't let them get close to you."

"Good advice," Gina said, shuddering. Like the monsters in the movies, only real ones.

"The half demons, the ones bred from humans, are

very similar in appearance to a human. The only difference is they're not quite as strong as the pure demons."

"So they look human, are stronger than humans, but not as powerful as the pure demons. Great," Gina said, rolling her eyes.

"Now the hybrid demons they create in their labs or whatever the hell they've got down there, the ones they genetically alter from humans they steal . . . these are big, ugly sonofabitches," Derek continued. "I don't know what the Sons of Darkness mixed up in the genetic soup for these fuckers, but it wasn't good. They're huge, incredibly strong, and they have a very thick skin. Almost like body armor. They're damned hard to kill, but they're also easier to fight because they're slow. They're the muscle for the demons. You don't want to get into a wrestling match or any kind of hand-to-hand combat with these guys because you'll lose. They can snap a man's neck with one squeeze of their hands."

Gina swallowed, not liking the thought of meeting up with one of those in the dark jungle. "Where are these things hiding?"

"They live underground, where it's cool and sheltered from the heat and light. They come out of portals in the ground, at will, whenever and wherever they choose."

"How?"

Lou smiled. "Well, if we knew that, we could predict when and where they'd show up and our jobs as hunters would be a lot easier. Portals are like heat spots that appear in locations where demons emerge. But they seem to close as soon as they open, and we have never been able to catch demons either emerging from or retreating into them. They don't seem to come and go in the same spots. But they do leave a lingering signature that we can pick up with a program I've developed on my computer."

"I'd like to see that," Jake said.

"It's a thermal imaging program. Tracks the heat signature left by the portal locations when the demons come and go. Given their aversions to high temperatures, I imagine they don't like the entry and exits much," Lou said with a slight curve of his lips. "But so far there's no telling where they'll come from, or where they'll reenter."

"Which is why you have to have sharp eyes and ears when you're out hunting," Derek added. "They're liable to pop out right behind you. And if it's a pure or half demon and he gets to you, you're dead before you even know he's there. At least with the hybrid demons you know they're coming."

"How so?" Olivia asked.

"They stink," Lou said.

Gina arched a brow. "Stink?"

"Really bad. Believe me, you'll know when they're around."

Demons with body odor. Fascinating.

"So how does this program help us in fighting them?" Gina wanted to know. "Is it only good for after the fact, to see where they've come and gone?"

"Good question, Gina," Lou said. "The imaging program can pinpoint hot spots when you're all in the jungle on the hunt, areas of ground that are heating up, indicating a demon has emerged. I can also track your locations and at least give you a few seconds' warning if one is in your immediate vicinity."

That was something, at least.

"How do we kill them?" Shay asked. "I really need to know how we kill them."

Derek grinned. "A very good question, and one I was just about to get to." He pulled the tarp off a long table behind him, revealing several incredibly foreign-looking weapons, including the one he was carrying last night when he found her. Long, black rifle with a laser sight and thicker than normal barrel, filled with a bluish liquid. Derek lifted it off the table.

"This is our UV laser light rifle. It fires a flash of concentrated ultraviolet light, which, as Gina can attest to, will melt a demon into a pile of liquid in an instant."

"Cool," Jake said, grinning.

Gina shuddered and made a face at the memory.

"That bad, huh?" Shay asked next to her, a worried expression on her face.

"Gruesome."

"It will also burn your retinas clean off if you don't have protective eyewear on when you fire it," Derek said, pulling the sunglasses he wore off the top of his head and slipping them over his eyes.

"These are specially designed to protect against the UV flash. They also serve as night-vision specs, replacing those unwieldy goggles you all wore during the game. They utilize a combination of light enhancement and thermal imaging technology, allowing you to see everything around you. And they're as light and thin as regular sunglasses."

That much was true. The lenses were nearly transparent. Gina could make out Derek's eyes quite clearly.

"You'll each get a pair. Keep them on you at all times and make certain you're wearing them when you fire the weapon. A blind demon hunter doesn't do us much good."

He set the rifle aside and grabbed what looked like an ordinary handgun, only when he dropped the clip, the bullets were thick, rubbery, and black.

"Demons have better senses than us. So higher concentrations of light or sound, like ultrasonic waves, can do some massive damage to them," Derek said with a smug grin. "These are sonic bullets. When you hit the target or the nearby vicinity of a target with one of these, they'll explode with sound waves. The waves are so strong it'll liquefy the tissue clean off a demon; their brains start to bleed and they're in some damn serious pain. It's a beautiful sight to behold."

He was actually enjoying this. As she looked to the other hunters, she saw them all grinning and nodding. Then again, after what these creatures had done, no wonder vengeance was on the mind of every demon hunter. No sympathy. They deserved none and they'd get none.

"Once again, if you get close enough to the shock wave it can also damage your hearing. You'll be given special ear devices that'll not only com you in to Lou and the other hunters, but will also protect your eardrums."

"You've thought of everything," she said.

"We try," Lou replied. "But believe me, the Sons of Darkness are as cunning as we are. As soon as we figure out how to hurt them, they come up with a way to defend it. We have to stay ten steps ahead to gain five steps on them."

"We also have sonic grenades," Derek continued, grabbing what looked like a regular grenade. "Same philosophy as the bullets, bigger sound wave in case you run into a horde of demons."

"Nice kick-ass weaponry," Gina said, itching to get her hands on the guns and grenades and take them out for a test run.

"Oh, we're not quite finished yet," Derek said, cracking a wicked grin. He reached behind the table and drew out a long, slender black rifle with a spiral barrel. "This is the microwave gun."

"What the hell does that thing do?" Ryder asked.

"Heats all the liquid in the body to boiling. Fire this at a demon and it'll shoot invisible microwaves. Cooks the sonofabitch from the inside out."

Gina's brows lifted. "You mean nuke them?"

"Holy shit," Trace said.

"Oh, I want one," Jake added.

"Every hunter does." Derek laid the weapon down on the table and turned back to them, hands on his hips.

"When you shoot at a demon, make damn sure of your target. Though both the laser and microwave weapons have pinpoint accuracy, hit your fellow hunters with one of these and it'll have the same effect on them. Be careful where you're aiming."

A sobering thought. But still, the weapons were incredible. Gina was shocked, amazed, and, she had to admit, excited as hell.

"Now that we have the weaponry, what's the plan?" Olivia asked.

"Today we'll work with you on the weapons. Tonight we'll break you up into teams with the experienced hunters and go out tracking demons."

He led them onto the beach and gave them instructions on the weapons. Of course they weren't going to be allowed to fire the real weaponry for target practice, using regular guns instead. Too bad. But still, guns were always fun to play with.

Weapons practice. Now they were talking. Gina was ready for it, primed and eager to get serious with firepower. Part of her was anxious to see how everyone else handled the weaponry and how she measured up, which was kind of amusing. Sort of like men comparing their "packages" to see whose was bigger.

She snorted.

"What's so funny?" Olivia asked.

"Just thinking about target practice today. Since we finally get to fire real weapons, you know, really get to see who's the best, it'll be like comparing dick sizes."

Olivia looked down at the ground, her lips quivering as if she fought her half-smile, then laughed softly. Shay snorted on the other side of her before saying, "Well, I can't wait to see who's got the biggest, then."

"The biggest what?" Derek asked, stepping next to them.

Gina turned and couldn't help but drink in the sight of him. He cut one hell of a figure, dressed in combat fatigues and a sleeveless shirt. Ripped to the max and sexy as hell.

She looked to Olivia and Shay, then back at Derek, and smirked. "The biggest dick."

Derek arched a brow and Gina resisted the urge to laugh. But then he made the connection when he saw the weapons in their hands. "We have some damn good marksmen here. What makes you think you'll qualify?"

She picked up the handgun in front of her, pivoted, aimed at the wooden target twenty-five yards away, and fired, hitting the bull's-eye point-blank center. When she was done, she laid the gun down, crossed her arms, and grinned.

Derek looked at the target, glanced down at the gun she'd used, then cast his gaze back at her. He nodded, crossed his arms, and said, "Nice dick."

"Thanks."

Hey, a girl had to score points where she could.

Though target practice was fun, what she really enjoyed was getting her hands on the high-tech stuff, even if they couldn't fire them yet. The real weapons were kick-ass and scary as hell. And every time she thought about wiring one up and cranking it out, she thought of demons stealing into her home in the dead of night and taking her mother, robbing her of her childhood, her warmth and security, her sense of love and belonging.

Everything had changed for her that night. The demons had screwed with her head but good twenty years ago.

And tonight, she'd start making them pay.

Chapter Eleven

"Are you scared?"

Gina looked to Shay, not sure how she should answer that question.

Dusk had begun to settle on the island, sprinkling a dusty orange glow over the horizon. She looked out to sea, then back at Shay. There was a tightness in her stomach, but she felt that before a major shoot, too. Then again, she wasn't in Hollywood and this was no movie. Any blood spilled wasn't going to be the special effects variety. "Not really," she finally replied with a casual shrug.

"How can you not be scared?" Shay asked.

"I guess because I'm more angry than frightened." Which was the truth. "So rather than cower in fright over what might happen to us, I'm going to do something about it. And stop these things from hurting anyone else."

Shay nodded, her shoulders relaxing a little. "I guess that's a good way to think about it. I'm angry about it, too. But I have to tell you, a part of me is scared as hell."

"I think that's perfectly normal," Olivia said, stepping up next to them. "We don't know what we're facing, and it's possible we could die out there."

"Oh, that makes me feel *so* much better." Shay sighed.

Olivia offered a soft smile. "Sorry. What I meant was, if you're prepared for the possibility of death, it makes you more aware of the things you need to do to avoid it. If you don't have a little fear about this whole situation, then you're not normal."

Gina supposed she wasn't normal, then, because she refused to let fear creep into her thoughts, refused to acknowledge that night so long ago when she was so scared she wet the bed, too afraid to get up and go to the bathroom for fear something was going to attack her while she huddled alone in the house without her mother.

No, she'd never feel that vulnerable again. And no damn monster would put her in the position of having those feelings.

"Fear makes you weak," she muttered, watching the orange sky shift to shades of gray.

Derek couldn't help but smile at the way Gina was loaded down, guns in holster, UV rifle slung over her shoulder, the sunglasses he'd just handed her pulling back her hair as she slipped them on top of her head.

"Any idea how many of them are on the island?" Gina asked, buckling on her ammo belt.

She looked sexy and deadly. A pretty lethal combination in black pants, a black tank top, her hair blowing back in the soft breeze created from the storm clouds floating in from the shore.

"No clue," he said, forcing his mind back on task. "But I'd bet there's a lot of them, so we're going to have to be sharp." He looked around at all six new hunters, wishing it didn't have to be like this. "We didn't want to do it this way. God knows you all need more time for weapons training, but you're not going to get it. Stay close to the other hunters and follow their lead. We have demons to kill here, and I don't want a single one of them leaving this island alive. I do, however, want all of you coming out of this breathing."

Derek surveyed the teams. His trained hunters, plus six new ones. Fourteen in total, counting himself, since he'd be leaving two with Lou tonight. Not very high numbers considering what instinct told him they were facing on this island.

Nervous energy skimmed along his spinal column. He shook it off and straightened, forcing whatever was rushing inside him to calm down.

He didn't like these damn sensations he'd been having lately. Focus was important in hunting demons. He couldn't afford a distraction right now.

"What's wrong?" Lou asked, coming up beside him and motioning him to the side.

"Don't know," he said as they walked off alone. "Been having some weird feelings lately."

Lou stalled and tilted his head. "What kind of feelings?"

"If I knew what they were, they wouldn't be weird, would they?"

"Funny. Now describe them."

Cracking a smile, Derek said, "I'm not really a 'share your feelings' kind of guy, Lou. But thanks for asking."

Lou rolled his eyes. "You always were difficult, boy. And you know what I mean."

"I can't really explain it," Derek said, trying to be serious, but it felt damn stupid to voice what he couldn't put into words. "They're almost like premonitions. Like something's off-kilter, or about to happen, but I can't pinpoint what it is." He shrugged as soon as he said it. "Anxiety probably, though if you tell anyone I said that I'll boil your insides with the nuke."

Lou snorted. "You know anything you've ever told me has always remained confidential. And you're not the anxiety attack type."

Lou studied Derek. He felt like he was being examined under a microscope.

"What?"

"Nothing. It's just that you've been doing this for a while. I think you've simply developed extra senses about the demons. You're worrying for nothing." He placed his hand on Derek's shoulder. "Listen to those feelings, Derek. They could save your life."

He hated when Lou got all otherworldly on him. Gave him the creeps sometimes. "Yeah. I'll do that. But I'd rather rely on my guns."

After gathering up the teams and splitting them into three groups, they headed off into the jungle. Derek's team had the fewest, the other two having five members on theirs.

But he had Gina and Ryder, in his opinion the strongest on the team of new hunters. If he was going in one man down, he wanted to compensate by having the best. And okay, he wanted to keep his eye on Gina, too, and he wasn't about to psychoanalyze the whys of that one. It just made him feel better to have her with him tonight.

Dalton as lead of team two had taken Jake and Shay, while Rafe as team-three leader had taken Olivia and Trace. The teams had a good mix of talent between experienced hunters and new recruits. Now Derek just had to hope his hunters could keep the new guys alive through tonight.

The game was on.

Battle plan laid out, fully armed and connected to Lou via their ear com devices, they headed into the jungle, each team branching out in different directions. Using the GPS hooked to his wrist, Derek led his team east and into the depths of the jungle.

"Stay tight and in formation," he said to Gina and Ryder. "Keep moving. If you see something, then say so. Listen for commands from me or Linc or Lou."

"What are we looking for specifically?" Gina asked. "Will Lou lead us to hot spots, or do you have a place in mind?"

"Lou will tell us immediately if there's a hot spot in our vicinity." They all wore thermal tracking devices so Lou knew their locations and could tell them if there was any demon activity in their area. "Otherwise, we're just takin' a walk. There's no way to figure out where these things are."

"So basically we wait for them to come to us," Ryder said.

"Yeah."

"That sucks," Gina mumbled.

Linc snorted. "You get used to it."

Gina nearly jumped out of her skin at the sound of Linc's exceptionally deep voice behind her. Though she didn't turn around since Derek was still walking, she asked, "How do you get used it? How do you do your normal hunting when you're not on an island?"

"Track 'em the same way we're doing right now. Lou does his thing, lets us know where they are, and we hunt until they make an appearance. Then we kill them."

"How do you do that in the middle of a major city?" She couldn't even imagine taking high-tech weapons like the one she carried into the middle of Chicago or New York City.

"They don't want to be seen any more than we do. They mostly hunt in smaller cities and towns. They use stealth, the cover of night, and inconspicuous areas where they're less likely to be spotted," Derek explained. "We hunt and fight at night. They want to kill us as much as we want to kill them, so once we spot them we'll either give chase or they'll come after us. We bring them to a secluded area like an alley or someplace where no one's around and do our thing."

"Still, it's not like there's no people around."

"You'd be surprised how people disappear when they

see guns drawn," Linc said. "Besides, not too many people are around in the middle of the night, even in the city. Only the bad element, and they see nothing. If there's nothing in it for them to profit from, they're not interested in getting involved. You point a weapon like these at them, they're gone."

Okay, that made sense. "But what about the police?"

"We make sure they don't see us," Derek said.

Amazing the hunters had been fighting so long without being found out. Just more proof they were good at what they did.

Would she ever measure up? Would she ever be that good? She hoped so. She'd like to think she could fit in well with these hunters. She'd already started to relax—a little. If it wasn't for the fact they were looking for evil monsters, Gina would enjoy this night walk. The jungle was peaceful, the oppressive heat and humidity of the day obliterated by a cooling night breeze wafting off the ocean. The only sound was the treetops shaking in the wind, crisp, like rattling paper overhead. She could almost relax.

Almost.

But then Derek held up his hand and they froze. Gina's stomach clenched, her grip tightening on her weapon as she waited, listening and looking for signs of anything around them.

"Turn your lights out and put your shades on," he commanded.

She flipped her shoulder lanterns off and put the sunglasses on. Just like the night-vision goggles she'd worn last night, only much lighter, they fit snug around her entire eye, no doubt to shield them from any UV blasts.

But she still didn't detect any movement or see anything.

"What's up, Derek?" Linc asked.

"Something's coming."

"Lou hasn't signaled," Linc came back.

"I know. He will. They're coming. Just north of us. Five of them."

How the hell did he know that?

"I'm tracking five that just entered north of your position, Derek," Lou commed. "And they're splitting."

Gina shivered like someone had just walked over her grave. Okay, that was damn spooky.

"Got it, Lou," he said, turning to them. "Linc, take Ryder and track west around those trees. See if you can intercept a couple of them. Gina, you're with me."

She nodded and followed. Apparently they were going to meet the demons head-on. Stepping up her pace, she sidled up next to him. He glanced at her. "You comfortable on weapons?"

"Yeah."

"Feel confident?"

Oh, right. She was about to meet up with demons. Creatures from Hell. Things that weren't human that she was supposed to kill with this futuristic flesh-melting weaponry. She'd never in her life felt less confident. "I'm fine."

"It's okay to be nervous."

She rolled her eyes. "I can handle this."

He stopped, looked ahead, then at her. "I know you can handle this. That's why I wanted you on my team tonight."

When he turned and walked ahead, it took her a second before she could kick-start her feet into moving.

He couldn't have complimented her more. With a wide grin, she hustled up behind him again, more determined than ever to prove him right.

"They're here," he whispered, taking a deep breath. "Pure or half demons, 'cuz I don't smell the stench of hybrids."

That was good to know. She wasn't sure she was ready yet for the big hulking stinky ones.

Then she saw it. A flicker of movement to her left. Like a flash of white lighting as it breezed by.

"They're fast, Gina. Get ready to run. He'll circle and pop up behind you before you know it, otherwise. Get your vision tracked and follow, but stay sharp. They like to gang up. And stay with me at all times."

She nodded and drew her weapon up rib high, acknowledging that her hands were shaking, forcing a calm she didn't feel.

It was just adrenaline. Not fear. She was ready for this fight. Prepared. Armed and strong. She could take these bastards.

"What scares you, little girl?"

For a split second, her eyes closed, and she was propelled back in time once again, becoming that frightened child all alone. As she gasped back a sob, reality surged and she pivoted.

The sonofabitch was fucking with her mind, and that

she would never, ever allow. She aimed and fired, the UV light surprising the demon. He threw his hands up, but it was too late. An unholy scream emanated from the creature as it boiled and bubbled, smoke pouring from its frying flesh before oozing to the ground in a gelatinous pile.

Gina walked over to it, watching the remains rise and fall as if it was still breathing.

"Don't ever fuck with me like that again," she whispered to the darkness around her. "You can't scare me."

Blinking back the moisture in her eyes, she turned. Derek was watching her.

"You okay?"

"Yes."

He focused on her for a second, then nodded. "Nice shot. Now let's move."

It didn't take long for another to dart by them. Like ghosts, they flew by, almost as if they were taunting them, playing a game of cat and mouse. Derek took off in a fast run, Gina right on his heels, digging down when she was nearly out of breath. When he increased his speed to nearly inhuman levels, Gina almost lost sight of him. For someone she'd easily kept up with just a few days ago, he'd sure stepped it up all of a sudden. She was wheezing, her lungs were on fire, and if he didn't slow down soon she was going to be left behind.

God, these things were fast, zooming around trees and through the bushes with lightning speed. Relentless, Derek refused to let go of his target, but finally halted so suddenly Gina almost ran up his back. She dug in her heels and stopped just in time to see him aim at a demon coming right at them. The gun whirred with a low humming sound, but she couldn't see anything coming from the barrel.

Nevertheless, the microwaves had obviously hit their intended target. The demon flew in the air, shimmying and shaking as the waves hit it, its eyeballs protruding from their sockets, white and bulging. When it hit the ground it began to sizzle, bumps popping out on its skin like a bad case of hives. Its skin turned bright red and began to bubble.

"Stand back, Gina," Derek said.

She did, and he took several steps backward, too.

Gina watched in horror and fascination as the demon began to expand, its skin stretching like a balloon filling with air. Wider and wider it expanded, more than skin should be able to inflate.

"This is where it gets really messy," Derek said.

Suddenly, the demon blew apart with a loud pop, parts of it flying all over the jungle.

Gina grimaced and looked at Derek. "Oh, that's so gross."

Grinning, he said, "Yeah, isn't it? Now, let's go get the last one."

Strangely, it seemed that the last demon was hiding. Or maybe it was stalking them, ready to pounce from behind a tree or thicket of bushes.

Gina and Derek combed the area, communicating back and forth with Linc and Ryder, who were engaged with their own set of demons.

"See anything?" Derek asked as he looked left and she looked right.

"Not yet."

But suddenly it was right there in front of them, appearing out of nowhere. Derek dropped his rifle as the demon lunged for him, its clawed hands and dripping fangs reaching out, trying to bite, to scratch, to insert its paralyzing toxin.

Human-looking in every way except for its hideous fangs and claws, it was just like the one she'd seen the night before. Nearly bald, with pale blue eyes, but emanating pure evil as its twisted, grimacing face glared at Derek.

Derek grabbed its wrists and held it back, struggling to keep it at bay.

Shocked for a second, Gina gaped at it, her mind scrambling for what to do.

Shoot it, dumbass!

Then instinct roared to life and she grabbed the handgun out of the holster at her hip, taking careful aim as the demon and Derek struggled in a fierce dance. She didn't want to hit Derek in case they moved suddenly, but she knew Derek didn't have much time. The muscles of Derek's arms bulged with the effort it took to keep the demon from sinking its fangs into his arm.

She fired a shot, striking the demon in the throat. It let go of Derek and reached for its neck, blood pouring over its hands.

Derek pushed back, panting and fighting for breath as he leaned over and braced his hands on his knees. Gina rushed over to him.

"Are you all right?"

"Yeah," he said, nodding. "Thanks."

She looked at the demon, horrified to see its flesh melting off its bones, a strangled, bubbly cry tearing through the night as first its flesh disappeared, then muscle, then organs disintegrated, until nothing was left but skeletal remains that dropped to the ground.

"You have some seriously kick-ass weapons, Derek."

"Yeah." He stood, inhaled, exhaled, and turned to her. "You did good. Thanks for thinking so clearly. You saved my life."

Beaming, she nodded. "You're welcome."

"Lou, we've hit all three here. Any other activity?" he commed.

"Other teams completed. Nothing else going on. Head back."

"Got it. Out." He turned to Gina. "We're done here. Let's go."

That was it? She was primed, exhilarated and pumped up with adrenaline. She wanted to kill more demons. Why weren't there more demons? What did he mean they were done?

Hell, she was just getting started. What was she going to do the rest of the night?

Chapter Twelve

The debriefing went well, Derek thought. All in all, they'd killed twelve demons tonight. Not too bad. But the best part was all of the hunters had come back alive and unscathed.

And pretty damn pumped up, from the looks of all of them.

If they had champagne lying around the new hunters would probably be spraying it over each other right now. Grins abounded, backs were slapped, war stories were told.

Derek and the other hunters just sat back and watched, amused. Hell, they'd all been there before, that first night of hunting. Kill a few demons, then think you could take on the whole world.

He'd let the new guys have tonight to celebrate and feel invincible. Tomorrow he'd hit them with the debriefing, remind them this wasn't as easy as it looked. In their business, hunters died. Unfortunately, all too frequently.

But they had done well and that was good. They needed more competent hunters. If this new team worked out, he'd be happy.

"I couldn't believe Derek chased down that demon," Gina said as they traded stories back and forth. "My calves were killing me trying to keep up. I almost lost him a few times."

"Dayum, Derek," Linc said, elbowing him in the ribs. "Since when did you become a speed runner?"

Derek shrugged. "Hell, I don't know. Maybe I had a slow demon tonight."

"Interesting," Lou said.

Derek rolled his eyes. "It wasn't that big a deal. I wasn't that fast."

"Hell you weren't," Gina argued. "I've never seen anyone run like that."

Derek tried to blow it off, but even he had to admit he was surprised by his own speed tonight. And his reflexes. And being able to sense the demons before Lou commed him. Maybe Lou was right and he'd been doing this so long he was just getting really good at it.

And maybe he believed in faeries and unicorns, too.

Fortunately, the conversation died down after awhile and everyone headed off to the bungalows to get some sleep, the first rays of dawn signaling safety.

But for some reason, despite the grueling night, he was still too keyed up. He tried a glass of whiskey, and still ended up pacing back and forth in his room.

He took a shower, but the only thing that did was dredge up memories of the last time he'd walked out wearing only a towel and found Gina leaning against his doorway. And that mental visual did nothing to calm his jittery senses.

"Damn," he whispered, stepping out of the bathroom and dragging his hand through his still damp hair. What he saw when he entered his bedroom made him wonder if he'd been hurled back in time.

Just like the other night, she leaned against his doorway. Only this time, the door was closed, and she wasn't wearing a pissed-off expression. Her eyes were smoky blue, her lips parted, high color spread across her cheeks. She must have just showered, too, because her hair was damp. Soft curls framed her face, the rest of her hair spilling over her shoulders and breasts. She wore a little sundress again. This time all black, silky, hugging every single one of her curves. His mouth watered and his towel started its own version of the tent dance. No way in hell was he going to be able to hide how felt about finding her here.

Then again, he got the idea she hadn't come to his room to discuss demon-killing strategy.

"I can't sleep," she said, resting her head against the wall.

"A little keyed up?" he asked, approaching.

"Yeah." She licked her lips and his mind went in a million directions. Like exactly where he'd like her to put her mouth. He could already imagine her sliding down the wall, grabbing his towel on the way, and taking his throbbing shaft between her sweet, full lips as soon as she hit her knees, her warm tongue sweeping around his hot flesh.

Yeah, there went the towel, but he didn't stop to pick it up.

Her gaze went south and lingered for a few seconds. She drew in a shuddering sigh, then dragged her focus back to his face, her eyes glassy and dark. "I can't sleep."

He planted his hands against the wall on either side of her head. "You said that already."

"I did?"

"Yeah."

"Then kiss me before I say something else stupid."

He leaned in and took her mouth, entering slowly, just the way he wanted to slide between her legs. Slow and easy, savoring every touch, every taste. He caught the flavor of mint from her toothpaste, imagined her showering, brushing her teeth, looking at herself in the mirror while she was readying herself to come to him. He liked thinking she'd been getting ready for him.

Oh, he wanted this slow for her, wanted to take his time to do it right. But then everything he'd been holding in took over, and it wasn't gentle anymore. All the pent-up anxiety and energy came pouring out in that kiss. He tunneled his fingers in the thick softness of her hair, dragging her closer. She whimpered into his mouth and met him eagerly, lifting her leg to wrap around his hip.

Contact. Flesh on flesh. Heat against heat. His mind became a foggy mist where only he and Gina existed.

With one hand he lifted her, pushing her against the wall as he settled himself against her hips, running his hand down the smooth silk of her rib cage, over one hip, dragging the hem of the dress up to reach the soft skin underneath. She wore only a tiny scrap of a panty that he eliminated with a fierce tug. She gasped, breaking the kiss long enough to cast him a shocked look, then a half smile, before groaning and grabbing his head to plant her lips more firmly over his again.

Desire took hold in a way that was overpowering, animalistic, and damned near hard to control. He'd never felt such a rush of hunger, a need to possess. Gina had been through something crazy tonight. He should pick her up, carry her to the bed and undress her slowly, then make love to her all night long. He was supposed to worship her, make her feel cherished.

But he couldn't. A raw need to brand her, to take her in some primitive fashion, had taken possession of him and wouldn't be denied. He searched the crevice between her legs and found her wet, swollen, ready for him. The first touch of his fingers made her cry out and arch against him.

And that made the madness even more intense.

Or maybe it was the sounds she made. Whimpers, moans in the back of her throat every time he rocked his hand over her sex, petting the bud that seemed to swell and tighten with every stroke of his fingers.

"Derek," she gasped. "Please."

"Tell me what you want, baby," he murmured against her ear. "You want to come?"

She shuddered, nodded, her entire body trembling against his. He loved having this power over her. He controlled her pleasure and he damn well enjoyed giving it to her. He wanted to make sure no other man would ever give her this much satisfaction again.

He slammed on the brakes, dropping to his knees and lifting the dress, balling the fabric into his fist. He kissed her thigh, her hipbone, glancing up to find her looking down at him.

"I like when you watch," he whispered, pushing away at the madness enveloping him, coaxing him to take her now.

She sucked her lower lip between her teeth.

God, that was sexy.

Her scent enveloped him. Primed, sweet, and musky. He lifted one leg and rested it over his shoulder, unveiling her altar for him. He wanted to worship her, to give her all his gifts, to show her a pleasure she'd never experienced from any man.

His first taste of her was a slice of heaven, her response even more as she moaned and shuddered, threading her fingers in his hair.

"Derek."

The way she whispered his name, in a throaty, pleading voice, was the sweetest music he'd ever heard. He leaned in and took her again, tasting her, loving her with his tongue, drinking all she had to offer until she was buried against his face, writhing against him and completely out of control.

Oh, he liked Gina out of control.

Gina knew she was tugging at Derek's hair, probably hurting him, but she had no power over her reactions.

He was killing her. His tongue and mouth performing a maddening dance. She never let a man do this. It was too intimate, took away her control. Yet she couldn't voice the words to tell him no when he'd slipped down there and taken possession of her.

And when he'd touched her with his tongue, so wet and warm, claiming what no man had ever claimed before, her legs had begun to shake and she wanted nothing more than to give him everything.

Everything.

Not that she had a choice in the matter. Already it was spiraling up inside her, tightening, a vortex of tornadic sensation that swept her along in a whirlwind, and she could only brace herself as he swept his velvet tongue along her folds and carried her away.

She'd come to his room without thought other than she was too pent up to sleep and his room was the first place she'd thought to go. She'd wanted to talk. Really, that was her intent. But then he'd walked out of the bathroom clad only in a towel and talk had been the last thing on her mind.

Now she had no mind at all, just a body that Derek was doing devilish things to with his tongue. And she was watching him, his dark head buried between her thighs, his tongue snaking out to twirl around the tight little pearl. He looked up at her, smiled, covered her with his mouth, and sucked.

"Oh, God," she cried, then she was lost, flying as Derek grasped her hips and latched onto her with his mouth, capturing her essence as she rocked against him. She tightened her hold on his hair and shivered uncontrollably, giving him all that he'd asked for.

She'd barely caught her breath before he stood and

claimed her mouth, letting her taste what he'd done. So erotic, so wickedly sensual it made her shudder, her body melting and warming inside.

Derek fought against the demons plaguing him, the ones telling him to forget slow and easy—to take, to ravage instead. The sweet strokes of Gina's tongue against his were maddening, the way she responded to him, the way she came for him. But he had to control his urges.

He slid two fingers inside her. Like a silk waterfall, she poured over him, and he almost lost it. It took every ounce of restraint he had not to let loose right there on the floor like some teenager getting it for the first time.

Control, his ass. He didn't have any at all where Gina was concerned.

With his free hand he jerked one strap of her dress down, then the other, freeing her breasts. The pink crests tempted him in the soft light spilling in from the open window of his bungalow. He dipped down and tasted her, sucked in the soft tip of her nipple and rolled it around on his tongue, relishing the sound of her sharp intake of breath as it hardened under the sucking pressure of his mouth. In return, he continued to gently dip his fingers inside her, teasing her with what was to come.

Her fingers danced in his hair as she held his head to her breast, arching her back to give him more.

"Oh, please, Derek," she whispered, rocking against his fingers.

She was close again, so responsive he could do this to her again and again, just to watch and feel her climax. But he didn't want her to go without him this time. He withdrew his fingers and stood, sliding them between his lips to taste her.

"Like honey," he said after he withdrew them, then kissed her again. She licked at his lips, taking her own sweet taste from his mouth without hesitation.

She was every man's dream.

The dress had to go. He wanted her fully naked. Yanking the material over her hips, it pooled to the floor and he kicked it out of the way.

She was so damn beautiful, her face devoid of makeup, her hair tumbled around her shoulders, her nipples hard, and the sweet musky scent of her sex entering his senses and driving him to madness.

"Spread your legs for me, baby."

He positioned himself at her entrance, then slid inside her in a slow thrust that made his balls quiver. He closed his eyes for a brief second and just felt her surround him.

She *was* a damn silken waterfall inside. Hot and pouring over him as she gripped him in a tight vise that had him struggling for restraint. Restraint that he had very little of right now. He grasped her wrists and pinned them over her head, then nestled fully against her so he could feel that little knot at her apex rubbing against his pelvis. Her eyes widened every time he brushed it with his thrusts.

Oh, yeah. If he had all the time in the world, he'd do this slow and easy, maybe even pull out and cover that sweet spot again with his mouth and tongue. He'd like to tease her a little, lap up every bit of her sweet honey, and drive her crazy until she was begging him to let her finish.

But there was a madness boiling up inside him, a driving need to thrust hard, to drive home, to possess her completely.

It was as if his blood churned and twisted, and it was damn painful. Voices inside him urged him to take this woman, to make her his.

Gina gasped as tiny pinpricks of pleasure splintered inside her. She'd like to say she hadn't come here tonight for this, but she'd be lying.

She wanted this, needed it, and was damn glad she hadn't had to resort to begging to get it.

And now Derek was inside her, and it was magic. A perfect blend of heaven and hell, ecstasy and torment as he moved slowly, then thrust hard, gave her an easy stroke or two followed by a punishing drive that nearly made her cry out with madness.

The things he did to her, the way her body responded . . . it just wasn't normal for her.

Just like the other night, her gaze was riveted to his, the intimacy almost too much to bear. A connection that went beyond their bodies, and that was something she never did. He'd made her connect with him the night before in the first-aid tent, and he was doing it to her again now. She was powerless to do anything but obey his silent command to look, to watch, to bond with him on this intimate, emotional level.

"Feel me," he commanded, whispering to her in a low, husky voice that made her shudder.

"I do."

"Feel me, Gina," he said again, thrusting upward, grinding against her.

Oh, God, she did feel it, and it was moving her to tears as the tension built, coiling around her center like a snake. Squeezing, tightening with every one of his exquisite thrusts.

He knew her body as if he'd been touching her forever. How could this happen? No man ever made her come as easily as he had the other night, as he had tonight. She was . . . difficult. And she never . . . not this way. Yet she felt it building, was almost afraid to hope it could happen.

"Let it go, baby," he said.

She shook her head. She never let go. It was too scary. This was madness. It had never happened.

"Gina, look at me."

She did, staring into gray eyes that were a vortex of stormy darkness. She was so lost when she looked at him. Yet she felt so safe.

"Let go," he said again, his voice demanding, gritty with the same need that she felt. Her belly tumbled with sensation and need.

And again, he ground against her, making her so wet she felt it trickle down her thighs. The quivering began then, and she went with it, digging her nails into his broad shoulders as he moved so expertly against her she quivered from the sheer pleasure of it and felt tears sting her eyes.

She was there. God, she was really there. "Derek!" she cried as her orgasm washed over her, making her shudder uncontrollably and tighten around him. It burst inside her and spilled over, a wild ride she was helpless to control. His jaw clenched and he groaned and went with her, emptying inside her while he gripped her buttocks, his gaze so intense it was almost painful to look at him.

But she couldn't tear her gaze away, locked with him in this amazing journey that tore her apart, watching his eyes go nearly black as he rode with her to dizzying heights. It was frightening and exhilarating. She couldn't let go no matter where it led.

He trembled then, too, holding tight to her and burying his head in her shoulder. She wrapped her arms around him and held him, feeling an inexplicable wave of tenderness, almost as if she had to protect him as he panted against her.

The unfamiliar emotional highs and lows she'd gone through the past few days were the weirdest things.

But right now was definitely a high.

"Whew," Derek said against her neck.

Gina smiled, grateful he'd broken the spell of intensity that seemed to hover around them. She needed light and easy right now. "Uh-huh."

He leaned back, grinned, then swept her into his arms, carrying her to his bed and depositing her there before crawling in next to her. The breeze from the open window and the fan overhead cooled her heated body, though not for long.

Not the way he was looking at her, scanning her body from head to foot. When he reached her eyes, he arched a brow and said, "I wasn't tired, either."

"Are you now?" she asked.

"No. You?"

"No."

"I had thought of dragging you away from that doorway and making love to you properly," he said.

"That seemed pretty damn proper to me," she teased.

Laughing, he said, "Well, thanks, but I had something different in mind. Something more slow and leisurely. A little time for exploration."

To prove his point, he began drawing lazy circles around her belly button. Her abdomen quivered and she laughed and slapped his hand away. "Exploration, huh? Yeah, I might be up for a little exploration, too," she said, reaching for his shaft and encircling it with her hand.

It pulsed to life around her palm. Amazing. Oh, yeah, she wanted to spend a really long time playing with every part of his body.

"Haven't you ever dabbled in fun and exploration with a man before?"

"Mmm, not really. I'm more about the release, not the relationship. No lingering, no conversation, no play, and certainly no exploration."

It took her a few seconds to realize he hadn't replied. She looked up to find a frown on his face and immediately let go of him. "What?"

He pulled her against him and kissed her. "You really never had much fun, did you?"

Oh, hell. She hadn't meant to launch into a "poor Gina" scenario. "I had plenty of fun," she said, shrugging.

"Bullshit." He sat up and leaned against the headboard.

"Doesn't sound to me like you even had much in the way of sex."

Rolling her eyes, she sat up and crossed her legs over each other, pulling the pillow onto her lap. "I'm hardly a virgin, Derek. I've had plenty of sex."

"Didn't sound like it from what you just said."

Sometimes she said too much. "I've been busy."

"You're what? Twenty-seven?"

"Twenty-eight."

"A woman who looks like you, with a career like yours, should have had a ton of men by now."

And that was exactly what everyone believed. Or what she wanted them to believe. "I'm selective."

"You're afraid."

So much for the afterglow. "You psychoanalyzing me?"

"Maybe."

She looked out the window, suddenly wanting to be anywhere but here right now. "Well, stop it. I don't like it."

"You just don't like it when someone gets close to the truth."

Her gaze shot to his, anger replacing the pulses of joy from a few moments ago. "I don't pick on your psyche, Derek. Leave mine the hell alone." She slipped off the bed and padded over to the door, grabbing her dress and tossing it over her head.

"Where are you going?"

"Back to my room."

"What about fun and exploration?"

She shot him a glare. "I think I've had enough of that. I'm tired now."

"Coward," he said, not even budging from his spot on the bed.

"I am not. I just don't want to talk about my past."

"Because you're afraid."

"Because I don't want to. This is stupid. I'm going to bed." She turned and walked out, slamming the door behind her and storming back to her own bungalow.

She closed and locked her door, took off the dress and threw it in the corner, then crawled between the sheets of her bed.

Dammit, she wasn't at all tired.

Now she was just irritated. She and Derek had had a wonderful time, right up until he wanted to talk about her past, about feelings and emotions, things she wasn't ready to get into.

Like fears.

Shit.

So much for getting any sleep.

Derek stared up at the darkness and drummed his fingers across his chest, wishing he could take the last twenty minutes back.

Great. Why did he have to open his big mouth and start asking Gina questions? Couldn't he have left it alone?

No, he couldn't. Not when she'd started talking about not having relationships, not having much sex, and not having fun with men.

Hell, a woman who looked like Gina, a famous actress, gorgeous. He just didn't get it. She should have had a string of lovers by now. But his sixth sense or intuition or whatever the hell it was told him she'd barely had a handful, and the guys she'd been with just hadn't melted her butter.

Yet she'd come apart for him tonight. And the other night. So it wasn't like she didn't know how to respond. She sure as hell responded to him.

Which made him feel like king of the world.

But it also meant mystery, and he just couldn't let a damn mystery go, could he? Why him and no one else?

So instead of spending the next few hours wrapped up in her arms and losing his mind inside her, he was staring up at a dark ceiling, coiled up tight with tension and pissed as hell at himself.

Because he had to go and ask questions, probe her, demand answers she clearly didn't want to give.

Because he had to go and start caring about her.

Chapter Thirteen

"Interesting development between the two of them," the second said.

The Master nodded and smiled, his chest expanding as he breathed in. "I felt his power. It energized me. It's raw and untapped, but we can use it to our advantage."

"Soon, I hope?"

The Master pondered, then shook his head. "Not yet. Let's give this time to develop and see where it goes. Do you see the potential here? We could have them both. Use one to obtain the other."

"Ah," the second said, nodding. "A bargaining chip."

"If necessary." He didn't think it would be. Not once the offer was made. No one turned down power such as this.

"Their hunters are mighty," the second said.

"But no match for us."

"They killed many."

"I'm not worried, and you shouldn't be, either. We will take care of them all, in good time."

Almost all of them, anyway. He had a plan.

Okay, she was avoiding Derek. Not really the most mature thing Gina could do, but right now her emotions weren't steady. She didn't want to put herself in the position where she might end up alone with him and possibly be forced to have a conversation about what had happened between them.

Wasn't it men who never wanted to open up and talk about emotions? Derek was the last man she'd thought would go all sensitive on her and start questioning her about her past.

She just wasn't going there, no matter how good the sex had been. No matter how she felt about him.

Since they fought at night, they slept at dawn and during the day. After she woke, she spent the early part of the day sparring with Olivia, then the afternoon on target practice with Dalton and Linc, which helped get her mind off Derek. Learning the subtle nuances of the weaponry was important, after all. And Derek didn't have to be the one to teach her everything. The other hunters were more than adept at weapons training.

It was almost like prepping for a film, learning the ins and outs of weapons, deciphering how they worked, how to handle them, the actual mechanics of each piece. Something they hadn't had time to do before they'd gone out hunting. And Ryder and Shay had joined her, working tirelessly dismantling these weapons.

Dalton and Linc were expert teachers, patiently showing them how the weapons worked on the demons. Before long, Jake, Olivia, and Trace had joined in, as well as two other hunters, Rico and Mandy. They had a full class in session.

"Who created these things?" Jake asked, playing with the liquid UV light.

"We have some wicked brilliant scientists in our corner." Mandy, an incredibly gorgeous Amazon with long raven hair and legs a mile long, demonstrated the ten-second approach to loading the liquid UV into the chamber. She didn't look like a demon hunter. She looked like a fashion model.

"How long have you been doing this?"

Mandy pursed her lips. "I came on board when I was fifteen. Lou wouldn't let me start fighting until I was eighteen. Which really pissed me off, but he was right, of course," she replied with a sideways grin.

"You were a huge pain in the ass, too," Linc said, taking a rag out of his back pocket to wipe the beads of sweat away from his bald ebony head. "Always in the way, asking questions, begging to go out and fight. It was like having a puppy winding in and out around our feet."

"You love me and you know it. I'm like the sister you never had."

"You're like the sister I never wanted," he teased, then winked and grabbed her in a huge bear hug. Of course, Mandy was almost six feet tall, and Linc about six foot six, so he still overshadowed her. She laughed and pushed him away.

The camaraderie among the hunters was strong. As was the bond. It was like being around a close-knit family who loved one another, who had each other's backs. It made her stomach hurt, made her want to get away from the familiarity, the feelings of love and togetherness.

She liked all these people. And she didn't want to like these people. Irritation sprang up. She had started to care about all of them, had so easily fallen into a comfort zone with them, both the experienced hunters and the new ones like herself.

What was going to happen when one of them died? There was a reason she hadn't allowed people to get close to her, had never established bonds or friendships or relationships over the years. There was a reason she hadn't allowed men to linger after sex. Hell, there was a reason she didn't have a lot of sexual experience for her age.

Sex meant getting close.

Gina didn't get close.

She got close with Derek, though.

And look what happened.

Big mistake.

Derek had read her right, and she hated that he knew so much about her. Things she didn't want him or anyone else knowing. She hadn't done a very good job of masking the real Gina with him, had she? Was she that transparent around him? So unguarded that he could see who she really was? People who'd known her for years didn't see that.

How could he?

By the time they'd packed their gear and the sun had begun its lazy fall over the tops of the trees, Lou shouted out he had detected a hot spot on the west side of the island.

"Demon activity. Portal location, about two kilometers west. Wait," he added, raising his hand. "There's also activity on the northeastern slope at the edge of the mountains, as well as several spots east."

"Busy fuckers tonight, aren't they?" Derek said.

"Very. We've got no fewer than six active portal spots. They're popping up everywhere. And each has a minimum of three demons."

Shit. Derek sighed. This wasn't going to be good. They needed to attack aggressively, which meant really whittling down the teams. He turned to his hunters, doing a quick calculation of how to divide them. Juggling them around and switching from last night wasn't a good idea. Symbiotic relationships formed quickly within hunting ranks. But he also wasn't going to send any of the new hunters out alone. Not yet, anyway. And he wasn't leaving any of them to guard Lou. They needed field experience right now.

"Ryder with Linc, Dalton with Jake, Mandy with Shay," he said, doing quick assessments. "I want you all on the east side. "Olivia with Nance, Trace with Rico to the west. Punk and Rafe, you stay here with Lou. Gina and I will handle the northeastern slope."

He walked away to grab his gear, passing by Gina, who

stood expressionless. Yet he saw the fire in her eyes, the anger she couldn't quite mask.

"You have something to say?" he asked.

"No."

"Did you think because you're angry with me about last night that I'd pair you with someone else?"

She shrugged and buckled her ammo belt. "Did I say that?"

"You didn't have to. It's written all over your face."

"There you go presuming again," she quipped. "I'm here, aren't I?"

"Look. Leave the personal shit in the bungalow, Gina. I need a fighting partner in the jungle tonight, not a pissed-off lover. Got it?"

If he could read her mind . . . well, it was probably a good thing he couldn't. Her firmly sealed lips and mutinous stare told him everything.

"Got it," she finally said. "We gonna stand around all night talking, or are we going to go kill some demons?"

Pissed-off lover. Whatever. Gina stalked through the jungle behind him, mentally drawing a big red target on Derek's back.

Okay, maybe she didn't mean that. But goddammit, he made her mad. Did he think she couldn't put aside her personal feelings while on a hunt for demons? Did he think she was so petty, so, so—juvenile, that in the middle of fighting she'd refuse to back him up because she was annoyed at him?

Dumbass. Men were stupid. No wonder she avoided them.

She should have continued to avoid them. Now she remembered why she didn't get involved with anyone. Emotions and entanglements led to arguments and hurt feelings and anger, muddying the waters with confusing emotion.

Vibrators and her own hand didn't talk back or cause emotional distress.

Then again they didn't provide the stellar eye candy Derek did. And he did have a mighty nice ass, which she could see just fine in the dark. And his back was broad, muscular, his waist devoid of any love handles as it tapered down into slim hips which led to very powerful thighs on long, strong legs.

She sighed, fully appreciating his fine form, then remembered his naked body pressed against hers last night as he took her up against the wall. The night heat was nothing compared to the quick flush of her body, the moistening between her legs as she recalled the pleasure he'd given her.

Like Jekyll and Hyde. Men should be sex slaves, there to give a woman pleasure, but never allowed to speak.

If only, she thought with a snort.

"You say something?" Derek asked, craning his neck around.

"No."

He frowned and continued fighting through the dense underbrush.

They had one hell of a long walk as they headed north

toward the mountains, the trees and bushes thickening as they moved further inland. The grass grew more lush under their feet, the air more dense the higher they climbed.

Loaded down with weapons and ammo, she was sweating and her thighs were killing her. Hell, by the time they found the demons she'd be too damn tired to fight them.

"Where are they?" she asked.

"No idea. Lou?" he commed. "Where the hell are the ones on the northeast slope?"

"They've disappeared, Derek," he replied. "I was just about to com you. They lingered for a while, not really going anywhere, then vanished."

Derek stopped. "Shit."

Gina dragged out her canteen and took a long swallow, grateful for a few seconds to catch her breath. "So what do you think that was all about? They wanted a little fresh air?"

Derek allowed a slight smile. "No idea."

"Do we head back now?"

He lifted his head as if he were sniffing the air. "No."

She waited while he searched the sky, then looked around, seemingly lost in his own thoughts.

Okay, don't tell me what we're doing, then.

"Derek."

"What?"

"What are we doing?"

"Waiting."

"For what?"

"Demons."

Well, wasn't he just master of the obvious? "There aren't any."

He finally looked at her, but his gaze wasn't focused on her. It was like he was in a trance, his eyes unfocused. "There will be."

"When?"

"Inhale."

"What?"

"Take a deep breath, Gina."

She did, and wrinkled her nose. "What is that? It smells like rotting garbage."

"Demons."

"Oh, shit." She knew what that meant. The demon hybrids. The really big ones. The ones who were really hard to kill. A shiver of fear skittered up her spine.

"Portal just opened again, Derek. Very near you," Lou commed.

"Got it, Lou. We're on it."

When he looked at her then, his focus was back. She didn't know where he'd been a few seconds ago, but the man had been lost in the ozone somewhere. Weird.

"You ready?" he asked. "These are the big, mean, ugly, smelly motherfuckers."

She swallowed past a lump the size of Ohio that had lodged in her throat. "Okay, I get your point. This is going to be bad."

"Stay close to me and follow my lead. They can't outrun you if you need to get away, but don't let them get too close, okay?"

She nodded, pulling her gun and resting her finger on the trigger. Another trial by fire. Another first.

She breathed in, then out, remembering to center herself, fighting for calm.

When Derek touched her shoulder, she nearly jumped out of her skin, but held her voice. "Dammit," she whispered. "Don't do that."

"You can handle this, Gina." His firm, steady voice was a lifeline in the darkness.

She nodded. "I know."

Just then the ground trembled under her feet as footsteps pounded.

Monsters. She tried to prepare herself for the visual, but her imagination worked overtime, scaring the hell out of her. The thick branches ahead rustled with movement as the demons crashed through them, pushing them out of the way with a loud snap.

"The UV laser works best," he said. "It stops them in their tracks."

"Got it." She already had the UV rifle locked and ready to fire.

She wasn't ready for their appearance when they crashed through the last thicket of branches.

Her worst nightmare come to life.

Thick-muscled, with gray, mottled skin. Hideous large heads, pointed devil-looking ears, and extra-large mouths with protruding fangs. No Hollywood-generated horror could compare to this. Their eyes glowed yellow in the dark—pairs of almond-shaped slits that exuded pure malice.

She started to shake, a cold chill entering her body, her feet frozen to the ground. She couldn't feel the tips of her fingers anymore. Was she even still holding the gun?

They were the monsters of every horrible dream. Hideous, dripping saliva everywhere, their long, clawlike fingers reaching out for her as they made their slow but deliberate approach, the thunderous sound made by feet that were three times the size of a large adult male's.

"No."

The voice was hers. She took a step back and wanted to run.

"Don't let them scare you, baby," Derek said, moving to stand beside her. "I'm right here."

The brush of his shoulder against hers shocked her into awareness of what she was doing. Her gaze shot to his, and she saw it in his eyes. The understanding, the acknowledgment.

He knew. Somehow, he knew how much they scared her. Damn, she didn't want to admit it, hated this weakness in herself, but she could swear she'd seen these things before. Maybe they were just the embodiment of an old nightmare.

"Gina, I won't let them hurt you. You're not alone."

Oh, God. She needed to hear those words. He had no idea how much they comforted her, strengthened her. She looked to him, forcing the fear away.

She wasn't a child. She wasn't alone.

Whatever it was, it passed, the chill evaporating and warmth returning.

"I'm fine. Let's get them."

He nodded, his expression determined as he moved forward. She stayed right at his side as they approached the demons.

"Aim for a wide burst. Stall them, then keep hitting them with the light. It'll take a little more than normal to bring these down."

"Got it."

The demons were close enough now that the smell was even worse than before, stealing her breath. "Oh, God, that stench is awful!" She gagged.

"Yeah. You'll get used to it."

"Not without a gas mask or clothespin on my nose. God almighty."

"Pick one and start hitting it. I'll get the other two."

"I'll take the one on the right." Without hesitating, she aimed and fired, the blue blast of light stunning the demon. It froze as if in suspended animation. Gina used the momentary pause to move to the right of the demon, then readjusted her settings to widen the UV array.

It didn't take the stun too long, advancing on her again. She clicked to fire, but her gun jammed.

Shit. She backed up, keeping one eye on the approaching demon while simultaneously trying to jimmy the mechanism on her rifle. Derek was too busy firing at two demons to be of any help to her, and no way was she going to distract him. She'd just have to figure this out on her own.

Thank God these things weren't fast, but she didn't like the way it was moving in on her. Taking a quick glance behind her, she realized she'd soon be out of room. There was a cliff behind her with a sharp drop-off, a wall of mountain to her right, and Derek and his two demons to her left.

And the goddamn gun still wouldn't fire.

The demon crept closer, its arms outstretched. She could really smell the thing now, her stomach rolling at the putrid stench.

She was out of options.

"Derek," she whispered.

He can't hear you if you don't open your mouth and yell, idiot.

She didn't want to bother him, but damn, the demon was drawing closer.

A blinding flash to her left drew her attention momentarily. One demon down, but the other was advancing on Derek. His gaze shot to her.

"What?"

"Trigger mechanism is stuck."

"Shit." He looked at her, the mountain, the cliff, and at both the demons advancing on them. "Shit," he said again.

Her thoughts exactly.

"What do we do?"

He fired on his demon again, the wide array slowing it, but not doing its intended job. The demon walked right through the UV light.

"That's not good," he said. "We need stronger UV light."

Hell of a time to figure that out. She felt off balance,

teetering on the edge of the cliff. The mountain to their right was sheer, with no footholds. Nothing to climb.

And sure as hell they weren't getting out straight ahead. The demons drew closer.

"We need to get out of here, Derek. Now!"

"I know! Give me a minute, goddammit. I'm thinking."

They didn't have a minute left.

Derek turned and peered over the cliff, then looked at her, determination fixed on his face.

When she caught his thought process, her eyes widened. "Are you serious?"

"I hear water rushing. It'll be fine."

"No."

"Now, Gina."

"Oh, hell no!"

"No time to argue."

Before she knew what was happening, he'd swept his arm around her and plunged them both over the cliff.

She left her stomach on the precipice, her high-pitched scream ringing in her ears as they plummeted over the edge into the abyss.

Chapter Fourteen

Instinct told Derek the water was deep, the fall not high enough to hurt them. He didn't know why his gut told him that, or why he believed it, but he did.

They landed feet first in the water, which was deep enough they didn't even touch bottom. Derek fought to the surface, clinging to Gina the entire time. She sputtered as her head shot up out of the water, muttering a string of curses.

"Are you deliberately trying to kill us both?"

"I told you we'd be fine."

"You're certifiably insane," she shouted over the sound of the waterfall.

He grinned, just damn happy to be alive right now.

They swam to shore and dragged themselves and their gear out of the water.

"It's going to take a while for all of this to dry out. Shouldn't hurt the weapons. Much," he said. Hopefully. He'd been out in the rain with the weapons before and it hadn't affected them. Then again, he'd never submerged them.

Gina swept strands of hair away from her eyes. "Uh-huh. And how are we going to get back up there?" She pointed. "Or contact Lou and the others? Do you even know where we are or how to get back to base?"

"Give me a minute to wring myself out and we'll figure it out, Gina. Relax."

"I can't relax. I just did a free fall into water whose depth you didn't know. You could have killed me."

"But I didn't, did I? Chill."

She shot him a look that was pure drama. He tried not to laugh, but couldn't help it.

"Don't you dare laugh at this. It's not funny."

"You have to admit it was one hell of a fun fall."

She shrugged. "Maybe."

"Come on. You, the no-fear action movie star who does her own stunts? You can't tell me you were afraid."

She squeezed the hem of her shorts and tilted her head to the side, a smile tickling her lips as she looked at him from the corner of her eyes. "It made my stomach flip. Like that first steep drop on a roller coaster."

"Mine, too. My favorite kind of ride. You gotta learn to trust me, Gina. I'd never purposely put you in harm's way."

She studied him for a second. "I'll work on that trust thing. You keep throwing me over cliffs, though, and it's going to be difficult."

Their shoulder lights were still functional, though their ear coms weren't. Since their eyeshades molded to their heads, they were still attached, thankfully. After testing the UV weaponry, they discovered Derek's gun still worked. Then he fixed the jammed mechanism on Gina's rifle and test-fired it. All good there, as well as the other weapons.

"Weapons check good. Unfortunately the only thing not working is the com system."

"Figures," Gina said. "Now we have no way of contacting Lou."

"First thing we do is figure a way out of here. Then, if we can't, we'll wait for Lou to realize we're out of touch and pick us up on his image program."

Derek studied their surroundings. They were blocked in on all sides by a steep rock face. No toe- or handholds with which to climb their way back up, and the waterfall on the north end wouldn't offer any help. Water surrounded them, as well as a short bank around the edge. That was it. They walked the perimeter of the area, but didn't see any openings.

"We're stuck," Gina said.

"Seems that way."

"So now what?"

"Now we wait until rescue arrives, and hope more demons don't show up in the meantime." Derek backed them up against one of the slopes and sat, resting his rifle against his thigh. Gina sat next to him.

"Why didn't the UV weapon work on the demons?" she asked.

"Need to strengthen the output, maybe reconfigure the concentration of UV light."

"It worked before."

"Yeah. On the pure or half demons. Haven't battled the hybrids for a while. Those fuckers are strong. And different. It's all about evolution, Gina. The way the Sons of Darkness create these hybrids, the genetics involved . . ." He dragged his fingers through his hair. "I don't know. It's not like we know everything. They adapt, then we adapt. It's war, know what I mean?"

Gina drew her knees up to her chest and wrapped her arms around them, not at all comforted by Derek's words.

War. Evolution. Adapting and learning on the fly. "I do know what you mean. But having to adapt in the middle of a battle when three hulking, foul creatures like that are a hairbreadth from killing you is a hell of a way to win."

"Sometimes we don't. Sometimes we retreat, regroup, and figure out another way."

"Great."

He looked at her. "This isn't the movies. The good guys don't always win."

"I'll keep that in mind."

"You should." He stared straight ahead. "It'll keep you alive longer."

What had she signed on for here? A chance to die young? A hopeless cause? "How do you do this, day in and day out, knowing that as soon as you think you've developed sophisticated enough weapons to beat them, they'll evolve enough to survive destruction?"

"Because we do kill them. Because they don't always figure out our weaponry fast enough, and because we're smarter than they are. And for every one of those nasty bastards that dies, there's one less demon out there to take some little boy or girl's mother. One less demon out there to steal a human male and turn it into a demon's slave. One less demon out there to throw the balance off. Because eventually, we will get them all."

"You believe that?" She wished she could. Maybe it was because this was all new to her, but as a relative newcomer looking from the outside, she had this vision of a demon factory in hell, churning them out faster than a small handful of human fighters could kill them.

"I do believe it. I have to. Otherwise, they'd win. Then we might as well just take our shit home and wait for Armageddon. And I'll be damned if I'll let that happen."

Gina turned her gaze to the waterfall, trying to lose herself in the sound of rushing water, to block out the sense of hopelessness enveloping her. But she couldn't leave it alone, her thoughts as restless as her body in these wet, sticking clothes.

She turned to Derek. "That night the demon took your brother. You were ten?"

He arched a brow. "Yeah. Why?"

"Weren't you terrified?"

He shrugged. "I guess. Confused more than anything. It didn't make sense. It was like a dream, only more tangible. You don't expect to see monsters really show up in your bedroom."

"Did your brother struggle?" She hated asking the questions, but they'd been plaguing her.

"No. He was asleep and didn't wake up."

"Didn't you find that strange?"

"Baby, everything about that night was strange."

"Of course it was. I'm sorry. I shouldn't bring it up." She started to turn away, but he caught her wrist.

"It's okay, Gina."

His fingers were warm on her chilled skin. Though the night was humid, her clothes were wet and there was a breeze coming off the water. The falls shot droplets in their direction with every gust of wind. She shivered.

"Come here." He pulled her into his arms. "You're shivering."

"I'm wet."

"So am I. We should get out of these clothes."

She tilted her head back. "What if someone showed up?"

"Then they'd see us naked, I guess. But it's getting cooler out here. Storm's coming in."

"What? You're a weatherman now?"

He grinned. "No, I can smell it on the air."

"So why get out of our clothes if we're just going to get wet again?"

"Well, first off, I'd get to see you naked again, and second . . . I guess there is no second," he teased.

She shook her head at his one-track mind. "That made absolutely no sense." But she still snuggled up against him. Just what they needed, a big tropical storm while they were out here with no shelter.

"We're just going to have to find a place where we can get out of it. These storms can get pretty bad. And if it rains hard, they aren't going to come looking for us anytime soon."

To prove his point, a big fat drop of rain landed on her leg. Then another.

"Come on." He stood and pulled her upright. "Let's head toward the falls."

Great. More water. Just what they needed when they were already wet and about to get wetter.

"Why?"

"Because there's something behind it."

"How do you know?"

"Quit asking questions and let's just go."

She followed, not sure what he thought he was doing. When they reached the waterfall it began to rain in earnest, soaking them through. Gina wished for wiper blades on her glasses, but without them she'd be blind in the dark.

"Give me your hand," Derek shouted. She reached for it, latching on as he pulled her against the rock wall face beside the waterfall.

The ground was slippery and she nearly lost her footing as he dragged her along the side of the slope, but then she saw what he was talking about. An opening, a ledge behind the falls. He let go of her to make the three-foot jump downward onto the ledge, and she followed, simply grateful to be out of the rain.

It was like a cocoon, the waterfall blanketing them from the storm outside. Lightning flashed, illuminating the small cave. Gina took a quick turn around and nodded.

"At least it's dry."

"Roomy enough, too. This will do until the storm passes." He shrugged the rifles off his shoulders, setting his lanterns on the ground and pointing them upward to bathe the cave in soft light. After discarding his boots and socks, he unbuckled his ammo belt and peeled off his wet shirt. "Better get out of those wet things."

He was right. Yet she felt strangely shy, even though they'd shared the most intimate of encounters last night. Getting naked for lovemaking was one thing. Standing around bare-assed with Derek while waiting for a storm to pass was another.

Derek rolled his eyes. "I'm not suggesting it to fuck you, Gina. A hunter with pneumonia does our cause no good. No one's coming for us in this storm, and even if they did they wouldn't find us in here. Now strip."

She shivered and realized he was right. This was no time for modesty or second thoughts about any other motives. She dropped her gear, toed off her boots, then pulled off her tank top and sports bra, unbuttoning her shorts with shaky fingers.

Dammit, her teeth were chattering. The wind howled outside, signaling an upsurge in the storm as it blew the waterfall back in on them.

She cursed when she couldn't manage the soaked buttons on her shorts.

"Let me help you," Derek said, shrugging out of his pants.

"I can do it."

"You're shaking and your lips are starting to turn blue." He brushed her numb fingers aside and deftly unbuttoned her shorts, then pushed the material down her hips. It clung to her skin, proving difficult. Derek squatted and dragged the soaked material all the way to her ankles, taking her socks off, too. She had to hold on to his shoulder while she stepped out of her shorts and panties.

When he looked up at her, she remembered last night, being in this same position, and her body began to warm. Especially the way he stared at her, his eyes darkening like storm clouds.

With a quick clearing of his throat, Derek stood and turned away to gather up their clothes, but the evidence of his desire couldn't be masked. His erection was full, prominent, and right out there for her to see.

She couldn't help but smile. At least she wasn't the only one thinking of last night. Waves of arousal heated her, warming her more effectively than if they'd built a fire right in the cave.

"The floor's a little cold," he said after he sat. "I don't want you on it."

She wrapped her arms around her middle. "What do you want me to do? Stand here?"

"No. I want you to sit on me."

Heat again, this time coiling around her belly. "You're kidding, right?"

"I need to get you warm, Gina. Now get over here and sit on me."

His voice was too husky, his body betraying the words that he was offering simply for her health. She knew his intentions were honorable, but she wasn't too sure about her own.

She needed his heat, and not just because her body was chilled. Flame had ignited already, and though her body was icy on the outside, it was hot on the inside, needing

Derek to stoke the fire. She walked over to him, watching the way his eyes darkened as she approached, the way he tilted his head back, his gaze gravitating to her sex as she placed it right in line with his full, oh so soft lips.

Then she straddled his thighs, and draped herself over his lap, facing him.

His wide-eyed look of shock was priceless. She wrapped her legs around his waist, the aching part of her making sweet, full-on contact with his erection.

"Damn, Gina," he whispered. "That's not what I meant."

She twined her arms around his neck. "You want me in a different position?"

He grasped her buttocks and dragged her closer against him. "Hell, no."

"Then warm me."

Shock didn't even begin to describe Derek's reaction to Gina's bold move. Straddling him. Naked, her wet center surging against his hard cock.

He hadn't expected this, his intent only to warm her body.

Well, hell, she was warm now. Hot, in fact, a flush returning to her cheeks, her lips no longer tinged with blue, but pink and lush.

He leaned in and brushed his tongue over her bottom lip. "Open."

She did, and he invaded, having taken the gentlemanly course for as long as he could tolerate. She offered, and he was damn well going to take. His lips pressed firmly to hers and his tongue entered her mouth, meeting hers in a desperate frenzy, licking and sucking in wild abandon.

He'd warm her all right. He'd get her so hot she'd be begging for a dip in the cool water.

Though frankly, at this point he was past worrying about her health and more concerned with getting inside her. She was wet, moaning and surging against him with blatant need that was hard to ignore.

His woman was ready. His woman. Yeah, she was his, at least for now. And now was all that mattered, wasn't it?

He'd never thought beyond the here and now. Anything more than that was dangerous.

She broke the kiss, sliding her lips down his neck and near his ear. "No foreplay," she gasped. "Fuck me."

More than ready, apparently. Suited him just fine, since he'd been hard from the moment he'd bent down to strip off her clothes, then looked up to see her naked beauty spread before him. She might have been shaking, blue and vulnerable, but even then she turned him on.

That kind of thing was hard to mask when you're naked. At least for a guy. And the look she cast down on him, her hair escaping her braid in wild disarray, her nipples pointed and begging for his tongue, and her legs widespread, her sex open for his view . . . a man could only offer so much chivalry.

He leaned back, finding her center, then slid inside her, groaning as he did. So tight, so hot, she sucked him into a vortex of wet heat. She surged against him, leaning back so he could watch as she moved forward, then retreated. The lanterns bathed her body in light, allowing him to see everything. Flickering shadows moved along her body. Like a dream, she undulated against him, teasing him with occasional glimpses of where they were connected. And each time, the visuals tore him apart, watching the way they were a part of each other and able to feel it at the same time.

Gina was a temptress.

"Do you know what you do to me?" she asked, her breasts swaying from side to side as she rode him. "It makes me crazy."

And she took him right to the bounds of sanity and beyond.

He lifted his finger and slipped it between her lips. She drew it in, sucking it, rolling her tongue around it, and his balls tightened, imagining her mouth on his cock, what magic she'd perform on him. "Yeah, baby. Suck it. Harder."

She drew her mouth over his finger the same way she slid over his dick. Slowly, inch by inch.

"You make me crazy, too, Gina. Goddamn, crazy."

Gina liked that, knowing she made him a little insane, knowing she gave him delirious pleasure. She saw it on his face as she sucked his thick finger into her mouth, as she imagined taking his shaft between her lips and pleasuring him that way.

He was tight inside her, hard and heavy, buried to the hilt and plunging even deeper. The chills and shivering cold had long since passed, leaving her burning, sweating, consumed with a fire that burned deep within.

She rocked that sweet spot between her legs against him, the hardened nub making contact each time she surged forward.

He withdrew his finger and cupped the back of her neck, drawing her close for a kiss. His tongue was liquid velvet sliding against hers, the words he murmured against her lips taking her ever closer to the release she so desperately sought.

"You want to come for me, baby?"

"Yes."

She'd never been one for conversation during sex. It was too . . . personal, brought her too close to her partner. But Derek whispered to her constantly, sometimes murmuring his approval as she moved, sometimes promising wicked things as he licked her earlobe.

He made her shiver. He made her do things she'd never ordinarily do.

He made her feel free.

"Ride me hard, Gina," he urged. She grasped his shoulders and lifted, then dropped down on him again, controlling both their pleasure. It was a truly heady experience, watching his face tighten, the shadows cast by the lantern giving him a harsh, roguish appearance.

His body was all hard muscles and planes. In this position she was free to touch him, run her hands over his shoulders and chest. When she grasped his chest hair and pulled, he cursed, but smiled at her in a way that let her know she was free to do whatever she wanted.

He could take it.

He grasped her buttocks, spreading them apart as he moved, positioning her in a way that was so perfect, as if he knew just what to do to take her there.

"Rock that pretty body against mine. Make yourself

come for me, Gina. I want to feel you squeeze me again. I want you to come on me, baby."

His words gave her hot chills. He gave her such power, such control, at the same time making her feel completely out of control.

She wanted to give him exactly what he asked for.

Derek watched the play of emotions on Gina's face. The ecstasy, the determination, the raw hunger that matched his own. She was a wildcat, scratching at him, pulling at him, and riding him with wild abandon.

But he'd held on as long as he could, waiting for the moment when he felt the contractions pull him deep, knowing she was about to launch.

That's right where he wanted her, primed and ready to rocket.

He drew her against him and buried his face in her neck, lifting his hips to bury himself deep inside her, biting down on the soft spot between her shoulder and neck as he did, feeling her tremble and come apart around him.

He loved to feel her come, shuddering against him, squeezing him, pouring over him with the sweetest, warmest rain. He growled against her and bit harder. She cried out and came again, and this time, he went with her, nearly light-headed with the lust that seemed to take over.

Damn, she brought out the animal in him.

He held her while she continued to rock against him, slowing until she stilled completely. He lay back and pulled her full on top of him, sweeping his hands over her back until she relaxed, her head resting on his chest.

He liked this, having her fall asleep lying on him.

A man could start thinking about tomorrow with a beautiful woman like Gina in his life.

He closed his eyes and pondered that thought.

The sun cast prisms of color through the waterfall, the last of the storm clouds blown away. Their clothes were mostly dry and they'd even managed to get a little sleep.

With their ear coms dried out, Derek had gotten in touch with Lou and gave them their location. Lou was dispatching a team with ropes to drag them out.

"You ready?" Derek asked, buckling his ammo belt on.

"Yeah." Gina turned to him. "Just need my guns."

He grasped her wrist and placed it on his crotch. "Got a big gun for you right here, baby."

She rolled her eyes and laughed, pushing at his chest. "Dumbass."

The high color on her cheeks made him feel better. Hell, he felt pretty damn good.

But now they had to get back to business. Reconfigure the UV weaponry, give Lou a report on the battle with the demons, and figure out what happened with the other hunters.

Playtime was over. Back to business.

Back to demon hunting.

Too bad he and Gina didn't live in another world, another place where demons didn't exist, where they could have a normal relationship.

Whatever normal was. He'd like to explore a normal

life sometime. He hadn't had normal since before Nic disappeared.

Only interludes of it. Like last night.

"Back to work, then," he said.

"I guess so," she replied with a reluctant sigh, slinging her rifle over her shoulder and turning to leave the cave.

He grabbed her then, taking in her gasp with his mouth over hers, kissing her deeply, with a longing that surprised the hell out of him.

Then he let her go, not sure why he'd done that, knowing damn well he shouldn't have. He didn't do emotional shit like that.

But Gina smiled, licked her bottom lip, and nodded, then climbed out of the cave.

Yeah, she understood.

Chapter Fifteen

While Derek was busy giving Lou a report on their failure with the UV weaponry last night, Gina took the opportunity to shower and change clothes. On her way back, she ran into Jake sitting on a secluded shady hill overlooking the beach, furiously scribbling on a notepad.

"What are you doing?" she asked, grabbing a spot on the ground next to him.

He glanced at her, then shifted back to his notepad. "Taking notes."

"Obviously," she said with a smile. "What kind of notes?"

"Laser notes."

"We had trouble with the UV last night."

"I know. I heard Derek telling Lou. That's why I'm making notes."

She peered over his shoulder to see a few drawings and

complex formulas that made absolutely no sense. "So what is that?"

"It's an idea I have about reconfiguring the lasers."

"Really? In what way?"

"Make a cutting tool out of the lasers instead of a flash weapon. I have the equipment here to do that. Just need some of Lou's weaponry."

"A cutting tool?"

He looked up at her again. "Slice and dice. Cut the demons in half."

"Yuck. But oooh, I like the sound of that." It would sure take care of the problem they'd encountered last night. "How long would it take to build the weapon?"

"Doesn't take any time at all. Just a matter of sending the laser through the mechanism, and the mechanism is easy. The key is whether or not Lou will let me build and try one."

"I don't see why he wouldn't. Have you talked to him about it?"

"No."

"Why not?"

"He might say no."

She rolled her eyes. "He might say yes. You need to tell him your idea."

"We'll see."

Geniuses. She'd never understand them. "Jake, are you afraid to make the suggestion to Lou?"

"I don't do people very well," he mumbled, his hair falling over his face.

Shy. The kid was shy. That was kind of cute. "Would you like me to go with you?"

He jerked his head up, flipping his hair out of the way. "You'd do that?"

"Sure. I think your idea has merit. Let's see what Lou says."

"And you can create this laser cutting machine in a day?"

Jake shrugged, pushing his hair out of his eyes again. "Yeah. Pretty much. I mean it's easy enough if I have the right tools, and I can create the remote controller easily. I can build it in a day, sure."

Lou looked over at her, lifting his brows and nodding. "Interesting."

"That means we lose weaponry," Derek said. "Not sure I like the idea."

"Only need a couple of the weapons," Jake said, jamming his hands in his pockets.

"I think it's a fabulous idea," Gina said. "And given that the UV light weapons didn't work for us last night, it's worth a try."

"They didn't work for anyone," Lou added. "We're reconfiguring them now. But still, I like your idea, Jake. I do agree with Derek that we can't really afford a shortage of weaponry, but if it's only two, then go for it."

"Excellent!" Gina was excited about this. "You need any help, Jake?"

Jake looked at her, wide-eyed. "Uh, yeah, if you want to."

"I'd love to be involved in this, to see how you build it

and to help you with the testing phase. Hell, I want to watch you kill demons with it."

"I'll bet you like those robot war shows on television," Derek said to her.

"As a matter of fact, I do."

Derek laughed. "You two go enjoy yourselves, then."

She did. Thoroughly. Building something with her hands wasn't something she often got to do. Jake really involved her in the process, and while she didn't understand everything, because God knows the kid was light-years ahead of her, she had a fundamental understanding of what he was doing. They worked all that day and into the night. Gina even got to stay behind as one of the guards for Lou while everyone else went out hunting. Gina and Dalton stood guard mostly while Jake worked, but she watched Jake.

He was fast. Scary fast. The remote control part she understood, but the whole laser array was out of her realm of understanding. She tried to ask him questions, but he might as well have been speaking Klingon to her.

When she wasn't watching Jake, she was watching Lou track demons and hunter activity. Derek and the others had managed to rerig the UV laser array, broadening and expanding the field. Of course it tested out as a stronger kill, but the only true test would be tonight. Gina had been torn between hanging out with Jake while he built the cutting laser and heading into the jungle to test the reconfigured UV weapon.

In the end, her geeky curiosity over the laser had won out. Derek didn't seem to mind, just shrugged and reworked the teams for tonight. He was probably happy not to have to drag her along with him.

Okay, so she hoped he missed her. A little.

Give it up, Gina. Other than screwing you, he's primarily interested in hunting demons. You're not his girlfriend or any permanent attachment in his life. You're a fellow demon hunter and occasional sex partner. So get over yourself.

To keep from obsessing about it, she turned to Lou. "How are they doing out there?"

"Holding on. All teams are engaged." He looked up at her. "That's all I can really tell you right now."

"Thanks." So no word yet on how the adjusted weaponry would work.

"I think the laser's ready for a quick test," Jake said.

"Seriously?"

"Yeah."

Gina looked to Lou. "Be my guest."

"What's the range, Jake?"

"Close is best. Say twenty-five feet."

Gina scanned the area lit by torches. "How about that tree limb right at the entrance to the jungle? That's about twenty-five feet."

"It'll do." He took the remote, which looked a lot like one of the devices used to manipulate a radio-controlled toy. After a quick flip of a side switch, the device lit up and began a soft whirring noise.

"It's supposed to do that, right?" she asked.

"Yeah. Don't worry."

She had been the recipient of too many high school chemistry class experiments gone wrong to believe that one. "Uh, I'll try. I'll just assume you know what you're doing."

He laughed. "Just step a little behind me in case this thing explodes."

He didn't have to say that twice. She moved back and held her breath while he aimed the handheld remote laser pointer in the direction of the branch attachment to the trunk. Once he had it in position, he pressed the button on the remote and a bright flash of light cut across the limb. It flamed for a second, then fell off the tree and crashed to the ground.

"Yes!" Gina jumped up in the air and threw her arms around Jake. "It works! It works!"

When she pulled back, Jake had turned beet red, but had the widest grin she'd ever seen. Gina pivoted and turned to Lou. "Did you see it?"

Lou was smiling. "I did. Well done, Jake. A very useful weapon."

"Thanks."

She couldn't wait for them to try it out.

Derek wasn't in the mood to argue.

And obviously Gina wasn't in the mood to see reason.

"You don't fight on Jake's team. You fight on mine," Derek said the next night when it was time to get ready.

"I understand that," Gina argued. "But I've been helping Jake since the inception of the laser. I would think you'd make allowances just this once. I want to go with him when he test-fires this thing."

"And he needs to be with experienced hunters who can back him up."

She blew out a breath of frustration. "Then put another hunter with us. Put two. You can go, too. I don't care. I just want to be there."

They stood on the beach face-to-face like Old West gunfighters preparing to draw. The other hunters were waiting, their rifles poised over their shoulders.

"Just keep things the way they are."

"I'm going with Jake."

"No, you're not."

"Yeah, I am. What are you going to do, shackle me to your ankle and drag me along with you into the jungle?"

"Don't make this difficult, Gina. It's important you understand one thing. I'm in charge of the hunters. I know what's best for all the teams. And your job as a hunter is to take direction from me. You're with me and Linc and Ryder tonight, and that's the way it is."

"This is important to me. I need to go with Jake. I want to be there."

He heard the silent plea in her voice, knew she was asking him based on their personal relationship.

Goddammit, that's the last thing he wanted, to feel anything for this woman that would cloud his judgment. He didn't like this. Not at all. And damn Gina for putting him in this position.

"Let her go with him, Derek," Lou said, stepping onto the beach. "She has a genuine interest in the laser and did help Jake build it."

"Fine. But I'm going on record against this." Derek

stalked away, content to leave his team one man short rather than restructure. And maybe digging in his heels at having her with him had more to do with wanting to keep her close, this unreasonable need to protect her.

At least Lou had taken the decision out of his hands. He'd have to remember to thank him later, as well as have a private talk with Gina about never doing this again. "Leave the extra man on that team. You might need him. Everyone get hunting."

Though he wasn't sure if he was more pissed at Gina or at himself, he was so goddamn livid he hoped they faced ten demons tonight. The way he felt right now he could probably kill them all with his bare hands.

Gina watched Derek stalk away and realized she'd just made a critical error, in both their personal and professional relationships.

What had come over her, pulling a diva move like that? Demanding her way or no way? She'd acted like a spoiled child, and that just wasn't like her. Why was it so important that she go out on Jake's team tonight and watch him fire the weapon? She already knew it worked.

What the hell was wrong with her?

She owed Derek an apology. Hell, she owed all of them an apology. But Derek and his team had already left and it was too late to tell him, at least. But not the rest of them.

"Hey, everyone. I'm sorry. I don't know what came over me there. A flight of movie star diva-ness, I think. My apologies for acting like a spoiled princess. That's really not me. Um, I dunno . . . PMS, maybe?" When they laughed, she exhaled, then turned to Lou, suddenly desperate to make this right. "I screwed up and stepped out of bounds. I can catch up with Derek and the team—"

Lou shook his head and grinned. "Don't worry about it. And we all butt heads with Derek now and then. Ask any of the hunters. You can go out with Jake's team tonight. Tomorrow, you're back with Derek."

If he'd have her. She nodded, feeling a little more relieved when the other hunters nodded back, some chuckled, and a few winked, diffusing the tension.

She'd tell Derek she was sorry later when he returned.

But for now she was heading out with a new leader. Dalton, a lean-looking muscle-bound warrior with surfer-boy shaggy, sandy hair and intense green eyes. Also on the team were Jake, Mandy, and a tough-looking hunter named Punk. She knew how he got that name: Had to be the hair, which stuck straight up. And he had the most interesting tribal tattoos on the back of his neck and around both biceps. But he looked like he'd cut your throat if you talked to him.

So she wasn't about to say a damn word. She was the interloper here. She stayed in formation and followed their lead. Jake remained silent, his newly created weapon tucked safely inside the pack at his side. He toted his rifle, but she knew if there was going to be any action, he'd be dragging the cutting laser out.

And Gina was dying to see how it worked.

Keeping her voice low, she asked, "You sure you're ready to use this on a real moving target, Jake?"

He slung the backpack over his shoulders, his lips curled in a half smile. She noted his nervousness, knew he tried to hide it behind his newly discovered bravado and maybe a little thrill at being the center of attention.

"It'll be fine, trust me. The system is untried, and while I would have liked more time for testing, I'm confident it'll fire." At her dubious expression he added, "I won't let the team down, Gina. This *will* work."

If ever someone needed a confidence booster, it was Jake. She nodded and squeezed his upper arm. "I know it will."

"Demons, your area, Dalton," Lou commed. "Four of them."

"Got it, Lou," Dalton replied, craning his head to look at Jake. "Looks like you'll get your chance, Jake."

She felt the muscles tense in Jake's arm.

"Gina, why don't you and Jake let us know what you want to do to set up," Dalton suggested.

At the look of uncertainty on Jake's face, Gina took over. "Let's have him stationary. Let the demons approach so Jake can aim and fire with the remote control."

She put Jake in front of two thick trees, positioning herself to his side so she could cover his back, and suggested the others work the front line defense. Jake should be well protected from the demons but still have clear line of sight to fire the laser.

"Jake, how's the vantage point?"

"Clear. I'm positioned and ready."

"All right everyone," Dalton said. "Stay sharp."

Adrenaline pumping and guns drawn, Gina scanned

the area for sign of approaching demons, eager for Jake to try out the lasers. All they had to do was draw the demons close enough for him to get a clear shot. Should be easy enough, right?

She hoped. Nothing was easy about these demons, but the whole thing seemed logical and straightforward. Right now it was all any of them could hope for.

The sounds came first, like an earthquake vibrating the ground under their feet. Then the movement along the tree line in front of them, branches swaying as the demons pushed them out of the way.

"Straight ahead," Mandy reported, already setting up her sights.

"Got it," Gina replied, taking aim. "Jake, you ready?"

"Lining up now."

"Mandy, Punk, you take the two on the outside. Leave the ones on the inside for Jake." Dalton looked to Gina, who nodded.

"That should work great," she said.

She turned and gave Jake the thumbs-up, wanting him to know she had every faith in him to do the job. The last thing she needed was for Jake to get nervous and freak out on them.

The sounds of the jungle simply died as animal life hid away from the unnatural forces making their appearance.

Gina spotted them, their gruesome appearance still making her shudder. God, those things were ugly. Giant movie zombies with glowing eyes, dripping fangs, and extended claws. Her skin prickled with goose bumps as fear inched its way up her spine.

Pushing her fear aside, she concentrated on the task. This was no time to be afraid. They had a huge task here—to kill these bastards. Unimaginable visions of these things running amok in a city or small town, creating havoc and killing the innocent, filled her with rage. They had to be stopped.

"Let them draw a little closer, wait them out," Dalton said.

Their menacing faces loomed into view, fingers uncurling to reveal their long, dripping claws. They were near enough for the hunters to see their red eyes and fangs, horrible, gruesome faces twisted in evil sneers.

She could smell them now, wrinkling her nose and trying to ignore how horrible it all was. Sometimes it seemed as if it was all a dream, that this wasn't real. But it was and she had to face it, had to fight them.

"You doing okay back there, Jake?" she asked, focusing only on the demons now, refusing to turn her gaze away from them.

"I'm ready, Gina. Just bring them to me."

She smiled.

As soon as the demons were in range, Mandy and Punk fired the UV lasers. The demons stopped, throwing their huge hands over their faces and twisting as if in great pain. But they kept coming. After firing again, the second and third shots took them down, boiling them down to a mass of smoking, gelatinous blobs.

Gina and Dalton backed up as the center demons continued their approach.

"Jake, ready?" she asked

"Ready!"

"Team down!" she commed.

They dropped to the ground and Jake fired the laser, a thin blue line arcing across the neck of one of the demons. Beautifully pinpoint, the demon stopped, tilting its head as if regarding them curiously. Then its head slid clean off its neck.

"Bull's-eye!" Gina yelled with an exuberant pump of her fist. She twisted halfway to give Jake another thumbs-up. "Way to go! All right, Jake, fire again!"

Another shot of the laser to their right and demon four was history.

Hot damn, this was fantastic! Exhilarated, Gina turned to give Jake another thumbs-up.

"Yes!" Jake said, standing up from his crouched position and pumping his fist in victory. He looked to Gina, his eyes sparkling in excitement.

"You did it, Jake!" She felt his thrill, knew how much it meant to him to participate, turned to Mandy and Dalton, who grinned back at her.

Hell, yeah, this new weapon rocked! When she looked back at Jake, her heart slammed against her chest, horror replacing her excitement.

Standing behind Jake was a demon, a human-looking one, a smug smile on its pale face, its long claws embedded in both sides of Jake's neck. Blood poured from the wounds in Jake's throat, sliding down his chest in lethal amounts. Jake's thin fingers fought against the claws embedded in his neck, but it was a fruitless effort.

It all happened so fast her mind barely registered it as

real, and yet it happened as if in slow motion, every single frame as vivid as a picture in a photo album. The look on Jake's face would be forever frozen in her memories. Shock, fear, disbelief, the light and life in his eyes quickly extinguishing as the demon lifted him in the air. Jake struggled, kicking his feet out for a few brief seconds, then stilled.

Noooo! Her mind screamed it, her voice frozen into silence. Oh, God, no, this couldn't be happening! There were four demons. They'd killed all of them. So where did the new one come from? Where was Lou's alert indicating another had surfaced?

Do something, goddammit! Her mind forced her body into action. Pulling her weapon, Gina lunged toward the demon, toward Jake, desperate to pull him away from danger, refusing to believe what she'd just seen. Punk grasped her arm, jerking her backward.

She didn't understand. Struggling to find her voice, she screamed, "What are you doing?"

"Look!"

She turned, horrified to see five of the hybrid demons appear out of nowhere. Rather than coming toward them, they flanked around the one holding onto Jake, as if protecting him. She didn't care; she'd take them all on if she had to. Struggling against him, she tried to pull away, but Punk held her firmly in his grasp.

"Woman, stop! You can't save him!"

The demon disappeared with Jake, dropping down into the ground. The other demons dropped down, too, vanishing instantly.

Gina wrestled away from Punk and started to run toward the spot where the demon and Jake had been. Punk tackled her to the ground. "Let me go, goddammit! I have to get to him."

"No," he yelled. "You'll only end up getting yourself killed. More of them could appear instantly."

She didn't care, had to save Jake. But Punk held on, refusing to let her loose, dragging her up to her feet by the back of her shirt.

"He's dead, Gina," Dalton said as he stepped up beside her, his calm voice belying the rage on his face. "There was nothing we could do."

She brushed tears away with the back of her hand, jamming her fist in her stomach to fight off the pain churning there. "Dammit, we can't just let them walk away with Jake! What if he's still alive?"

Mandy grasped her arm and turned her around, forcing Gina to meet her hard eyes. "The demon cut into his carotid arteries. He's gone."

"He's not gone! There's still a chance we can save him! We've got to go get him!"

"We can't battle the demons for Jake's body," Mandy said. "We've lost him."

Chapter Sixteen

Before Gina returned to camp, Derek and the others knew what had happened. Dalton alerted Lou, who in turn announced Jake's death to the rest of the hunters.

Shit. This wasn't going to go well.

Poor kid. Derek felt bad for Jake. Despite being a little pale and skinny, Derek saw something in him. He was a genius with weaponry. He'd have made a brilliant demon hunter who would have contributed much to the Realm of Light. They'd chosen Jake for a reason.

And the goddamn demons knew it, too. He'd bet his ass they targeted him first, deliberately set out to isolate and terminate him because they recognized him as a major threat.

He'd also bet Gina was blaming herself for this.

In fact, he knew she was as soon as the team walked into camp, Gina cradling the remains of Jake's crushed remote in her arms like the symbolic evidence of his body.

She laid it on the table, unshed tears pooling in her half-lidded gaze as she barely made eye contact with them all.

"This is my fault," she whispered, her voice shaky. "I take full responsibility for Jake's death."

She turned and walked away, heading to the bungalows.

Ah, Christ. He wished he could have been there. Maybe he could have prevented it. Right, and how could he have done that?

It wouldn't have made any difference anyway, whether or not he'd been there. Couldn't save the world all by himself. He'd learned that one a long time ago. They were all vulnerable.

After debriefing and dinner, Gina still hadn't returned.

"I'm going to go talk to her," Derek finally said, tired of waiting for her.

"You do that," Lou replied. "Don't let her go on thinking this is her fault."

He stopped off at his room for a quick shower and change of clothes, but he knew it was a stall tactic. He wasn't sure what he was going to say to her. He was the wrong person to offer sympathy. In the demon hunting business, people died. He'd seen it before.

It was bound to happen. Demons were smart and devious and couldn't be counted on to play fair. He'd warned all the hunters that death was a possibility, but he also knew none of them had really listened.

Most never do, until it happens. He'd been there and done that himself when he lost a team member. *So just shut up and offer sympathy.* No, he should make her talk about it.

Oh, right. Trying to get Gina to talk about her feelings had worked so well the other night, hadn't it?

But this time she'd have to.

He knew what it was like to try to run from your feelings. It didn't do any good, because they stayed right with you no matter where you went. Like demons, the memories were unshakable. She'd have to face them eventually.

He'd had to. A long time ago. Now it was her turn.

And that part he *could* help her with.

Stupid, stupid, stupid.

It was all her fault.

Because she was arrogant, thinking this was some kind of game. She'd been so excited, wanting to take the lead with Jake like she'd been the one to personally discover his new weapon. And then she'd gone off on Derek like she was Gina, queen bitch of the jungle, large and in charge.

Only this wasn't Hollywood, and it wasn't a game. The monsters were real. They could all be killed.

Correction—someone *had* been killed.

Jake. And it was her fault he was dead. Her responsibility. She'd taken him under her wing, but instead of protecting the kid, she'd let her overconfidence and giant ego blind her to the reality that she had no idea what she was doing.

She was an actress who dabbled in extreme sports, martial arts, and weaponry. She thought she could easily step in and manage demon hunting. Right. She didn't have a clue what she was doing.

God, what a mess she'd made. She dropped her head in her hands and wished she could crawl into a hole and pretend today had never happened. If only she hadn't encouraged Jake to build the weapon. If she'd left him alone . . .

She startled at the knock on the door. Wasn't everyone in bed by now? Shay had already come by. So had Olivia, and Dalton and Mandy. She'd sent them all away. The last thing she wanted to do was talk this out. Nor did she want anyone's sympathy.

She wanted to feel awful, deserved a lot worse than a twisted stomach and shaky limbs.

"Go away."

Whoever it was turned the knob and walked in. She whirled to find Derek closing the door behind him.

"I don't want company."

"I know. But you're getting it anyway. And you should lock your door."

"Why?"

He tilted his head to the side and arched a dark brow as he approached. "What if I'd been a demon?"

"They knock?"

"You know what I mean."

Shrugging, she started to head past him, intent on grabbing water from the minifridge. "I guess I would have been dead."

He slipped his fingers around her wrist, stopping her from moving away.

"You've been crying."

Dammit. He wasn't supposed to notice that. With a quick turn, she shot him a "no shit" look. "Well, Derek, one of my team members was brutally murdered today. Forgive me if that got to me just a little."

Now he looked even more uncomfortable than she felt.

"Hey. I'm sorry. I didn't mean you weren't supposed to cry." Jamming a hand through his hair, he added, "Dammit, Gina, I'm not very good at this sensitivity shit."

"I noticed." She smiled. She didn't want to, but she did. She extricated her wrist from his hold and grabbed the bottle of water, unscrewing and rescrewing the cap.

"You can't blame yourself for what happened with Jake."

This was a conversation she didn't want to have. "Who do you think I should blame, then?"

"The demons, Gina. They're cunning and vicious. You're new to this game. Hell, even those of us who've been fighting them for years still lose. You can't predict them. They show no mercy."

She'd witnessed that firsthand today. "I hadn't expected them to be merciful, Derek. But I should have known better."

"How would you have known?"

"I don't know." She fiddled with the cap on the bottle, finally putting it back, needing something stronger than water. But even alcohol wouldn't dull her senses enough tonight. "I shouldn't have let him build that machine."

"He still might have been killed, weapon or not." Derek sat on the chair next to her bed and stretched his legs out. "They'd have figured out eventually that Jake was a threat to them."

"So I expedited his death, then." Great. That made her feel so much better.

"Do you really want to make this about you?"

She sat on the bed and gripped the edge of the mattress. "It is about me. And the mistakes I made."

"You're wrong. You're a good warrior. All of you are good warriors. It could have happened to any of us. It could have happened on my team today. Lou didn't even get the hot-spot warning on those demons that appeared and grabbed Jake until they were already out. It was instantaneous, and that has never happened before."

"Really?"

"Yeah. It was a portal blast of some sort. Like an express elevator, if you will. From the way Lou explained it, one minute there was no new demon activity, the next they were right there, killing Jake. It was so fast Lou didn't even have time to warn you."

She leaned forward and clasped her hands together. "And a sudden appearance like that, one without a heat warning, had never happened before."

"No. The demons appear fast, of course, but never without a heat signature, the increased temperature warning that registers on Lou's program. This was so fast it didn't even log on his scale. He's looking into it now, to see if they've developed some new method of appearing, one that doesn't project a thermal signal."

That, at least, offered her some comfort.

"If you're going to be a demon hunter, if you're going

to fight alongside us, you have to get used to people dying. You have to learn to deal with it."

"How do *you* deal with it?"

She could see the lines etched alongside his eyes as he blinked, trying to mask the pain. Memories of people he'd lost, maybe?

But just as quickly as it had been there, it disappeared, replaced by a shrug of indifference. "I don't let myself care about anybody."

Ouch. Talk about listening to her own inner voice. Except hearing it from Derek sounded heartless. And she wasn't heartless. She wished she was—then she wouldn't be hurting so bad inside.

And Derek did care, no matter what he said. He was as good at trying to hide his feelings as she was.

"I can't do that anymore. I can't pretend I don't care."

He frowned. "I didn't say you shouldn't care. But you're going to have to toughen up. You can't do this job and fall apart every time you lose someone on the team. It'll tear you up."

It already had. She knew caring was a huge mistake, knew getting involved with these people was going to screw her up. Where had the hard Gina gone, the one who never got involved, never got emotional, never developed ties? When had she gotten so wrapped up in these people?

"Think out loud."

She looked up at him. "Huh?"

"Your mind is processing. It helps to do it out loud."

"I don't want to." She didn't want him there. She didn't want anyone there.

"You just want to wallow in your misery all by yourself. Feel sorry for yourself. Blame yourself."

"Actually, yeah, I do. So if you wouldn't mind leaving . . ."

But he didn't. Instead, he climbed onto the bed behind her, stretching his long legs out on either side of hers.

"What are you doing?"

His warm hands reached for her shoulders, digging into the tension that had knotted there.

"Massaging your shoulders."

She tightened, trying to shrug him off. "Don't."

His chest brushed her back, his heartbeat strong and rhythmic. Relaxing.

Dammit, she didn't want to relax. She shifted, trying to look around.

"Stop, Gina," he said, his voice soothing.

"Why are you doing this?"

"Because I've been where you are. Beating yourself up isn't going to bring Jake back. It's not your fault."

He continued to dig into the tight muscles of her shoulders, pulling her back against his chest. Though she struggled at first, it was clear he wasn't going to let her up, so she finally gave in and rested against him, letting his fingers work their magic.

Blissfully silent, he didn't speak, just melted away her tension with his magical fingers. Gina closed her eyes and for a few moments, everything was okay.

"Let it go," he finally whispered in her ear. "A good hunter mourns a loss, then lets it go. You can't dwell. It'll eat you up inside."

She shuddered a sigh. "I know you're right. The logical part of me, anyway."

"I talked to Dalton and he filled me in on what happened, step by step. I'd have done everything you did."

She tilted her head back and looked at him. "Honestly?"

"Honestly. I wouldn't have done anything different. You set Jake up so he'd be protected, you had him covered well. I would have been shocked as shit, just as you were, when that other demon showed up and killed him. And I'd have blamed myself, too."

"You would?"

"For a few minutes, yeah. But then I would have realized it wasn't my fault. They came out of nowhere in that portal blast." He squeezed her shoulders. "Now let it go."

"You're right. I guess. I feel horrible about this, Derek. He was just a kid." Damn tears. She swiped them away.

"I know, babe." He wrapped his arms around her. "There are times I just want to walk away from all this. Times I feel like we're never going to make any headway, that the demons are going to win no matter what we do."

"What keeps you going?"

"Nic."

She shifted in his arms so she was cradled sideways, allowing her to see his face. "Your brother? Why?"

"Because they took him. Because a part of me holds out hope, stupid as it is, that someday I might be able to find him."

"You think he's still alive, that he's still . . ." She couldn't say the word.

"Human? I don't know. Probably not. But the thought of it drives me. You have to have hope, ya know?"

No, she didn't know about hope. After her mother had disappeared and they'd wrenched her away from her home and dumped her into foster care, she'd given up on hoping she'd ever see her again. And now to find out the demons had taken her and made her a vile baby-making machine . . . what kind of hope could she have knowing that?

She shuddered.

Derek tipped her chin up. "What's wrong?"

"Nothing."

"Secrets," he said, his gaze boring into hers. "Dark demons."

"What?"

"We hold all this shit inside and never share it with anyone. It's like a cancer eating away at us."

"Do you ever share your feelings and emotions with anyone?"

The corners of his mouth tilted in a wry smile. "I never used to."

Touché. "I never had family, Derek. I never had people to share my feelings with. I lost my mother when I was a child. She was the only family I had. You have no idea what I went through after that." She pushed back from him. "I don't do this 'opening up' thing well."

The lines at the corners of his eyes deepened as he frowned and jammed his fingers through his hair. "Do you think it's easy for me? For any of us? We're all fighting our pasts. My mother went off the fucking deep end after Nic disappeared. She lied to me about him, then went crazy trying to hide us from my dad. We moved around constantly until she died and I joined the Navy. I had no friends, no relationships, no other family to talk to. No one to confide in about this demon I saw taking my little brother out of his bed. Hell, for the longest time I thought I was crazy, too. Not quite what I'd call a stable family life."

"You're right. I'm sorry. I have no right to complain."

"That's not what I meant at all. Of course you have a right. You have every right. All of us do. I'm just trying to get you to open up, to share the pain with me. You're not all alone in this. You're not the only one this has happened to."

She turned her head to look out the window. Moonlight filtered through the trees. "I can't share that with anyone."

"Why not? Because it'll show you as less than the tough, ballsy, fearless woman you portray on the screen? Well, guess what, Gina—your cover is blown. I already know you're nothing but a big, toasted marshmallow."

Her wide-eyed gaze shot to his. "That's not funny."

He wasn't smiling. "It wasn't meant to be. I read you the first day. Crispy on the outside. Creamy inside. My favorite."

"Now you are teasing me."

"Yeah, I am."

"I hate that."

"No, you don't. You've just never experienced it before so you don't know how to handle it. Most people cater to you, treat you with kid gloves because they're afraid of offending you. I just treat you like an equal."

She crossed her arms. "I don't like it."

His lips twitched. "Are you going to pout?"

"I might."

He pushed back against the mattress and rested against the headboard of the bed. Lacing his fingers behind his head, his wide chest expanded as he arched his back. "Go ahead. I'll watch."

"Derek!" Dammit, he was mean. "Get out of my room and let me get some sleep."

"You don't want to sleep," he said, his eyes darkening.

"Since when do you presume to know what I want?"

"Since I've decided we're so much alike it's damn scary."

She slid off the bed and grabbed for that bottle of water again, unscrewing the cap and taking a long swallow. She threw one to him and he caught it one-handed. "We are nothing alike," she said. "You're a bullheaded, opinionated, have-to-have-things-your-own-way pain in the ass."

"Exactly."

"Oh, that's not fair. I'm nothing like that."

"Aren't you?"

She was really going to have to start locking her door. "Go away, Derek. I don't want you here. Seriously."

"You're just mad that I'm not kissing your ass and giving in. But that's not my style, Gina, and you know that. You don't always get to have your way. Now come lay down on the bed with me and I'll make you forget all your troubles."

"You have an enormous ego."

"Overshadowed by your gigantic one."

She tossed the empty water bottle in the trash and placed her hands on her hips, leveling a glare in his direction. "Neanderthal."

He arched a brow. "Brat."

"Bastard."

He was smiling now. "Bitch."

She snorted. No one ever talked to her the way he did. No one ever gave her shit or threw her own attitude back at her. Admittedly, she found it rather invigorating. She approached the bed, resting the front of her thighs at the edge of the mattress.

"I'll have you fired," she teased.

"I'll have you spanked."

Her eyes widened. Now there was a challenge. She crawled onto the bed. "You wouldn't dare."

"Try me."

The flare of arousal sparked inside her, her body flaming like an unchecked wildfire. The thought of his hands on her, touching her, spanking her. God, the places her mind went just then.

"Come here, Gina."

"No."

Poised for flight, she still wasn't prepared for his quick reflexes. When he lunged at her, she let out a squeal, but he caught her around the waist and dragged her, face-down, over his lap.

"Derek, let me up!"

"Oh, I don't think so. You've been a very bad girl."

She squirmed, but it sure as hell wasn't to get away. Desire coiled heavy along her limbs and in her belly, especially when Derek dragged her shorts down to her thighs, baring her buttocks.

"Don't you dare!"

"You want me to."

His voice had gone dark, dangerous, just the sound of it enough to inflame her senses. When he touched her skin, she jumped, her body anticipating and needy. But he caressed her butt, smoothing his hand over her flesh, sliding between her legs and tempting her by purposely evading the parts she wanted him to touch.

She bit down on her lower lip, refusing to beg him to touch her there, wondering what he was going to do next.

When he swatted her buttocks, she let out a yelp. But he hadn't spanked her hard. Oh, no, that was a love tap, meant to excite, not punish.

Damn, did it ever excite her. She grabbed a fistful of blanket and held on as he did it again to the other cheek, then smoothed the area he had just swatted with a soft caress, once again sliding his fingers between her legs.

"Open for me, Gina."

Insinuating his hand between her thighs, he pushed them further apart, tugging her shorts all the way off. But still, he didn't touch her sex, which throbbed in anticipation.

Please.

One spank, another tingle of lightning excitement, another sweet caress. And still, he didn't touch her where she craved it most, didn't answer her unspoken pleas.

It was the sweetest, most agonizing punishment she'd ever received. And she knew that when he did touch her, when he did caress her most sensitized areas, she was going to explode.

Derek had never spanked a woman in his entire life, had never engaged in this kind of sexual play. But with Gina, everything came naturally.

This need to claim her in unusual ways was overpowering him. The need to dominate her, the animal urges inside him growing stronger.

Forcing a gentle calm he didn't feel, he played with her, enjoying the way she squirmed and moaned on his lap. He was so hard he was ready to explode, but he enjoyed teasing her, loved watching her, inhaling her musky sweet scent, feeling the trickle of arousal seep from between her legs.

Her sweet, firm ass was pink from his swats, though he took care not to hurt her, knowing his own strength. When she shuddered, he knew it was from pleasure, not pain. No, not the way she was undulating against him, brushing his cock with every movement.

He was dying all right, but he was waiting for her to utter the words.

Finally, she did.

"Derek, please," she whispered, her face buried in the rumpled blankets.

"Please what, baby?" he asked, teasing her inner thighs with swirling fingers, aching to touch her weeping center but forcing himself to wait.

"You know what."

"Tell me what you want."

"Touch me."

"Where? Here?" He rubbed the small of her back, loving the little dimple where her body indented there.

"No." She arched against him and he bit back a groan.

"Here, then?" He rubbed her buttocks. So firm, her skin so unbearably soft.

"Well, yeah, that's nice. But not there. Lower."

"Oh, here." He smoothed his hands over her firm, taut thighs.

"No, dammit." She flipped over and grabbed his hand, placing it on her sex. Fire blazed in the dark blue of her eyes. "Here."

She was wet, slick with desire, and he'd just found heaven. He cradled her head in the crook of his arm and brought her head up to his. "Oh," he said, smiling down at her as he moved his fingers through her folds. "There."

She hiccuped a gasp and he swallowed it with his lips as he kissed her, then slid his fingers inside her, licking her tongue, sucking it gently into his mouth. Her body convulsed around his fingers like a vise while he circled the small knot with his thumb, massaging her with gentle strokes until she gasped.

A sense of urgency overrode his desire to take her slow and easy. He laid her on the bed and removed her top, discarding his own clothing in a hurry. Then he flipped Gina onto her belly again. She went willingly, offering a saucy smile as she lifted up to accept him.

God, the woman was as hot as the fires of hell itself. Which did nothing to quell the madness surging inside him. Her wild nature only stoked the flame to blistering level as he kneed her legs apart and plunged inside her, rewarded with her shriek of approval as he buried himself deep.

He paused and took a few sweet seconds to feel her pulse around him, her body accommodating him, drawing him in.

He could die right here and be one damn happy man.

But then the urge to move took control. The time for sweet tenderness was over. The hunger had returned full force, beating against him with urgent pulses, forcing him to power inside her like a beast in mating. He wrapped one arm around her waist and thrust deep, retreating, and each time trying to crawl deeper and deeper inside her. Her body accepted each stroke, squeezing the very life out of him until he simply couldn't gasp a breath anymore, had no control over the monster within him and just had to let it out.

He roared and let it free, the cries of her climax compelling him to let loose. He pinned himself against her and shuddered, biting down on the back of her neck as he shook with the force of his own orgasm and took her with him again.

Such a sweet release. Panting, sweating, they stayed glued like that for minutes while the only sounds were of their own breathing.

God, he needed to do this with her more often. He held her close, realizing that the madness, the boiling tension that lived inside him seemed to disappear for a while whenever they made love.

The first thing he remembered when he crawled out of the red haze was Gina underneath him. God, she probably couldn't even breathe. Sometimes he wondered if he hurt her. He was so lost in sensation, his mind focused on her body and being joined to her, that it was like he became someone else.

Sometimes he forgot to be gentle with her. He purposely held back, but he wondered if it was still too much for her.

He rolled to his side, taking her along and keeping her nestled close, her back against his chest.

"You okay?" he asked.

"Mmm-hmmm" was her only answer.

He blew out a sigh of relief. Each time it got harder and harder to maintain his control. He had no idea what kind of mental trip he took when he made love with Gina, but it was like nothing that had ever happened to him before. She was like a drug in his system, and she took him on one hell of a ride.

Spent, Derek wrapped his arms around Gina, falling in and out of consciousness, content to hold her next to him for as long as he could.

Chapter Seventeen

Gina was huddled in a dark corner. Demons were all around her, searching. If she curled herself into the smallest little ball possible, maybe they wouldn't be able to find her.

She was shaking nearly uncontrollably now, fear snaking its way up her spine, every nerve ending in her body primed with terror.

"Gina?"

At first she could barely hear the soft voice. She strained to listen.

"Gina, sweetheart, can you hear me?"

She shoved her fist against her mouth, batting back the tears. *Momma?*

No, it couldn't be. She was dead. Gone. They'd taken her a long time ago.

"Gina, where are you?"

She closed her eyes, refusing to believe. It was a trick

the demons were playing on her to get her to come out of her hiding place.

No way. She wasn't going to fall for it.

Yet she could smell her mother's lotion, so familiar, so comforting. The urge to leap from the dark corner and run to that scent was so strong she had to force herself to stay put.

They'll hurt you if you move. Don't do it.

"Let me get you out of here. I know the way."

Don't do this to me, Momma. Please.

She heard a scraping noise against the floor, then shuffling, growing ever nearer her location. Her heart thudded, her blood pounding in her ears. She covered her ears with her hands, willing the nightmare to go away.

"Gina, come to me."

She wasn't real. She wasn't. Yet she could still smell her, could feel her mother's presence.

"Sweetheart, let me take you out of here. Let me take us someplace safe."

Her hands dropped to her sides and she stood, then, needing this. To hell with demons and nightmares. She wanted her mother. "Momma. Where are you?"

"I'm right here. Listen to my voice. Follow it."

She did, winding her way through the darkness, ignoring everything but the sweet call of her mother. Soon she'd fall into her arms and everything would be all right.

The light. She saw the light, and a shadow in front of it. Long hair falling over her shoulders, her arms outstretched.

"Is that you, Momma?"

"Yes, it's Momma. Come to me."

She was almost running now, afraid to look back, afraid the demons would get to her before she reached her mother.

Almost there, her arms outstretched. The fog was lifting now, the light illuminating the shadows around her mother.

Gina skidded to a halt only inches away from the woman whose arms she'd almost thrown herself into.

That . . . thing was not her mother. Hideous, its face was twisted into a demon's mask.

It was her mother's voice, but not her mother's face. It was ugly, with fangs dripping blood, clawlike fingers reaching for her.

"Come to me."

Revulsion filled her. Gina shook her head, tears flowing from her eyes. Her stomach hurt. Her heart hurt.

"Momma, what did they do to you?"

"They made me better. Stronger. Let me hold you. I'll make you just like us." Her mother lunged for her, evil filling her eyes.

"No! Don't touch me!"

"Gina."

"Stop it! Get away from me. Don't touch me!"

"Gina, wake up!"

She shot up in bed, a part of the dream still with her, her face wet as she blinked back tears. Derek was right there, his arms tight around her.

"Baby, it's okay. It was just a dream."

A dream. Her mother was gone. It was just a dream.

A horrible, awful nightmare.

"I know." She brushed her hair away from her face and allowed Derek to pull her back down. The room was dark, though she knew it was daylight outside by now. Somewhere during the early dawn hours he must have pulled the window shades and closed the shutters, blanketing the room in cooling darkness.

The dream had been so vivid, she still shuddered as she recalled every detail. She hadn't dreamed of her mother in years. Why now?

"Tell me about it."

"I was in a dark place, hiding from demons, and my mother called out to me. At first I didn't believe it was her, but then I went out to find her, and when I did, she had the face of a demon." It hurt again just to think about it.

Derek pulled her tighter against him. "I'm sorry. I know how painful it is to think about them taking her."

For the first time, she realized someone really did know how she felt. She turned around and switched on the bedside lamp, then faced him. "How have you coped all these years, knowing they took your brother?"

He swept her hair away from her face, then smoothed his hand over her shoulder and down her arm, continuing to caress her skin. "When I was little, it was mostly fear that they would come for me next. Then I felt safer when we moved. But when I spotted one as an adult, it all came rushing back."

She lifted up on her elbow. "You spotted one? You mean in public?"

"Sort of. I was in the Navy and out on leave in Chicago

with some of my buddies. It was about three in the morning and I'd just left a bar and was heading toward the parking lot by cutting through an alley. There it was. Same kind of ugly fucker I'd seen the night Nic was taken. At first I couldn't believe what I was seeing, thought it was the alcohol. I hid behind a Dumpster, scared shitless and shaking, convinced I was having some kind of psychotic break. But when I watched it take a human and disappear down a manhole cover, I knew damn well I wasn't drunk and seeing things."

"Oh, my God. I can't believe it."

He nodded, squeezing her hand. "Then I saw Lou and a few hunters go in after it, and I followed them. They fought off a bunch of demons, and Lou found me. He didn't seem surprised to see me there, almost as if he'd been expecting me."

"Well, he did say he had psychic abilities. Maybe he had a premonition about you or knew about your background like he did ours."

"Yeah, something like that. I just wanted to kill those bastards. Not too long after I met Lou I got out of the service and joined up with the Realm of Light and have been doing this ever since."

Whenever he talked about demons his face went hard, the lines of his forehead more pronounced, the gray of his eyes darkening like an approaching storm. She smoothed the furrows on his brow with her fingertips. "It's been a difficult life for you." Would she become the same way? Would the drive for revenge against the creatures who'd stolen her mother become what she lived for?

"It's a choice I made a long time ago, even before I saw the demon and found Lou. I knew I had to find the thing that took Nic, had to figure out what happened to him. Even if just to prove to myself it hadn't been a dream, that Nic hadn't died that day like my mother claimed."

She stared at the smooth expanse of his chest. "I never searched."

"What do you mean?"

"For my mother. I never looked for her."

"You were a child, Gina. What were you supposed to do?"

"I don't know. Nothing at first. But when I grew up, I never hired anyone to try and find out what happened to her. I had just pushed it all out of my memories. The authorities had no leads and had closed the file on her by then. I just gave up. It was so painful, thinking about that night, waking up alone and not knowing where she was."

He reached for her chin and lifted her head, forcing her to meet his gaze. "You were a child. It was a trauma. What happened to you after that?"

"Since I had no other living relatives, I was sent to foster care. Hated my foster parents, hated the other kids. Of course they were all nice enough, not abusive or anything. God knows they tried to reach me, but I didn't want them to. I'd already had a mother and didn't want another one. All I wanted was to be left alone."

She hadn't wanted anyone to love her ever again, hadn't wanted to risk the possibility of opening her heart to anyone, to take the chance that they, too, would be taken from her.

Her stomach clenched as the memories flooded back.

"Where was your dad?" he asked.

"He died when I was a baby. Brain tumor."

Derek rubbed his thumb over her cheek. "So you decided you'd just tough it out on your own."

"Yeah."

"So did I. My mom had no other family, either. When Nic disappeared and my dad did whatever the hell he did and we moved, it was just the two of us. And of course, she was pretty much just a shell. I was taking care of her after that."

"Aren't we a pair?" she stated.

He smiled and palmed her cheek, his voice filled with soft tenderness. "Kindred spirits, in a twisted kind of way. We've been through hell and back, and we're survivors. We don't let anyone hurt us. Nothing could be as bad as what we've been through."

Which was probably what drew her to him. That he had a tough exterior, yet underneath a tenderness that surprised her.

Something she was learning to adapt to.

"It's strange," she murmured, not realizing she'd said it out loud until he responded.

"What is?"

"Oh. Nothing."

"Come on."

"You, I guess," she said with a light chuckle.

"Oh, thanks."

"No. That's not what I meant. Well, I guess I did. You're unlike any man I've ever met." And she was getting uncomfortably close to revealing emotions she wasn't certain she was ready to uncover. Either to him or to herself.

"In what way?"

"I'm not very good at this, Derek. I told you I don't do relationships with men. Hell, I don't do relationships with people, period."

"Try me. I won't bite. Well, I might, but you'll like it."

She snorted. "It's terrifying to feel close to you, to want to confide in you. I never had friends or family that I talked to about her, about what was going through my head after she was gone. I never talked to anyone about anything important."

"I know exactly how you felt."

"You do."

"Yeah. Scared, alone, and isolated. Like no one loved you and no one ever would again. And if you allowed yourself to care about someone, they'd hurt you."

Whoa. Derek couldn't believe he'd just said that. Why not just purr for her and complete the utter pussy transformation?

And the way she looked at him right now, her big blue eyes growing wider . . . she'd probably toss him out of her bed any second.

He pushed away and sat up, jamming his legs into his pants. Something about Gina drove him to tell her things he'd never told anyone.

"What are you doing?"

"Leaving."

"Why?"

"I don't know."

"Because you're the one who's afraid now."

"I'm not afraid, Gina. It's just time to go."

"You want me to open up, but when you do, it scares you. What does that say, Derek?"

He paused and half turned, his gut tightening as he looked at her sprawled out across the bed.

She looked so goddamn beautiful she took his breath away. And vulnerable, with unshed tears glistening in her eyes.

Tears. Shit. Now what?

"What's wrong?" he asked.

She held out her hand, and like the dumbass he was, he took it and allowed her to pull him back down on the bed.

"I don't know what's wrong. Everything's wrong. Nothing's wrong." She drew her knees up to her chest and wrapped her arms around them. "I'm never weepy. It's weak."

He swiped at a tear rolling down her cheek. "Yeah, well, I never admit to women that I might have felt lost, alone, and scared. It's weak."

"It is not weak to admit that. If it is, then I was weak, too. I was so afraid the night my mom disappeared I couldn't get out of bed to go to the bathroom. I wet the bed, Derek, because I was afraid of someone or something getting me if I left it."

Her voice wavered as she said it, her lip trembling.

"Ah, God, Gina." He jerked her against him and she let loose, her body shuddering as she released huge, wracking sobs she probably hadn't allowed herself to cry in years. And he remembered that shaking fear, though he'd long ago come to grips with it, used it to his advantage when he fought the monsters.

She'd learn how to use it, too. But for now, he let her cry it out, held her while she sobbed against his shoulder until she had nothing left.

"It's not weak to cry for your mother, baby. It's not weak to mourn for her again, especially since we just dredged it all up, making it fresh."

She sniffed. "I guess."

"And it's okay to care." He didn't know if he was trying to convince her, or himself. "It's okay to care."

"Caring about someone scares me. I want to care, Derek, I really do. But God, it scares me so much."

He pulled her away, wiped her tears, then kissed her lips, licking away the salt as he covered her mouth.

God, he did care. Too damn much.

And that was more frightening than the demons.

He wanted to lose himself inside her again, spend the day forgetting where they were or what they had to do. But they'd already hidden away long enough.

"We need to get something to eat, and figure out the plan for tonight," he said, after reluctantly releasing her mouth.

"I'm a mess. I'm going to take a shower and get rid of these swollen bags under my eyes."

"You look beautiful. But take your time. I'll see you outside later."

"Thank you."

She kissed him again, and his heart clenched. By the time he walked out of her bungalow, he realized he was well and truly screwed.

He'd fallen in love with Gina, and that had just made his job ten times more difficult.

The Master watched the transformation take place. So painful for these humans. Though this one was almost dead by the time they'd brought him in. It took all the enjoyment out of the process when they weren't fully cognizant of what was happening to them. They had gone overboard during the capture and hadn't listened to his instructions. Now the human's mind was gone and he was useless to them. Those who had done so had been punished severely.

But this one would still prove useful in other, more entertaining ways.

It didn't take long, though the final changes would take weeks to perfect. But they had transformed him enough to send him back out with the others.

"So soon, though?" the second asked.

"Yes. For . . . psychological reasons," the Master said.

"Of course," the second replied, his dark eyes gleaming. "You are so evil."

The Master grinned. "I am the best at what I do. I know what frightens them."

He turned away from the second to regard the beast in transformation. Chains secured its arms and legs to the wall, holding it as its muscles broadened and its body strengthened with the hormones and chemicals they'd implanted within it.

Such hideous creatures, yet such utter perfection.

"You may not survive what I have planned for you, but you will be mine in so many other ways."

The creature lifted its lids, barely aware of what was happening, yet finally regaining consciousness. Not really the same consciousness it had before, but still, a mindless awareness, susceptible to command. As it opened its mouth, the Master saw fangs beginning to emerge where teeth used to be.

The Master swiped a sharp claw down its torso from left to right, cutting a thin swath of flesh open. Blood trickled from the wound and the Master's eyes widened in excitement. He knew those behind him scented the human part of it that still remained. Yet they would not approach.

No, this one belonged to the Master and they knew better. Bringing his fingers to his lips, the Master licked the blood from them. So sweet, so innocent, so sad to have his life cut so short.

The Master laughed.

The wound bubbled, a frothy white substance pouring forth where blood appeared. The cut would scar, forever marking this one as special. The Master slid his claw inside the open wound, emblazoning his own version of a tattoo along its abdomen as the sizzling sound of burning flesh echoed throughout the chamber. The creature didn't even flinch. When he removed his claw, the wound had already begun to heal, but the mark would remain.

Yes, he knew these humans, knew what terrors lurked within their minds.

And their horrors were only beginning.

Chapter Eighteen

Team organization was back to normal. Gina was ready and in fighting spirit. She was determined to be a good soldier tonight and do as she was told. That meant being on Derek's team and not deviating from instructions in any way, shape, or form.

At least not tonight. Tomorrow, she'd see.

She actually felt good. Really good, surprisingly. Of course, great sex, a good talk, and a good night's sleep, even with the nightmare, had helped.

For the first time in her life she'd opened up about the night her mother disappeared. She'd expressed her fears about getting close to someone.

And nothing horrible had happened.

"You okay?" Shay asked, approaching her with trepidation as if she was afraid Gina would bite her head off.

Smiling, Gina nodded. "I'm fine. And thanks."

"I don't know how you do it."

"What?"

"Bounce back so quickly. I don't think I could."

"Oh, I think you could," Gina said. "You're stronger than you think. We all are. Look what we've already survived. Sometimes I think we all forget that." She had, for a while. But the toughness inside her had returned, thanks to Derek. If he could weather the trauma he'd had to deal with, then so could she.

Shay nodded. "I never thought of that. I guess you're right."

"Everyone ready?" Derek asked, slipping his shades on.

Gina did the same, slinging her weapon over her shoulder and following Derek into the jungle, Linc and Ryder behind her.

The full moon cast a silvery glow over the jungle, lighting their way through the path. It was hot and muggy, and they hadn't ventured more than a half hour before she was soaked through her clothes and fighting to drag in a breath of air. Even that was thick with humidity and she reached for her canteen to grab a quick swig of water, since Derek seemed determined to run a race tonight.

"You in a hurry?" she asked.

"No. Why?"

"Because I'm panting here. It's sweltering, and you're hustling us like you're on some kind of personal timetable to get somewhere."

He halted and pivoted, frowning. "Didn't realize."

Hell, the man wasn't even out of breath. Maybe it was just her. She turned to Linc and Ryder. Sweat poured off their faces, their chests heaving with their labored breathing. They glared at Derek.

Okay, so it wasn't just her. And she'd kept up with him easily when they'd raced each other just days ago. So what was up with his sudden gust of inhuman energy and strength?

"Where you goin' in such a rush, man?" Linc asked, panting out each word.

Derek's brows lifted. "No idea, actually. I just started walking."

"Running was more like it," Ryder grumbled through heaving breaths.

"Sorry, okay? I didn't notice. I'll slow the pace."

"'Bout damn time," Linc said. "I'll need oxygen by the time we run into demons."

Derek snorted and turned, trying to hide his own confusion. He felt like he'd just woken from a daze. From the minute he'd entered the jungle he'd been on a mission with a purpose, as if he knew exactly where he was going.

Only he had no idea. Just that he had to get somewhere, and in a hurry. His legs were moving of their own volition, as if something else had been guiding him.

And he didn't like it one damn bit. Even now he felt jittery, like he had to keep going, as if he was being drawn.

He knew where. But not why.

"What's wrong?"

Gina stepped next to him, concern etched on her frowning features.

"Nothing."

"You look angry, or preoccupied, or something. Are you okay?"

"I said I was fine," he snapped back. "Let's just get going."

He knew he sounded brusque and didn't mean to, but he had to get to whatever the hell it was that compelled him. It was making his skin crawl, this need to reach an end.

They pushed on, deeper into the jungle where all sounds had gone dead silent.

"I don't like this," Linc said.

"Me, either," Ryder added. "The birds have gone quiet."

"Derek, where are we?" Gina asked.

"Something's up ahead," he answered.

"Where?" Linc asked. "I don't see anything."

"Ahead. A shimmering."

"I don't see it either," Gina said.

"Then you're all blind. Follow me."

The energy was growing stronger as they drew nearer. He felt empowered by it, his blood surging with strength.

Gina's hand on his arm stilled him. They didn't have time for all these interruptions. He jerked around to glare at her. "What now?"

"Stop, Derek. What's wrong with you?"

"Don't you see it?"

"No. None of us do. What do you see?"

"It's a light."

Linc moved to his side. "Man, there's no light out there anywhere."

"You need to shake this off, Derek. Whatever's gotten hold of you can't be good."

He heard Gina's voice, but it was far off, as if she were

in a tunnel. He shook his head, trying to clear the cobwebs.

"Derek, look at me," she said again. "Focus."

He blinked, the shimmering light calling to him. The more he resisted, the more it pained him. Like electric shocks every time he tried to fight off its effects.

Goddamn. Gina was right. This wasn't good.

"Derek, you've got a mess heading your way," Lou commed in.

And that cleared his head, finally.

"Shit, look!" Linc hollered.

Derek turned and saw a wall of demons heading in their direction, but the rumbling under his feet told him the second team were hybrids.

"How many, Lou?"

"The clusters are so dense I can't even count. It's nothing but a big red blotch on my screen."

Fuck. "Lou, you'd better send the other teams this way. And hurry."

"Already have," Lou said. "Hang on, they're on the way."

Hang on. Yeah. If they could. Four hunters and a hell of a lot more demons than they could handle alone.

What a fucking nightmare.

What had he been thinking leading them into this? Because that's exactly what he'd done while he'd been sleepwalking or whatever the hell he'd been doing. He'd led them into an ambush.

He turned to his team. "We gotta retreat until the others show up. Run like hell and stay alert."

He hated it, but they had no choice. No way could they

face that army alone. Not until backup arrived. Linc led the way, and he'd never seen anyone so big run so fast. Derek kept the pace easy, wishing he could pick them all up and zip out of there before the demons caught up.

And they *were* catching up. He sensed them closing in, the hairs on the back of his neck rising with every step he took. He glanced over his shoulder, unable to see them anymore, yet feeling them drawing near.

"Hurry up, dammit," he yelled.

If they could close the gap between themselves and the others, they at least had a fighting chance.

How many goddamn demons were on this island, anyway? Did the Sons of Darkness bring them all?

If one of them tripped and fell, the demons would be on them. Derek prayed they'd stay upright, but he focused on Gina, ready to swoop her up at a second's notice if she should stumble.

He wasn't going to lose her.

Fortunately she was agile, hopping over logs, lifting her legs and maneuvering her way swiftly through the jungle. He heard her, felt every one of her sawing breaths as she fought to keep moving. He pulled his laser and fired on a demon who had moved to his line of sight, obliterating it in a melting flash. Then another. He blasted it, too.

Not one of those goddamn things was going to get past him and get to Gina or the others. This was his fault.

"Dalton, where are you?" he commed.

Dalton gave his location. Okay, not far. They could do this. They were going to make it.

"We're at four point six," he commed back to the

others. "Everyone keep your fingers on your triggers, but no firing. We don't want you shooting each other."

Finally, he saw the other teams and breathed a sigh of relief.

They were going to have to fight first. His team was winded and needed a break. But as soon as they met up with the others his hunters surprised him, pulling their weapons and turning around, aiming and firing at the demons who were already within reach.

It was like an explosion of light as they blasted all around him. Derek did the same, taking aim at the first demon he saw.

His hunters formed a circle, knowing the demons would attempt to flank them and come at them from behind. The UV lasers flashed all around them, a display of screaming demons, bright light, and melting flesh.

Derek heaved in big gulps of air, grateful to be standing, his team still alive. Sonic bullets whizzed past him, finding their intended targets as the first wave of hybrid demons made their way in. Their gelatinous flesh exploded around them, their tortured screams of pain music to his ears.

"Stay in formation!" he commed. "Don't break up yet!"

Gina fired the UV as a whirlwind of activity scattered around her. Cocooned within the safety of the other hunters, she'd never felt more protected. Earlier, fear like she'd never known before had hit her when she'd heard from Lou that a mass of demons was headed their way, and then she'd seen the ominous look of foreboding on

Derek's face. When he told them to retreat, she knew it was bad.

Really bad.

But now it was awesome, banded together with the hunters and kicking some serious demon ass. Thank God they'd managed to backtrack with the other teams in time before the demons had caught up with them. She'd never run so fast in her life, had never felt such fiery pain in her lungs as she squeezed out every bit of air she could, forcing each breath, forcing her burning legs to keep pushing past the pain.

She'd heard Derek fire behind her before they'd teamed up with the others, knew the demons were that close, but was too afraid to turn around and look, not wanting to waste a precious millisecond on finding just how close they really were.

She worried for him, but she did what she was told and kept running, knowing it was what he wanted her to do.

And now she could only hope that they'd manage to fight off these demons before they drew close enough to start taking on the hunters one by one.

The stench of so many of the hybrids was awful. She'd never grow used to that smell.

And for every demon they killed, two or three more advanced. They weren't making any headway.

"Branch out," Derek commed. "Form a line and start targeting."

There didn't seem to be any more pure and half demons. Just the hybrids now, slowly approaching. Gina shuddered at the thought of one of them getting close enough to grab her. And every hunter was busy fighting his or her own cluster of demons.

Forcing revulsion aside, she pretended she was at an amusement park and the hideous creatures approaching were cute little ducks. She aimed her weapon and fired at one. It paused and looked right at her, tilting its head to the side before grimacing in pain. Its features twisted, its mouth opening wide and showing her its long fangs. She shuddered as it continued to approach. She hit it again and it began to melt into itself, feet first, smoke pouring from it as it oozed into nothingness.

How much firepower did these UV laser weapons have, she wondered? One of those things she'd never asked and should have. She hoped it was a lot, because more were coming.

How many of these damn things were there?

Now that they had branched out, she felt more isolated. Pushing the thought aside, she concentrated on the ones near her, the ones she needed to kill.

She had two dispatched when one came toward her. This one looked different, but she couldn't put her finger on it until it drew closer.

It wasn't as bulky as the rest of them. And it appeared to be more human. It had a long wound running across its chest from its left pec to its lower right abdomen. It looked like it'd been injured recently.

And it was determinedly heading straight for her, its arms outstretched, its claws reaching.

Gina backed up, the hairs on her arms rising as the niggling sense of familiarity assaulted her once again.

What was it about this demon, this haunting sense of déjà vu?

She aimed her weapon and rested her finger on the trigger, positioning its horrid face in her sight.

Then realization hit her.

Something in the eyes, the shape of its mouth, the bridge of the nose.

The scar scrolling along its abdomen. Like a name had been carved on its belly. She squinted, trying to read in the dark, daring to allow the creature to approach so she could read the crude scrawl on its stomach.

J-A-K-E.

Was this some kind of sick joke?

She looked again, certain that had to be some kind of mistake. It wasn't; the spelling of his name was crude but legible.

No. She let the weapon drop, blinking fast to clear the tears clouding her vision. It couldn't be him. He was dead.

But the eyes, the mouth, even the way the thing curled its lips upward.

It was Jake.

Goddammit, it was Jake!

She shuddered a gasp and watched it approach, looking to her left, searching for Derek. What should she do?

He was rapid-firing round after round of sonic bullets into several demons. She couldn't scream for him.

Everyone around her was engaged.

It was just her and Jake. No, her and this *thing* that was not Jake anymore.

It wasn't.

Logic, Gina. Use your logic. These Sons of Darkness are screwing with your head. Where's the cool, kick-ass Gina Bliss?

On a movie screen, that's where she was. Not here in the middle of a jungle, watching the demonic resurrection of someone she had considered a friend.

But that wasn't right. Because her friend Jake was dead. This creature coming at her wasn't him. She didn't need Derek or anyone else propping her up, holding her hand or telling her that. She knew it in her heart.

They were fucking with her in a huge way, those sonofabitches. They'd sent out this thing that used to be Jake specifically to screw with her head. She didn't know why, and frankly she didn't care.

I'm sorry, Jake, but I know you're already dead, or at least the soul of you, the heart of who you were, is.

She grabbed her guns and pointed both of them at the chest of the thing and fired. One round. Two. Then three.

The demon threw its shoulder back, its arms flailing, its skin beginning to bubble. It ceased advancing, just looked at her with the saddest expression as if it couldn't believe she'd shot it.

"You are not Jake," she said, then fired another bullet into it. It swelled like it was having an allergic reaction.

In short order its size tripled. Gina stepped far back as it exploded, feeling a sad triumph as pieces of it littered the jungle.

Gina watched it with a detached eye. It was just another demon. Whatever it had been at one time, it had been transformed into a mindless twisted hybrid programmed to do the bidding of the Sons of Darkness.

Which meant it had to die. If she ever ended up like that thing, she'd hope to God one of the hunters would put an end to her fast.

She knew Jake would have wanted the same thing.

"I'm sorry, Jake," she whispered to the darkness. "May you rest in peace."

"Gina? What happened?"

She turned to Derek, looking around to see the rest of the demons were gone, either returned via a portal or dead. Her gaze flitted back to Derek.

"They sent Jake back," she said.

He frowned. "What?"

The others approached. "It was Jake. Changed into one of the hybrids. I killed him."

"How do you know it was Jake?" Ryder asked.

"He hadn't completely changed yet. His face still bore the resemblance. And they'd marked his stomach with his name."

"You serious?" Trace asked, his eyes widening in disbelief.

"Yes. It was Jake, I swear it. Same eyes, same mouth, same nose. I killed him." She almost said "again," but stopped herself.

"They sent him back. The sonofabitches sent him back," Derek said, his voice low. "I'm sorry, Gina."

"It doesn't matter. It wasn't really him anymore. I know it wasn't. They sent him to screw with me."

"Yeah, they did," Derek said, shaking his head.

"Doesn't matter. I took care of it. Jake would have wanted me to."

"You did good. Now holster your weapons, babe."

She didn't even realize she still held a death grip on her guns until Derek slipped his fingers on her wrists, then slid his hands down along hers to pry her fingers from each weapon.

"Bastards," he said as he slid them back into her holster. "It's a mind game. They've done it before when they've taken our hunters. Sometimes they don't kill them."

She didn't want to hear this. Not right now. Inhaling deeply and blowing it out, she looked at Derek. "We done here?"

He looked around. "Appears so."

"I'm going back to camp. I've had enough." She turned and walked away, not really caring if the rest of them followed, if more demons appeared, or if Derek yelled at her. Emotionally, she was toast. She was tired and needed to scrub the stench of demon from her body.

And if she was lucky, maybe she could wash away the memory of Jake from her mind.

Chapter Nineteen

"It's time," the Master said.

"The attack didn't generate the outcome you desired?" the second asked.

"Yes and no. But it's time to step it up."

"Many of ours were killed in that last attack."

The Master turned slowly to face the second, who didn't flinch. "Do you think I'm unaware of this?"

"No. Just reiterating that we can't afford to lose so many while you play this game."

Normally he'd punish such insolence. But this was his brother and one of the Lords, his counsel. He could not. Besides, his brother was correct.

With a sigh he said, "Soon it will be over. It's time to play our most important card."

"And what is that?"

"Bring her to me. Where she is, he will follow. Once we have him, we can end this charade."

"You mean we can finally kill them?"

"Yes. You can kill them all."

Gina picked at her food, staring out over the ocean and watching the sun slip down behind the trees on the west side of the island. Almost dusk, which meant dark would come soon.

Sunset meant preparation time. Arming the mental stamina for what was to come tonight.

More battles. And then what? How long would they be at this? Night after night after night. How long would they stay here and fight these things? How many of these damn creatures were on this godforsaken island, anyway?

Hundreds? Thousands? Millions?

She wanted to go home.

No breeze lifted the heat that had settled over them. Suffocating humidity, bugs everywhere, souring her mood even further. She couldn't breathe.

"You look tired," Olivia said after dumping her trash and grabbing the seat next to hers.

"I am."

"Maybe you should stay behind tonight and do guard duty with Lou."

"That bad, huh?" She probably looked as awful as she felt. And she was damn tired of feeling this way.

"I think we're all worn out," Trace said.

"I know I am," Shay chimed in from across the table. "How much longer are we going to be doing this?"

Derek looked up from his plate, finished chewing, and

took a long swig from his bottle of water. "Until they're all dead."

"And how will we know when they're all dead?" Gina asked.

"When no more of them come out at night."

Ryder shifted, pushing his chair back. "So we could be stuck here indefinitely?"

Derek stood, plate in hand. "You all agreed to be hunters. This is what we do. Hunt demons."

He left the tent without another word.

"Great," Trace said. "We could be here for months."

"I don't think it'll be months," Lou said.

The veteran hunters had all departed, leaving only the new ones alone with Lou. "How do you know?" Gina asked.

"The Sons of Darkness have a plan, and I'm sure we're going to find out very shortly what it is."

"Is this one of those Realm psychic things? You know they have a plan because you can feel it or something?" Trace asked.

"I can sense it. The other members of the Realm also know this to be true. There's something big going on with the Sons of Darkness."

"Like a disturbance in the Force kind of thing?" Gina quipped.

"Something like that," Lou replied with the hint of a smile.

"So how many others are there like you?" she asked. "And where are they?"

"There are two dozen of us left. Spread around the world."

"That's it? And how many of the Sons of Darkness?" Ryder asked.

"There are twelve Lords of the Sons of Darkness. As far as their minions—we don't know. Thousands, perhaps. Maybe more."

"How many hunters?" Gina asked.

"Several hundred."

"We're outnumbered." She shouldn't have asked.

"How can we be expected to win when we're so outnumbered?" Shay asked. "It's impossible."

"Because you're better and smarter," Lou replied. "Because no matter how many of those things the Sons of Darkness manufacture, our weaponry—the skills, heart, and tenacity of our hunters—has always and will always win out." He stood and scanned all of them, his eyes lighting up with a look of fierce determination. "Don't give up hope. You all have an inner strength, a light that gives you special power over these evil beings. You are more than mere humans, capable of amazing feats. You simply haven't realized your potential yet."

"C'mon, Lou. We're just people," Trace said, jamming his fingers through his hair. "We're not special."

Lou's lips turned upward, as if he held a secret. "You have no idea what you're capable of. Time will tell."

Gina barely felt capable of making it through tonight's battle, let alone feeling special in any way. Lou had given them a pep talk. Total bullshit manufactured to pump them up, nothing more.

They weren't special. They were human. And they could die.

She'd seen how easily they could die at the hands of the Sons of Darkness.

But she kept her thoughts to herself, because maybe what Lou said would empower the others, keep them going for a while longer.

It hadn't helped her a bit.

And Derek had avoided her since they returned to base camp last night. Was it because he didn't want to deal with her angst over having killed demon Jake, or was it because of the way he'd been acting when he led them so far into the jungle before that?

She didn't know, and he still wasn't talking. To anyone.

Well, fine. If he could withdraw, so could she. She didn't need a confidant, a lover, a friend.

She'd spent years without someone to rely on.

She could easily do it again.

In fact, she preferred it. She liked isolation.

Liar. She hurt inside. Missed his touch, missed talking to him. She'd just opened her heart and he'd withdrawn, and goddammit, she missed him.

So what prevented her from going to him, asking him what was wrong?

Because something sure as hell was bugging him. She started over to him, wanting to figure this out before they went out hunting tonight.

"Hey," she said, watching him inventorying the gear.

"Hey," he replied without looking up.

"Got a second?"

He looked at her then, but he scowled. "Kinda busy here. Need something?"

This was a big step for her. She wasn't used to rejection, so she wouldn't normally put herself out there like this. "Uh, yeah, I do. Can you come over here?"

She motioned him toward the supply hut and inside. Once there, she dragged him in and shut the door.

"Gina, what are you—"

She silenced his protests with her mouth, fisting her hands in his shirt and drawing her body up against him. Would he understand how much she needed him, how much she'd missed his touch? Would he know that if he pushed her away right now, she'd never survive the rejection?

She shouldn't have worried. He growled into her mouth, wrapped his arms around her, and slammed her against the wall, devouring her lips in his hungry response.

Whoa. Okay, maybe he had missed her, too. This kiss was not a brush-off by any stretch of the imagination, his hard cock pressing insistently between her legs and telling her exactly what she needed to know.

He wanted her, he needed her. Right here, right now. Something was bothering him, but he didn't want to talk about it. Instead, he wanted to forget.

She knew all about "forget." They could talk later.

No time to shed clothing. Instead, she slid down the wall and reached for his zipper.

Derek sucked in a breath. "Christ, Gina." The room was pitch-dark and he wanted to see her. But he couldn't find words as she unzipped his pants and slid her hand inside, fondling him in her warm palm, encircling him, stroking him until he bit back another oath and palmed the wall, letting her do what she wanted.

Words? What words? Stark need for her was all he could manage. He was speechless.

Her hands were a soft balm against the gritty reality of what was happening around him, the fear that what had happened last night would reoccur tonight. He shut it all out for the moment, needing this brief respite, this sweet interlude of Gina's soft hands caressing him, her breath against his thigh as she drew closer.

Acceptance. No matter what was going on inside him, she still wanted him.

"Gina." He sighed as her lips covered his cock and she took him into her mouth. Her tongue was a salve against the wounds within him, bathing him in tender, velvet strokes that made his balls quiver with impending release. If anyone could heal his pain, it was Gina. He moved his hips, feeding her, his need so deep it was almost too much to bear.

But he didn't want to end it this way. He wanted to be buried inside her, bringing her the same pleasure she brought him. He bent down and reached for her, lifting her, fumbling around in the dark until he found a table and bent her forward. He jerked her shorts down until they were pooled around her ankles, then wedged his knee between her legs, parting them.

Reaching around to search her soft center, he found her wet and caressed her, rewarded by moans of acceptance.

Thank God she was ready, because he was in agony and couldn't wait. He drove inside her, pinning her to the table with his body, reaching for her wrists to hold her steady as he banged against her.

He was rough and didn't care. She didn't either, slamming back against his thrusts, which only served to heighten the wildness building inside him.

"Gina," he warned.

"Fuck me," she growled, her harsh words arousing the hell out of him.

Oh, man, did he love her wild streak.

He gave her exactly what she wanted. She cried out, her body pulsing around him. He couldn't hold back and let go, climaxing with her and leaning around to ravage her mouth, sucking at her tongue as the last of his control left him.

Spent, he tried to make up for the way he had behaved by gentling his kiss. When he stood and pulled her up, they fumbled in the dark to clean up and right their clothing, the only sound their panting breaths.

"I'm sorry," he finally said. "I'm sure that's not what you wanted when you came in here."

"Um, I think I started it," she teased, but then grasped his hand and squeezed. "I was worried about you. You've been distant since last night."

His chest tightened. "I'm okay."

"No, you're not," she whispered, wrapping her arms

around his middle and laying her head against his chest. He held tight, absorbing her warmth, her comfort.

God, he could stay in here all night. Just hidden away, holding Gina like this. "I'm fine, babe. Really. Just a little weirded out by last night. I didn't feel like I had control over myself."

"In what way?"

Being in the dark helped. He wouldn't be able to see her reaction when he told her. "It was like I wasn't the one guiding us to that spot last night. Like something was making me take us there."

"Maybe something did. You said we don't know everything about the Sons of Darkness. Maybe they can do some sort of mind control thing."

"Could be." And wouldn't that be just fucking great? As if odd shit wasn't already happening to him, now he had this to worry about?

"You're strong, Derek. Now that you know it happened, you'll be on your guard against allowing them to do it to you again."

She'd responded so matter-of-fact. Not with shock or with blame. It seemed so clear when she said it. "You're right. It won't happen again. I'll make certain it doesn't."

"See?" She clasped her arms tighter around him and sighed. "I guess we should get out there before someone comes looking for us and gets suspicious."

He smiled in the darkness. "Gina, I don't think our relationship is a very big secret."

He heard her soft laugh. "Oh, who cares."

Tonight, Derek handled things differently. He waited at camp until Lou found the hot spots.

Gina thought that was a really wise choice.

"No fucking way are we walking into an ambush like we did last night."

And like last night, the demons all came out in one centralized location.

"Just like I thought they would," Derek said, a smug smile on his face as he looked over Lou's shoulder at the swarm of red blotches on the screen. "We're heading west," he said to all of them.

Geared up, she'd been standing around waiting over two hours since dusk for this, feeding off everyone else's impatience. Anxious and eager to go, they hustled into the jungle. Gina was primed and ready for a fight, having cast aside her doldrums over the night before.

This was her job now. She was going to kill demons. If it took the rest of her life, she was going to obliterate every single damn one of them.

"We've got another mess of demons up ahead," Dalton commed.

Derek and Dalton led the way. Derek wanted them all close tonight, so they stayed in a tight formation.

"Don't spread out until I tell you to start firing. Then I want you in groups of three like we talked about earlier."

She'd be with Derek and Dalton tonight, sandwiched between two of the big, muscled he-men of the group. She smiled at the thought. And also felt safe.

There wasn't anything wrong with feeling safe. Especially knowing what was coming. Then again, once the fighting started, they'd all be battling their own demons and it wouldn't matter how the teams were broken out.

Once again, the flash of demons could be seen, like lightning streaking horizontally throughout the jungle grounds.

"Why are they coming at us with so much warning, approaching from so far away?" Gina asked.

Derek shrugged. "Who the hell knows? Fucking with our heads, no doubt. They like to do that. They want to show us their numbers, scare the shit out of us."

"It's working," she whispered.

"They're close enough now," Derek said. "Spread out into groups and get into position."

Their group was on the left, with Derek on the outside and Dalton on the inside, her in the middle. She moved forward and drew her weapon, tracking the demons as they approached.

Damn, they were fast. She blinked, trying to focus as they zipped back and forth across her field of vision.

"They're coming in fast," Derek said. "Be prepared for anything."

She prepared to fire, but she got the idea they were going to come in too quick for her to sight them. She slung her rifle over her shoulder and pulled her guns out of the holsters.

One was coming right at her, seemingly hell-bent in her direction. She swallowed hard and pushed aside her fear, aiming and firing one of the sonic bullets at it. It flew into the air and immediately began to swell, screaming in pain. She couldn't stop to watch because another came at her and she fired at it, too.

All around her the demons attacked. Fast, swirling.

"How many?" she shouted, though she didn't even know who she was asking.

"Too many! Fight them back any way you can," was Derek's only reply.

Now they were close enough to touch—a danger zone. But they weren't attacking with claws and fangs. Why?

Gina's pulse raced, adrenaline at high speed. There weren't as many of the demons, but they were engaged hand-to-hand with these things. She felt them all around her, the air vibrating, the high-pitched whine of their nearly invisible movements causing her to pivot three hundred sixty degrees.

She was firing constantly, reloading and firing again, making herself dizzy with turns and attempts to focus on first one, then another.

She felt an icy cold hand on her wrist and dropped her guns. She jerked, tried to pull it away, but it was like a steel shackle had clamped down on her. Something was dragging her away.

"No!" she screamed. "Derek!"

But in the melee surrounding her, no one responded.

"Get the hell off me!" She kicked at them, but they had her pinned, surrounding her with their icy bodies like an arctic blanket. She couldn't breathe, couldn't move.

Oh, God, no. Not like this. "Derek! Help me!"

More cold hands held her now, and she was falling,

helplessly falling as the ground opened underneath her feet and oblivion took over.

Derek, help me!

Derek shot a demon, then another, pivoting around to search for Gina as her cry for help reached his ear comm.

Shit. Where the hell was she?

"Gina!" He looked to his right, but she wasn't in position. Only Dalton. "Dalton, where's Gina?" he commed.

He sighted Dalton to his right, but he didn't answer, too busy battling back his own horde of demons.

Too damn many of them again. His hunters were gaining the upper hand, though. He twisted and searched the area, firing his laser with one hand and the sonic gun with the other, obliterating demons in his path.

Where was Gina? Panic gripped him and he swiveled, determined to find her. He took one step and damn near tripped over a hole in the ground.

A hole that was rapidly closing up.

"Dalton, Linc, need you here now!" he commed. "Straight south, twenty yards. I need backup!"

Dropping to the ground, he felt the spot with his hand.

Hot to the touch. He closed his eyes and breathed in, swearing he could pick up Gina's scent.

She'd been here. Just now. She had screamed his name, begged him for help.

Goddammit, they had taken her.

"What?" Dalton asked. "We've got them beat. They're gone."

"They fucking disappeared, man," Linc said. "What are you doing?"

"They took Gina. Right here."

"You saw it?" Dalton asked.

"No. But I know it happened."

"How do you know?" Punk asked.

His gaze shot to Punk. "I just know!" He couldn't explain that he'd heard her, felt her, still felt her right at this spot.

He looked up. The others assembled around him, their faces covered in dirt, sweat, some bloodied from the battle.

"Anyone scratched or bitten by the demons? Any paralysis? Rafe, you and Mandy do a count and check for injuries."

"And what are you going to do?" Dalton asked.

Derek was already on his feet. He reached into his pack and took out a flare, marking the spot where she disappeared. "Let's head back to base."

"What do you mean you're going in after her?" Lou asked, a concerned frown on his face.

As soon as Derek had returned to base, he took the launch to the ship, packed up his explosives, and headed back to the beach, where Lou stood waiting for him.

"I'm going to get Gina."

"How?"

"I'm blowing the portal."

"Again, how?"

Derek placed the items he'd need into a bag and zipped

it up, tossing it over his shoulder, then reloaded his weapons, packing extra ammo. "Explosives. I'm blowing it down and then I'm going in after her."

Lou clasped his hands behind his back. "Alone."

"Yeah."

"How do you even know you can explode the hole and reveal anything? We've tried it before."

"I just know it'll work."

"Becoming psychic like me?"

His gaze shot to Lou's. "Gina and I are connected. I know where she is."

Lou studied him for a few seconds, then said, "Take some of the others with you."

"No. I'm not compromising anyone else on the team. It's me and me alone."

"How are you going to face all those demons by yourself?"

Hearing Lou say it, it sounded like a no-win situation. He was still going. "I'll figure it out. You know me, Lou. I always win."

"I can't afford to lose you, Derek."

And he couldn't afford to lose Gina. "You're not going to. I'm coming back, and I'm bringing Gina with me."

Lou let out a forceful sigh, then stepped back. "I have never stood in your way, and I'm not going to start now."

"You think I'm making a mistake."

"I didn't say that."

"You didn't have to." He started to turn away, then paused. "I'll find her. And I'm coming back."

"You'd better. The Realm needs you. So do I."

He nodded and headed back to the spot where Gina had disappeared.

Moving fast, he dug a well in the spot, then took a brick of explosive, poked a hole in it, and gently slid the blasting cap in, squeezing the brick to close it back up. Then he carefully laid it in the hole and unwound the wire back to the remote.

He muttered a fervent prayer this would work. Theory was great, but all the stuff he'd worked out in his head didn't mean squat if he ended up with just a hole in the ground and no way to get to Gina.

The sun had risen, beating down through the open spots in the trees, sweat pooling in his eyes. He swiped it away and continued working, using instinct as a guide.

Getting to their portals this way had never worked before. But this time it *had* to.

He positioned himself behind a wall of thick trees and pushed the button.

The explosion wasn't noisy, but the ground shook like an earthquake. Mounds of dirt flew up like a geyser, then outward toward him, soil flying in all directions. Derek crouched down, covering his head from the scattered debris.

He waited a few seconds while the air cleared of the remnants of smoke and dirt, then moved over to the hole.

Sweet. Just as he'd planned, the opening left behind after the explosion was huge, a rounded-out shell that looked as if a massive excavation crew had just come in and dug it out.

Grabbing his shovel and gear, he slid down the steep

slope. He walked the perimeter, stomping the ground to feel for anything that might signal an entry into their tunnels.

Nothing. Shit.

This had to work. If he had to dig with his hands until he reached her, he was going to find Gina. He dug in and started shoveling, scooping up dirt and tossing it over his shoulder.

But then he felt it. A rumbling under his feet, like an earthquake. He wobbled, struggling to maintain his balance. A strange energy surrounded him as the earth shook.

He knew what was happening. He dropped the shovel and grabbed his gear, trying to maintain his balance.

The ground opened up underneath him like a chute and he went sliding under.

Chapter Twenty

It was like an instantaneous trip to the coldest zone in the universe, an icy chill filling Derek's body as he zoomed through nothing but wintry darkness. Dizziness rolled his stomach as he fell, but mercifully the fall was short and he landed feet first into a pile of . . . something sticky.

Pitch-black. He didn't want to turn on his lights because he didn't know if he was alone, so he grabbed his shades from around his neck and slipped them on, illuminating the room he found himself in.

Interesting. God, it smelled awful down here—like the hybrid demons' stink on the surface times a million. He wrinkled his nose at the stench and surveyed the tiny room. It looked like they'd excavated and plastered some sticky wet shit on the walls and floor to keep the dirt from caving in. His boots stuck in the slime. He lifted them, and the muck was a mixture of dirt and something clear and stringy.

He probably didn't even want to know what it was, but it reminded him of something he'd seen in ghost movies. Ectoplasm or something like that.

The room narrowed and led to a tunnel on the right, but it was dark, and he couldn't make out anything beyond. There was nothing in the room. And the room was small; no more than two or three people, or creatures, could fit in it.

When he heard movement, he grabbed his laser, his gut tightening in anticipation. He stilled, waiting, but no one appeared. Instinct told him he'd been allowed down here, that they'd brought him. If these creatures had wanted him dead, he'd be dead already. Maybe they wanted to change him into one of them and that's why he was still alive. It didn't really matter what their agenda was. He had one of his own. Find Gina and get both of them out of there. In the meantime, this was an opportunity to gather whatever information he could.

He started moving, lifting his boots and shaking off the muck as he left the narrow room and headed down the tunnel. It was wide enough for the hybrid demons to move single file through it, but that was about it. Reminded him of studying ant colonies in those narrow glass cases when he was a kid. The tunnels snaked this way and that, and he had no freakin' idea which way to go next. But he did make a mental note of which way he'd come in, because as far as he was concerned, that was the way out.

The further he moved through their tunnels, the more he realized no one was around. No demons rushed at him, no hulking hybrids blocked his way. It was as if they had been ordered to let him pass.

As if he were purposely being allowed to move freely.

But why?

He hated when someone fucked with him this way.

And that weird energy he'd been feeling for weeks now was growing stronger. Uncomfortably stronger. He liked that even less, because it was powerful. An ugly power, unsettling, like voices in his head. Was he going crazy?

Maybe.

But before he did, he was going to find Gina and get her the hell out of here. No way were these assholes going to use her as a baby-making machine.

Not the woman he loved.

I'm gonna get you out of here, Gina. Hang tough.

He moved down the tunnels, knowing they were aware he was here.

Oh, but they didn't know what he was capable of.

They were about to find out.

Gina woke with a start, confusion fogging her brain. Her entire body was ice cold and she was shivering. She wanted to turn around to curl up for warmth, but she couldn't. When she tried to sit up, something held her back.

Her eyes shot open, but it was dark and she couldn't see. She blinked to focus, allowing her eyes to adjust to the lack of light. She wiggled her fingers, trying to feel what had her bound at her middle, but she couldn't reach.

Dammit! Where the hell was she?

She remembered the battle with the demons, and being surrounded by cold hands, frozen bodies, a sudden drop like falling in an elevator without brakes. Then everything went black.

Which meant she had to be in the tunnels. With the demons.

Ceasing her struggles, she let her head rest on the flat surface. Fear snaked along her spine, her breathing shallow and quick. Nausea rolled in her stomach and she swallowed, breathing in through her nose and out through her mouth, trying to slow down her breaths.

Okay, don't panic. Forcing a calm she didn't feel, she had to relax. Terror wasn't going to get her anywhere and what she really wanted right now was out of here.

She struggled against the bindings but they wouldn't budge. And she was cold. So damn cold her teeth were chattering.

If only she could see. She hated not being able to see.

Then she heard a sound and she stilled, stopped breathing for a second, paralyzed with fear.

Something was in the room with her. She heard a squishing sound, like someone stepping in and out of mud.

Squick, squick, squick.

And breaths. Rhythmic, in and out, drawing closer.

So much for don't panic. She started to shake. The

pitching in her stomach increased and she was certain she was going to throw up.

"Don't be afraid, my dear," came a voice behind her head. "No one is going to harm you."

Soft, deep voice. She shuddered. Just like the one from that demon the first night. Not harm her? Oh, sure. That's what the demon had said that night, too.

"Gina, isn't it?"

He knew her name. How did he know her name?

When he reached out and caressed her hair, she recoiled, scooting as far away as she could. Damn these bindings!

"I'm sorry it's so cold in here, but we find it quite comfortable. You will, too, in time."

She was going to die. Tears slid from the corners of her eyes and fell down her cheeks. She sniffed them back, refusing to show fear.

"Don't cry, Gina. He's coming for you."

Who was coming? A demon?

Oh, no. It was worse. *He* was coming. Which meant one of them. She was going to be forced to . . . not that. Please, God, not that. Not like her mother. She began to cry in earnest now, hating her own weakness but unable to stomach the thought of being turned into one of those creature-making machines. Her mind filled with visions of what she'd have to endure. No matter how hard she tried to clear her head, she couldn't block them out.

She'd rather be dead. Somehow, she'd figure out a way to kill herself. She could not, would not go through the same thing her mother had.

"Don't cry, Gina," the voice said, smoothing his hand over her hair. His fingertips brushed her cheek and the frigid cold shot right through her. "You will grow to love it here. All the women do."

She grimaced in disgust, wishing she could see him, could leap off this table. If she could, she'd wrap her hands around his frosty throat and squeeze the life right out of the bastard.

But she couldn't. And it was dark and she hated this blindness.

Then he laughed. A dark chuckle that shriveled her soul.

It was, purely and simply, evil. The sound left her ears ringing, her heart pounding, and her body shaking.

She squeezed her eyes shut and prayed for death.

The tunnels seemed endless, but Derek finally found, literally, a light at the end of one of them. He followed it, tired of running into one dead end after another.

And still he hadn't found any demons.

What the hell was up with that? He was packing enough ammo to fight off hundreds of them if he had to, which slowed him down considerably, but he wasn't taking any chances. Once he found Gina, he wanted to make sure he had enough firepower to get them both out of there.

Plus he'd brought the explosives.

These bastards were going down. Especially if they hurt her.

As he drew closer to the light, he realized it wasn't anything man-made. By the time he got right on top of it, he looked up and found the source. It was a break in the ground above. Sunlight, from the surface. That was a good thing. A very good thing. It meant a possible way out.

The tunnels finally widened, then ended in a huge open space. With about six more openings for him to choose from.

"Shit," he whispered, frustration eating away at him.

He closed his eyes and inhaled, letting the power he was fighting against flow through him.

Third tunnel from the left. Definitely. He felt her.

Goddamn, that was some scary shit.

But he knew it was correct. He headed through to the tunnel and was instantly hit with the thick stench of demon. Oh, yeah, much more powerful now. He readied his laser, finger poised on the trigger, muscles tensed in anticipation.

Gina's presence grew stronger.

She was alive. Relief washed over him.

He didn't understand how they were connected, or what this strange power was that seemed to be growing stronger down here, but he wasn't going to look the psychic gift horse in the mouth. He followed the invisible thread that led him through a hallway and into a room. As soon as he rounded the corner, he caught sight of her.

She lay on a rectangular slab, bound.

Her eyes were closed and she wasn't moving. His heart slammed against his chest. Was she even still alive?

She was. He'd know if she wasn't.

At least she was alone, but he smelled ambush. There was a reason he'd gotten through the portal this time, and he didn't think it had anything to do with the explosives suddenly deciding to work. He'd been allowed down here for a reason.

Keeping his weapon at the ready, he hustled over to her, circling the dirt table where she lay and reaching into his belt for his switchblade.

Her eyes shot open, her gaze flitting nervously left to right.

He exhaled a sigh of relief. She was alive!

And scared to death. Of course. She was blind in here since it was pitch-black.

He leaned down to her ear. "Gina, it's me."

She sucked in a breath and turned her head in his direction. "Derek?"

"Yeah."

"Oh, God," she whispered, tears falling. Her lower lip trembled. She looked miserable and scared. Really damn scared.

"Did they hurt you?"

"No. But I'd really like to get the hell out of here. Now. Right now."

"Hold still, baby. Let me cut these ties." He sliced through the bindings across her body and legs, then lifted her up. She latched onto him, burying her face in his neck. After sheathing his knife, he wrapped his free hand around her waist and hoisted her off the table, grateful to have found her alive.

God, she felt good. But she was still shaking.

"You're freezing."

"I don't care. You're warm."

"Let's get out of here. It's hot enough topside."

"Oh, what a sweet, tender reunion."

Derek froze, releasing his hold on Gina. The intruder stood in shadow at the entrance to the room. "Get behind me and hang onto me," he ordered her.

She did, her hands never leaving his waist. "I recognize his voice. He spoke to me earlier."

Derek could only make out a tall, broad, shadowy figure, partially obscured by a pole at the room's entrance. He lifted his weapon to take a shot, but the figure moved behind the pillar.

"Too dark in here, Derek, don't you think?" the figure asked.

Hey! How'd they know his name?

Instantly, Derek was blinded as the room lit up. He jerked the shades off and blinked to adjust his vision.

"Let there be light," the man said with a smile and a shrug, entering the room.

Derek raised his weapon to fire, but something stopped him from pulling the trigger.

"Oh, you don't want to do that."

He didn't, but he didn't know why. Oh, screw that. He needed to get Gina out of here. He raised his weapon and aimed.

"You look good, Derek."

His finger stalled. Again, the man had said his name.

"Derek," Gina whispered. "Fire!"

Ignoring her, he tilted his head to the side. Who the hell was this guy? Dressed in light camouflage pants and a tight brown T-shirt stretched over well-developed shoulders and chest, he was several years older than Derek. He appeared normally human in all aspects, right down to his dark, lively eyes and black hair peppered with gray at the temples. He seemed robust, fit, healthy, and more importantly, completely human.

But looks could be deceiving and Derek didn't trust anything having to do with demons.

"Okay, so you know my name. Who are you?"

Gina tugged at Derek's gun, but he pulled it away from her grasp. He wasn't ready to kill this guy yet. He should be, but something was stopping him.

God, he was confused.

The man smiled, showing off even, white teeth, not at all like those snarling fangs the demons sported. "Look again, Derek."

What kind of game was this asshole playing? "I am looking. Still don't know who you are."

"If you let your guard down I think you could figure it out."

Derek studied the man and frowned. There was something familiar about him, but he couldn't put his finger on it. Maybe he and Lou had run into him before, but it wasn't likely. The Realm of Light was a close-knit organization. Derek had met them all, and he'd have remembered this guy.

"You want to tell me what's going on here?" *Starting with who you are?* It was driving him crazy. The familiarity, the niggling sense of awareness and foreboding. Gina moved to his side and he glanced down at her pale, tear-streaked face. She slipped her hand in his.

"You don't recognize me, do you?" The man paced slowly in front of Derek, studying him by tilting his head from side to side. "We never did look alike. You always favored your mother's side of the family."

Derek let his eyes drift closed for a fraction of a second, wanting this all to be a bad dream. Denial was a good thing, right? This man couldn't be who he was beginning to suspect he was. He was supposed to be dead, or in jail. Anywhere but here. Why here, and for what reason?

"You're not him."

One corner of the man's mouth lifted, as if he were just letting Derek in on a private joke. "Yes, I am."

"You left. Or died." He refused to believe it. It was some kind of trick, or illusion. Hell, it had been so long Derek didn't even remember his face anymore. And twenty-five years had changed him.

"Is that what your mother told you? That I died?" He stepped so close Derek felt the man's breath across his cheek. "She was always afraid of me. That's why she took you and ran, hid you away so I couldn't find you. Because she was scared of me. But you never were. Then or now. You don't fear me at all, do you?"

"No."

"Good. A boy should never be afraid of his father, Derek."

Derek's heart crashed to his feet. Despite inner denial, he couldn't refute the truth.

He heard Gina's gasp, but he couldn't tear his gaze away from his father, Ben.

"What are you doing down here, with . . . them?"

"They are my brothers. I belong here."

So what he suspected all along had really happened. All those years ago, when the demons had taken his brother, Dominic, they had also taken his father. He had asked his mother about it but she refused to talk about Ben.

Maybe the Sons of Darkness had taken his father before they'd taken Nic? Maybe he'd even been part of Nic's capture. Derek wished he could remember. He'd only seen the demons take Nic.

He had such vague memories of his dad, of the times before Nic disappeared.

Did his mother know? Was that why she'd been so obsessed with running after Nic had been taken?

"How are you associated with these things?"

"We have a lot to talk about, Derek. Will you put your weapon down and listen?"

A dozen demons appeared, filling the outer room, standing behind Ben. He could take some of them down, but not all of them. And he had Gina to consider. "Do I have a choice?"

"Not really," his father said, amusement in his voice.

Derek tried not to shudder. "Then I guess I'll just listen

to what you have to say." For starters. Then he'd think about what he had to do, what his options were.

"Derek!" Gina urged in a fervent whisper.

"It's okay," he said, not even looking at her. He had it under control.

He'd listen, but no matter who the man claimed to be, these things were going down. And if Derek had to take himself and his father with them, so be it.

All demons had to die, no matter who they were.

He just had to get Gina out of here first. As soon as he figured out a plan.

"I don't suppose you'd care to hand over your weapons," Ben suggested.

"No. I think I'll hang on to them for now."

Ben nodded and motioned through the doorway. "Then you and Gina can follow me."

The demons parted and allowed them to pass. Derek didn't like it, but he and Gina were surrounded and they had little choice.

As they followed Ben, it occurred to him there were no light fixtures, but low-level light allowed him to see where they were going. And as they moved from room to room, the dirt walls became real walls. He ran his fingers across them. Real, painted walls. This wasn't at all like the other room. Solid floors and sterile, gray walls, like a laboratory, with computer gadgetry that belied his expectations about demons. He hadn't expected tech stuff. Who the hell used these things?

"What is all this?"

"We'll get to that later," Ben said, motioning him into

yet another room, an expansive, elegant living area with sofa and table and chairs. Gleaming silver swords lined the walls over one sofa. "Take a seat."

Derek's eyes widened at how . . . normal this all seemed. If he didn't know better, he would think he was in somebody's house.

"How'd you get all this stuff down here?" he asked, he and Gina taking a seat on one of the love seats across from the sofa, noting as he did so that all the slimy muck had disappeared off his boots.

He looked to Gina, who appeared shocked. She had yet to say a word, just stared at Ben and then back at him as if she couldn't fathom it all, either.

"Think of it as wish fulfillment," Ben said, slipping onto the sofa. "Want something to drink? Beer? How about a cigar?"

In an instant an ice-cold bottled beer appeared on the table in front of him, along with a humidor. Derek lifted the lid, somehow not surprised to find it filled with his favorite Cuban cigars. He inhaled the sweet aroma, then shook his head, certain neither of those items had been there before. "How'd you do that?"

"Like I said," Ben said with a sly grin. "Wish fulfillment. Anything you can think of, just wish for it and it can be yours."

Uh-huh. He'd seen too many people sell their souls to the devil to fall for that shit. "No, thanks."

"How about you, Gina. Can I offer you something?"

"Our freedom," she shot back.

He laughed. "I'm afraid I can't do that."

"Then you can go straight to hell."

Ben laughed. "Interesting choice of words, my dear."

"What are you doing down here?" Derek asked again.

Turning his attention back to Derek, Ben said, "It's my home. At least for now. And soon it'll be yours."

"I'm not going to become a demon."

"We'll see. It's not as bad as you think."

"Tell me how it happened, Da— Ben." He couldn't bring himself to call him Dad. It just wasn't right. He didn't know exactly what his father was, but he didn't have that kind of familial feeling for this man. Ben was nothing more than a stranger now.

Ben quirked a brow. "How what happened?"

"How the demons got you. Was it before they took Nic?"

His smile grew wider. "You don't understand yet, do you?"

"I guess I don't. Why don't you explain it to me?" He hated playing games.

"I'm enjoying letting you figure it all out yourself."

Derek scanned the room, conscious of demons lurking in the dark recesses surrounding them. He counted four so far. "Well, while we're playing twenty questions, why don't you get rid of the Frankensteins. They give me the creeps."

With one quick nod of his head, the demons vanished into the darkness. Ben leaned forward and clasped his hands together, staring at his fingers for a second before looking up at Derek. "Ask and I'll tell you."

"I want to know everything. And I want the truth."

"The truth is, no demons captured me. Ever."

Derek frowned and shook his head. "I don't understand."

"Of course you don't, because you were too young to notice and I didn't want you to know until I was ready to fully assimilate you. I took your brother first, but your mother got smart and spirited you away before I could get to you. I should have taken you both at the same time, but I couldn't."

"So I was right." Ben had been turned before Nic. He had taken his own son.

But wait. The thing that took his brother had looked a lot like one of the hybrids. Huge, imposing, with red glowing eyes and scary as hell. His father didn't look anything like one of those.

Shit. Now he was more confused than ever. Blood pounded in his temples. Derek scrubbed a hand over his face, trying to make sense of everything. Gina scooted closer and wrapped her arm around his shoulders.

"Just spill it, Ben," Gina interjected. "Tell Derek the damn truth."

"Because I wasn't *turned* into a demon, Derek. I was born one. And when I took Dominic, I came to claim what was rightfully mine. You and Dominic are as much mine as you were your mother's. Half of my blood runs in both of you."

Derek stared at Ben, not wanting to make that connection. "That's not true."

Ben smiled, looking so human Derek couldn't believe the words that spilled from his mouth. "Yes, it is, son. I'm a demon. Not just a demon, but a demon Lord. Your friend Louis has told you all about the Sons of Darkness."

A black haze filled his mind, every word Lou had told him about the Sons of Darkness slamming into his consciousness.

"I *am* the Sons of Darkness, Derek. One of the twelve leaders. My blood is your blood. It's time for you to face what you are."

Chapter Twenty-One

Gina's heart stuttered, and if she could have taken Derek anywhere but here right now, she would have.

She couldn't believe what Ben said, and yet she knew it was true. Her heart ached for Derek, yet she could do nothing to help him, just listen in horror and shock to Ben's words.

Derek's father was a demon Lord, one of the twelve leaders of the Sons of Darkness.

A descendant of the great evil.

What did that make Derek?

She didn't want to wrap her mind around it right now, couldn't fathom what Derek was thinking.

"You're lying," Derek said, his voice laced with hatred. His entire body vibrated with violence.

"Why would I? Consider where you are, Derek. What I have shown you so far. I have no reason to lie, and in your soul you know it to be true."

"I don't believe it." Derek stood, his weapon falling to

the floor, forgotten. He jammed his fingers through his hair and paced.

Gina picked up the discarded laser and trained it on Ben. Ben smirked as if he saw her as little threat.

Big mistake, asshole.

"Derek," Ben continued. "Search yourself, the changes you have experienced within your body the past few months. Your strength, speed, your own psychic visions. You have abilities a normal human doesn't possess. Though you've fought against them, they have been overpowering you."

"Bullshit," he said, his voice an accusation.

"What about control when you fuck this woman?" he asked, his glance flitting to Gina.

Gina's eyes widened at Ben's callous mention of what she and Derek shared. Derek looked to her, then back at Ben.

"Leave her out of this."

Ben smirked. "You know what I'm talking about. She's your chosen mate. That's why sex with her is so powerful, why it's so hard to control. You have yet to unleash your full lust on her. It will truly be something to behold when you do. You will tear each other apart like beasts when you fully realize what you are and make her one of us."

Oh, she could so kill the bastard right now. How dare he make something so intimate between her and Derek sound so . . . disgusting and depraved.

"You make me sick," Derek growled.

Ben laughed. "You'll soon see what I'm talking about. Even now the lust for her burns inside you. You think I can't sense how you feel? The change is happening, Derek. You can't avoid it forever."

Derek had a feeling this whole demon thing his father talked about was more real than he wanted it to be. At least as far as his ability to sense things, the surging power he felt within himself, the weird sensations he'd been trying so hard to control, especially around Gina.

And he had felt the surge, the strange sensations growing within him since he'd been down here. They'd led him right to Gina.

Could those feelings be the demon blood inside him trying to burst free?

Then again, maybe none of it had anything to do with him being part demon, and everything to do with his connection to Gina. Had he even seen any proof about this demon stuff from Ben yet? "I don't believe you," he said to his father.

Ben arched a brow. "Don't you feel it?"

He so wasn't going to play this game. "I don't feel a goddamned thing."

"It's the truth."

"Prove it."

With a sigh, Ben said, "If you insist. But I'm not big on show-and-tell."

Derek stared at him, waiting for his father to turn into one of the hulking demons he fought on the surface. Instead, nothing happened. For a second, anyway. Then his father's eyes changed, swirling colors that went from the darkest of browns to a pale amber and then to an eerie red. Ben grinned, his straight, even teeth turning into long fangs, dripping with that same sticky substance Derek was all too familiar with.

It was more than the physical appearance though. It was the sensation of evil surrounding them. Gina must have felt it, too. She grasped his hand and inched closer to him.

"That's enough," Derek said, his stomach churning.

In an instant, his father was wholly human again, but Derek had seen the darkness and wondered how much of it he carried. Would he become like his father? Is that what burned inside him, desperate to break free? Is that what he felt every time he made love to Gina? Those animalistic, dark urges, voices telling him to let go with her, to set his hungers free? The thought of what he might have done to her if he'd let the beast loose made him sick to his stomach.

"Don't be afraid of it," Ben soothed, reaching for him.

Derek flinched and moved away. "I'm not afraid. I just don't want any part of it. I've spent my entire life killing your kind."

Ben's lips curled in a wry smile. "Kind of ironic, now that you know you've essentially been eliminating *your* own people, isn't it?"

"You're not my kind. They're not my people." Derek was human, at least for now, and he intended to remain that way.

"You'll learn to embrace what you are. It will make you more powerful. You are one of very few half human, half demons able to live among the humans without recognition. They will never know what you are. You are the beginning of a new species. Do you know how long I have been searching for you, how long it has taken me to find you?"

"How *did* you find me?"

"Pure dumb luck. You killed one of ours and I happened to be there and recognized you. Your face, so much like your mother's. If you hadn't become a demon hunter I might never have found you again. Your mother did a good job hiding you."

"You mean with all your skills, both . . . otherworldly and technologically, you couldn't manage to locate one little kid?" Granted, it wasn't much, but it was the only dig he had right now.

Ben's brows knit in a tight frown. "There were reasons you could not be located."

"No sixth sense or magical mumbo jumbo you could use to find me? No psychic connection between us? You can conjure up beer and cigars out of thin air but you can't locate one single offspring?"

Ben laughed. "You carry much of your mother's blood in you, Derek. And much of her brand of righteous anger. It's a very potent force. Yes, I do have a connection to you, but your denial of who and what you are blocked my efforts. You have much power in your own right, especially the strength to resist me."

So, maybe demons weren't as powerful as he'd thought. Derek filed that information away for later. Lou would want to know this.

"But I found you," Ben added. "Consider it destiny."

Great. Because of Derek's zeal, his burning need to hunt and kill demons, he'd led his father right to him. Not that it really mattered, anyway. Now that he'd been told what he was, whose blood he carried, he knew what he had to do. Destroy the portal and everything underground, kill his father and all the other demons, and make sure he was down here when it all happened.

It was the only way to assure no demons would escape the island and wreak more havoc on humans.

His father was a key player in all this, had been for a very long time. Eliminating him would remove a major component to the Sons of Darkness.

His thoughts strayed to Gina, to what they'd shared, to what he felt for her and what could have been. Anguish burned in his chest, an unfamiliar tightening inside him. He had to protect her, not only from the evil inside him that would surely escape one day, but also from what he had to do down here.

He loved her. He had to get her out of here.

"Let Gina go," Derek said.

"Oh, I don't think we can do that. She is your mate."

"She's not my mate. Let her go and I'll stay."

"Derek!" Gina protested. "I'm not going anywhere without you!"

He turned to Gina. "Quit arguing with me. You're going."

"So touching, this little lover's spat. Sadly, you're both staying."

"Look, asshole," Gina said, standing and pointing her weapon at him. "I don't care who the hell you think you are, but with one pull of this trigger you're dead."

In a flash Ben moved, his hand striking the end of the rifle, sending the gun flying out of Gina's arms. She scrambled to grab it, but two demons appeared out of nowhere and subdued her. Derek lunged for them, but more demons surrounded her, caging her.

"Let her go, Ben," Derek warned, pivoting toward his father. "Let her go and I'll do anything you ask."

"Love. Such a misguided and disgusting emotion. It can be so easily used to manipulate humans. It really is your downfall," Ben said with a shake of his head. "Of course you will do anything I ask. Because if you don't, the woman you love is going to begin suffering."

To prove his point, Ben nodded to the demons surrounding Gina. They opened their mouths and began closing in on her, their outstretched claws going for her skin. Gina backed away and began turning in circles, but there was no escape. Soon they would reach her, touch her, puncture her.

"Stop," Derek said, knowing exactly what would happen if that toxin entered her bloodstream. "What do you want?"

"Your full cooperation and acquiescence, of course."

"You have it."

"Excellent." Ben nodded to the demons, who halted and spread out again, leaving Gina caged within their circle.

"But only if Gina stays unharmed."

Ben smiled. "The only harm that will come to Gina is from you. And you would never do that, would you, Derek?"

Chapter Twenty-Two

"We can't just stay up here and do nothing," Ryder said, pacing the beach and glaring at Lou.

"I agree," Dalton added. "I can't believe you let him go down there without us."

"We're a team of hunters," Punk complained. "Not singular. A team. Goddammit, I'm itching to get down there and kick their asses."

Lou crossed his arms and sighed; he'd known this was coming. He should have alerted them right away, but he wanted time to communicate with the Realm first. The other Keepers were outraged that he had allowed Derek to attempt to breach the surface and head underground in search of Gina.

Gina's life was undoubtedly forfeit, the Realm had surmised.

A hunter could kill thousands of demons, save thousands of lives.

A valuable hunter should never compromise his own life in search of one lost soul.

Sometimes the Keepers didn't have a grasp on reality, either.

And the Keepers didn't understand how much Derek loved Gina.

Lou did, though. So he listened to them argue, accepting their recriminations for what they considered his bad decision, and in the end nothing had changed. Derek had done the right thing. Maybe not what he should have done for the good of the Realm, but he'd done what was right.

And dammit, if Lou had done that years ago, his beloved Anna and their children might still be alive today. If he had put his wife and children ahead of his duties as Keeper, if he had walked away from all this and hidden them, they would be alive now. But he had put his duties as Keeper first. He had put the Realm first, and his wife and children had died because of it.

The painful memories twisted his gut. Burying them deep, he focused on the hunters.

"You realize you could all die down there," he stated.

Mutinous expressions greeted him. Even those of the newest hunters.

"We could all die up here," Trace argued.

"If it were one of us down there, and there was a chance we were still alive, he'd have sent the whole team down after us," Shay argued. "And you know damn well Gina would be the first one in line to go."

"We succeed or fail as a team," Olivia added. "If Gina is

down there and alive, and Derek is obviously convinced she is, then we all need to help."

They had all bonded. He couldn't be prouder of them.

"Pack as much ammo and weaponry as possible."

"Now you're talkin'," Punk said, grabbing his gear and loading up his weapons.

"Just one thing before you go," Lou said, stepping up to the table where the weaponry was stored.

Dalton paused and raised a brow. "What?"

"I'm a little rusty on the weaponry, so while we're traipsing through the jungle, give me a refresher course. I've a mind to kick a little demon ass myself."

"Oh, hell yeah!" Linc said, clapping Lou on the back.

It was time to reenter the world of demon hunting.

Lou wanted Derek back, and he was damn well going to face the bastards himself.

Okay, this whole captured, damsel-in-distress bit was wearing thin. Gina had grown tired of being tied up and used as a pawn in whatever sick, twisted game Ben was playing with Derek.

She'd rather be dead than used this way.

"Derek, just let them kill me," she pleaded as they bound her once again to an icy cold dirt table.

Derek stood next to Ben, his gaze unfocused as he shook his head. "I can't let them hurt you, babe. Sorry."

Well, this just sucked. Ben was going to have to die, and soon.

As soon as she figured out how. Maybe pleading with

Derek, convincing him they weren't going to let her off unscathed, would do the trick.

"They're going to use me to make more of those half demons. Use my body to make more of them."

Derek looked to Ben, who shook his head. "You have my word she will not be used that way. She is your mate, and you are a child of the Sons of Darkness." His lips curled. "We do hold some things sacred, you know. We would never use the mate of one of the Sons that way."

She didn't believe a word he said. Surely Derek wasn't buying into his bullshit. The Sons of Darkness thought very little of females. "What about my mother, Ben? Where's my mother? You turned her into a baby-making machine for your twisted creatures."

Ben moved to her side, running his cold fingers along the inside of her arm. Refusing to curl away in revulsion, she kept her gaze focused on his.

"Ah yes. The lovely Rebecca. She turned out quite a few half-breeds for us before she had to be destroyed."

It couldn't have hurt more had he plunged a knife in her heart. A part of her had always held out hope that her mother was still alive somewhere. Foolish, but childish dreams faded slowly.

Ben's words shattered that dream.

Her mother was dead.

This pain was unbearable, a hollow ache so deep she really did want to die. But she refused to let him see it, unwilling to shed a tear in front of this monster. Instead, she let the hatred inside her flow, so that was the only thing he saw.

He arched a brow and inhaled. "The sweet scent of anger. It fills my soul, lovely woman. You will be an asset to the Sons of Darkness."

Gritting her teeth to fight back the tears, she said, "I will kill you."

He looked down on her and smiled, patting her arm in a patronizing manner, treating her as if she were nothing more than a tiny bug. "If you say so."

Turning his attention to Derek, Ben said, "It's time."

Derek stepped forward, resignation rendering him expressionless. "I have questions first."

"Go right ahead."

"Who are the Sons of Darkness?"

"Twelve demon Lords originated the Sons of Darkness, charged with entering the human world to disrupt the balance of good, to gain souls for, I guess you would say, our side," Ben finished with a smile.

"Soul stealers?"

"Sort of. Darkness and evil require much feeding, my son. They always hunger."

Derek felt sick, unable to fathom being blood kin to this vile creature. "How did you choose my mother?"

"She was purity and innocence. We are most attracted to those whose souls are either troubled or incredibly white." He looked pointedly at Gina.

"You feed off corrupting goodness?"

Ben folded his arms. "Of course. And soon, so will you."

He'd kill himself before he ever allowed that to happen. But he'd rather kill all of them, instead. "Where's Dominic?"

"You'll find out soon enough. Your brother is an amazing young man. You'd be quite proud of him."

"Is he one of you?"

"He is just like you. And not at all like you."

Cryptic much? That told him nothing. "Where is he?"

"Soon, Derek. First we must bring you into the fold. Then we will reunite you with your brother. There is so much you have to learn about us. Our power grows stronger every day."

"What about limitations?"

Ben grinned and clasped his shoulder. "As I said, one step at a time. All will be revealed soon enough."

He wasn't going to get all the answers right now, no matter how many questions he asked. "Just tell me what you want me to do and let's get this over with."

"Release her," Ben said to the demons watching over Gina. They untied her bonds and dragged her up, thrusting her back against Ben's chest.

Derek clenched his fists when Ben smoothed his hand over Gina's throat, her collarbone, letting his fingertips rest just above the swell of her breast. It sickened him to see Ben touching her that intimately. His father would pay for that.

Through it all, Gina kept her gaze on Derek. Her eyes were clear, trusting.

Trusting in him. She smiled at him, nodded, and he knew then she would accept whatever it would take to get them both out of this mess with their souls intact.

If that meant they both had to die by Derek's hand, so be it.

"What do you want?" he asked Ben.

When Ben raised his head and looked at Derek, the darkness within him was evident. Derek had to force himself to stand firm and not back away against the malevolence reflected in his father's glowing eyes. He'd never felt a force so powerful.

"Accept what lives within you," Ben said, his voice deepening. "Acknowledge the demon blood that is part of you. Let it out, use it to transform Gina."

"I won't do that."

"Then she dies." Ben's claws extended, a thick, sticky substance dripping down along Gina's skin. Derek saw the horror on Gina's face, even though she tried to mask it.

Derek could feel her fear, as well as the pure evil surrounding them. Darkness closed in, clawing at him, cutting off his air. His blood burned and he ached to dive for Gina. But not to save her. To take what was his, to ravage her as he'd wanted to do each time he made love to her, to drive himself inside her and possess her.

"No!" he yelled, clutching his head, squeezing his temples to force the darkness away. Fighting it hurt, the pain so intense it nearly dropped him to the ground.

"You can't resist the urges," Ben crooned. "They've been with you your entire life, but not until you met this woman did the physical urge to mate, to let the beast roar inside you, claw its way to the surface. Now you realize what you might be capable of. Take the pleasures offered to you. Become one of the Sons of Darkness. There is so much about us you don't know. You only know the demons you've seen, but there is more. Much more. You will truly never have another experience like this. And you will be able to keep Gina by your side forever."

Derek's mouth burned, his teeth tingled, pain like a strike of lightning electrifying his insides. Evil surrounded him, more powerful than anything he had ever fought. Fangs tore through his gums and replaced his teeth, and the snarl that tore from his throat wasn't human.

"That's my boy," his father said, loosening his grip on Gina as Derek approached. Ben's claws traced a line across the top of Gina's left breast. A thin trail of blood appeared, and Derek stilled.

"Now take what is yours. Make her one of us or I will kill her."

Frustrated, powerless, and blinded by the haze of lust threatening to consume him, Derek knew he had no other choice. "You win, goddammit. Give her to me!"

With a loud roar, he spread his arms wide and finally let loose the beast he'd fought so hard to harness. A sudden gust of wind moaned and ripped through the room, nearly lifting him off the ground. Anger and violence sailed in on the wind, a haze of red covering his eyes like bloody blinders. Every muscle in his body popped, his blood surging with lust for blood and flesh, a hunger nearly uncontrollable. His gaze tore to Gina, to the thin line of blood above her breast, his stomach churning with a need so violent he could barely control it.

"Don't fight it," he heard Ben say. "Let the pleasure and pain envelop you, then do what the voices urge you to do."

If he did that, Gina would be in pieces by now.

"You will learn to control your urges in time," Ben said.

"Take her. Do it now!" Ben pushed Gina into Derek's arms.

Derek's fingers dug into Gina's skin and he knew he bruised her, but had no control over that. His mouth opened with the need to bury his face in her neck, to taste her flesh, her blood. He bent down and licked the thin trickle of blood at her breast. So sweet, but it burned on his tongue. Shuddering, he fought against his dark needs and swept her into his arms, instead taking in the scent of her hair, the shampoo she used.

Normal, human, the sweetness of her. He clung to those lifelines like a rapidly shredding rope, the only part of humanity left in this blinding vortex that was quickly sucking his soul from his body. He prayed his love for Gina was more pure, stronger than the demon blood coursing through his veins, prayed that he could fight this off and maintain his humanity.

If not, he mentally begged forgiveness for what he would do to her. Gathering her close, he whispered raggedly in her ear.

"I love you, Gina."

Gina would have sworn she'd misheard Derek's whispered words, especially considering what she'd just seen. The transformation had been horrifying, yet through it all she still believed he retained his soul, that he hadn't yet given up the fight.

But then she heard a growl. Tilting her head back, the sight that greeted her had a shriek tearing from her throat.

That *wasn't* Derek gripping her, his fingers gouging her skin. His eyes were blood red like a demon's, his teeth elongated. A scowl of demonic anger marred his normally perfect features. His cheekbones had hollowed, lending him a gaunt and ghostly appearance. That same ugly visage she'd seen every time they'd fought those . . . creatures.

"Don't do this, Derek," she whispered.

His lips moved, but no words came out. She knew he was struggling to maintain his humanity as he bent low, his lips touching her ear. "Holding on by a goddamned thread here, Gina. Scream. Fight me. Now!"

Instinct kicked in and she did just that. "No!" she cried out, kicking and struggling against him. It wasn't too hard to do considering the way he held her, his claws scraping along the flesh of her back and hip. She tried to extricate her arms but he'd pinned them at her sides, so she kicked his legs. It was like battling against a giant redwood tree, her attack on him having no effect at all. Nevertheless, she screamed at the top of her lungs.

"Her struggles will arouse you, Derek," she heard Ben say. "The more she fights, the better it will be for you."

What a disgusting animal Ben was. It was hard to believe that man was Derek's father. She leaned into Derek's chest, trying to get close enough to his ear so he'd hear her.

Derek breathed heavily against her, the sound more animalistic than human. She shuddered, realizing the man holding her wasn't really Derek anymore.

She was losing him. Tears slid down her cheeks. This could not happen. She tilted her head back and rested her neck on his forearm, no longer fighting him. "Look at me, Derek."

He did, and this time she didn't flinch when she met his gaze. Ignoring the swirling red haze in his eyes, the dripping fangs, the horrible grimace on his face, she remembered laughing and sparring with him, arguing with him, remembered the way he touched her and kissed her.

Dammit, she wanted that Derek back.

"I love you," she whispered, her heart hurting with the swell of emotion. "Do you hear me? I love you. Don't let these demons overcome you. You fought them before, you can do it again. Don't leave me."

He frowned, his thick brows arching together in a point. He looked angry, but not at her. Then he shook his head and growled.

She worked one of her hands free, but instead of fighting him, she ran her palm against his cheek, nearly sobbing at the feel of his beard stubble against her hand. "I love you."

Then he shocked the hell out of her by bending down and kissing her. Only it wasn't a demon kissing her. It was Derek. Her Derek. The man she loved, kissing her with gentle sweeping motions of his lips against hers.

When he raised his head, everything about him was normal. His face, his eyes, his mouth . . . it was all Derek. Her Derek.

He pulled her upright, then turned to Ben. "This game is over. You're going to die, asshole."

Ben's eyes widened. "This is not possible. You are one of the Sons of Darkness."

Derek folded his arms. "Apparently not, old man. In this case, *not* like father, like son. I want no part of you or the Sons of Darkness. I am my mother's son. You can all go back to hell where you belong."

"I witnessed your transformation."

"No, you didn't. Derek's transformation happened a very long time ago, Ben. You weren't there to witness it. I was."

Derek whirled at the sound of Lou's voice, shocked to see all the hunters poised, guns drawn, at the entrance to the room.

His spirits soared as they surrounded the demons. The demons backed away, growling, rushing to surround Ben.

Dalton sidled up next to Derek and Gina, handing off weapons and shades. Derek took them, feeling much better now that he was armed and with his hunters again.

His brothers.

His family.

"Ah," Ben said. "Louis. Welcome to my domain. How nice to see one of the Keepers of the Realm of Light again. It has been a very long time."

"Again?" Derek turned to Lou. "What does he mean, again?"

"You never told him, did you, Louis?"

"No, I didn't," Lou said, his gaze narrowed. "He didn't need to know what you'd done."

"Sins of the father are always wonderful burdens to carry, though."

Okay, what the hell was going on? Derek looked to Lou

and then to Ben. The tension rocketed between them, a powerful force building in the room.

"It wasn't his responsibility, Ben," Lou said. "It was yours. The boy shouldn't suffer for your sins."

"Always the protector, aren't you?" Ben said, shaking his head before turning to Derek. "Louis never told you about the night I visited his home in Scotland. The night I took care of his lovely Anna, and sweet little Henry and Edward."

Derek's gaze shot to Lou and saw the truth in Lou's eyes. He felt sucker-punched. "Why didn't you tell me? You knew, didn't you? You knew who my father was all along."

Lou sighed. "Yes. I knew. But I hoped you would never have to know."

"Why?"

"Because it didn't matter. I knew you had power beyond that of a human. I watched you. From the time you were a boy the Realm has kept its eye on you. But I never once thought you would turn out like your father. You have your mother's strength within you, Derek. You proved that just now."

What the hell was he supposed to think? How was he supposed to react to this bombshell? His father had killed Lou's wife and children. Lou had known what he was all along, and yet had treated him like his own son for years, had taught him, sheltered him, trusted him. He'd brought Derek into the Realm of Light, knowing he carried demon blood.

Lou had been more of a father than Ben had ever been.

And Ben had wreaked more havoc in their lives than could ever be punished.

But he would be punished.

"I'm sorry, Lou," Derek said, his voice low. He'd never felt such pain before, such anguish.

"It's long ago. And it wasn't your fault. Don't take the blame for this, Derek," Lou said, pointing his weapon at Ben.

"No, I know exactly who to blame," Derek said as he looked to Ben.

The demons took a step forward, their growls menacing. They tightened their formation around Ben.

The coward.

"Spread out," Derek ordered, readying his laser. "Cover the exits." No fucking way was this asshole going to escape.

The lights faded and darkness descended. Derek slipped on his glasses, clarifying the room. The demons started toward them, but Derek knew who he wanted.

His father was going to die.

Derek was going to kill him.

Gina flipped her shades on, grateful to once again have a weapon in her hand. She didn't play helpless very well, which was why she didn't take those roles in her films. On top and kicking ass suited her much better, and there were demons in the way of her ultimate target right now.

Her heart hurt for Derek and for Lou. She didn't even think of Ben as Derek's father anymore. She knew Derek, or at least knew him better than she'd known any other person, and no part of Ben lived within him. There wasn't an ounce of evil within him.

But Ben? Ben had to go down.

Way down.

She raised her weapon and targeted an approaching demon, melting it before it could launch at her. She'd never felt so empowered before. Tie her up and make her feel like a helpless ninny, will they? Man, she hated that shit. Another went down. Then another. The hunters were in sync, blasting in a protective circle, eliminating row upon row of demons as they worked their way through the line toward Ben.

And Ben stood against the wall, watching with a smug smile on his face, no doubt assured of his own victory.

Ha! Ben didn't know his son at all, did he?

But Gina did.

She blasted another demon, watching it fall. She'd do this as long as it took, but the numbers of demons were dwindling, and they were drawing closer to Ben.

She knew Derek wanted to kill him, to destroy his own father. But she wanted to help him. She wanted revenge for her mother's death, for the death of Lou's wife and children.

As they fought back the demons, she noticed Ben moving along the wall toward one of the exits.

Oh, no. That was not going to happen. They had a demon Lord in their midst and they were not going to let him go. Her gaze shot to Derek, then Lou, who were busy firing off their lasers. No one else noticed Ben.

She did, though. And she was in the back of the group. Skirting behind the line of fire, she bent low and snuck around the edge of the action, intercepting Ben just as he was about to hit the doorway. Derek reached him at the same time.

"You're not leaving us, are you . . . Dad?" Derek asked with a smirk.

Gina blocked the doorway, raising her laser and pointing it directly at Ben's chest.

"He's not going anywhere," she said.

In fact, Ben was going to die.

Chapter Twenty-Three

Ben's gaze shifted to Derek, then to Gina.

Derek could swear he saw a flicker of fear in his father's eyes.

"You afraid of me?" Derek asked. "Need your minions here to shelter you while you make your escape? I thought you were the great and powerful demon Lord, yet you were trying to sneak away. You're nothing but a pussy."

"I don't need to run away. I could kill you right now."

Derek shrugged. "Then do it. Show me."

Ben shook his head. "Such a waste. You could have been so valuable to the Sons of Darkness. You and Gina both. The children you could have created together would have been so powerful, would have sat at the right hand of the great ones."

"Uh-huh. Still waiting for you to do the killing thing."

"Can we just shoot him now?" Gina asked.

Derek smiled. God, he loved her.

Around them, the battle continued, but Derek felt the

shift of power. The stench of toasted carcass was strong in the room as one demon after another went down. His hunters had gained the advantage.

Ben's eyes began to change, becoming darker, his body thickening. Malevolence spread out as the force of his evil blanketed them.

Derek looked to Gina and nodded. Without even blinking, she fired her laser at Ben's chest. His eyes widened and he flinched, but his transformation continued. Derek fired, too, and kept at it, pounding Ben's flesh with wave after wave of UV light, enough blasts to take down ten demons.

But Ben was no average demon, and Derek knew he wasn't going to go down easy. His human skin began to bubble and melt, but still the evil advanced on them.

Derek and Gina backed up.

Gina kept pumping pulse after pulse into Ben, but it seemed not to faze him. She took a quick glance at Derek, his expression determined as he rapid-fired the trigger of his rifle.

This wasn't working. She slung her laser over her shoulder and grabbed for the microwave, hoping that cooking him would have an effect. She blasted him with waves and he halted, looking at her.

God, he was gruesome, half his flesh melted. Still, an evil light glowed in his eyes, and he was laughing at them.

Laughing! The bastard, as if he knew their weapons would have no effect.

Yet the microwave was starting to work. Not as much as it did on the other demons, but his skin, what little there was left, began to bubble, his muscles expanding and contracting as if they were breathing. Ben frowned.

"You cannot kill me. I am a Lord of the Sons of Darkness," he said, his voice echoing deeply throughout the chamber.

Uh-huh. Everything could die. Maybe if she shot him up with enough of this stuff, he'd explode.

She pulled her guns and pumped him full of sonic bullets. His body flew backward with each shot, and yet he recovered, this time heading directly toward her.

She wasn't afraid of him. But Derek pushed her out of the way, stepping in front of her and emitting a low growl at Ben. She moved to Derek's side, intent on continuing to fire at Ben until she had nothing left to shoot him with. Her gaze shot to Derek's, and she gasped at the look on his face.

Just like that, Derek had transformed into a demon, his eyes glowing in the darkness, claws extending from his fingertips, his mouth filled with hideous fangs as he faced his father.

She shuddered and stepped away as Derek launched at Ben, the two of them flying out of the smaller room and into the one they'd occupied earlier. Furniture went crashing around them as they fell to the floor, righted themselves, and dove at each other again.

Derek dug his hands into Ben's body, tearing away the flesh that had been melted by the weapons. But Ben was regenerating, muscle reappearing as quickly as it disappeared.

Gina swallowed past the revulsion. They weren't going to be able to kill him. The bullets were tearing him apart, bubbling and baking him from the inside out, and still he was fighting off their effects.

"You can join me, Derek. We will rule the world."

"You can rule in Hell for all I care," Derek growled, then reached into Ben's chest, grasping his ribs and crushing the bones to dust. "I won't let you hurt another person I care about."

Ben grunted, then laughed, shoving Derek away. The bones reappeared and the wound closed up, flesh rematerializing where moments ago Gina had been able to see clear through him.

He might be regenerating, but he was tiring, his breath sawing in and out, his chest heaving with the force of his efforts.

"If you kill me, it will end nothing. The Sons of Darkness will go on," Ben said.

"But you'll be dead!" Derek rushed his father, pushing him back against the wall of the room with a grunt of effort. The ancient swords on the wall crashed down around them, clattering to the floor. Gina stared at them, remembering the movie scene she'd shot just before she left to come to the island. The sword scene.

She holstered her guns and slung her rifles over her shoulders, sidestepping the two men grappling against the wall. Picking up the broadsword, she held it over her shoulder and positioned herself behind Ben.

Derek made eye contact with her and nodded, grasping Ben's throat with both hands and squeezing hard. Ben reciprocated by doing the same to Derek.

Dammit, that wasn't going to do at all, considering

what she had in mind, but she couldn't very well tell Derek to remove his hands from his father's throat without giving herself away. Right now Ben's attention was on Derek, since he no doubt didn't see Gina as any kind of threat. She stayed in position behind Ben, moving when he did. The noises the two of them made were so loud she doubted he even heard her.

But then Derek let go of Ben's throat, positioning his arms underneath his father's and trying to pry Ben's fingers from his neck.

But Derek was still too close, and Gina wouldn't take the chance on hurting Derek, too.

"Do it!" Derek croaked.

"You want me to kill you?" Ben asked. "Is this how you want to die? By my hand?"

Gina knew Derek wasn't talking to his father, but to her. But Ben didn't know that. She raised the sword over her head, sweat pouring down her arms, her face, fear causing her limbs to shake.

"Just do it, goddammit!" Derek choked out, struggling against the tightening hold of Ben's grasp around his throat. "Now!"

Ben shook his head, squeezing tighter. Derek's face lost the look of a demon and now turned a dark, mottled purple. He didn't have long. With all her strength, Gina swung the sword in a careful arc, realizing at the second it touched Ben's neck that this was no movie.

The sword sliced clean through the bone and muscle holding Ben's head to his neck. For a split second, nothing happened. Then Ben dropped his hands from Derek's neck. Derek coughed and fell to his knees. Ben turned around slowly, his eyes narrowed.

He said nothing, just tilted his head as if he were pondering who stood behind him and had the audacity to come at him with a sword. Gina watched in horror as the head slid from his shoulders onto the ground, followed by the rest of him a few seconds later.

Nothing happened. Gina waited for his head to pop back onto his shoulders and regenerate, just like the rest of his body had before.

It didn't.

A howling roar sailed throughout the room as a swirling black cloud rose from Ben's body. The floor rumbled underneath her like an earthquake, shaking the contents of the room. Fixtures rattled as the invisible moan whistled, grew in intensity, then dissipated. Ben's head and body burned in an acrid cloud of ash and disappeared.

"Holy shit," she whispered. He was gone. Really gone. Dead. She glanced at Derek, who shook his head at her and shrugged, obviously just as shocked as she was.

She looked down at the sword she still held in a tight grip and lifted it up over her head, resisting the urge to roar in triumph.

A sudden peace settled over her, as if an evil had been lifted. She sucked in a breath of clean air, then exhaled. Dropping the sword, she ran over to Derek.

"Are you all right?"

He coughed and nodded. "Fine," he said, his voice hoarse. "Just fucking fine."

The rest of the hunters dashed into the room.

"Demons are done for," Dalton said, then looked around. "Where is he?"

"Dead," Gina said, keeping her gaze focused on Derek.

Derek stood, and Lou approached.

"You see that?" Derek asked.

Lou nodded. "You did well. Both of you."

Gina looked to the dark spot on the floor where Ben used to be. "All the technology we use on these things. One ancient broadsword and a beheading did the trick." She looked back to Lou for an answer.

"They're my swords," Lou answered, picking up the sword that Gina had used to kill Ben. He grabbed a cloth from his pack and wiped Ben's blood from the blade.

"Yours?" Derek looked as surprised as Gina.

Lou nodded. "Actually, they were passed down from those who started the Realm of Light. Ben took them from my home the night he killed my family. I suppose he kept them as trophies." Lou glanced to the dark spot on the floor. "He never realized their power. To him, they were just keepsakes from his kill. To the Realm of Light, they are the embodiment of the power of the light."

"They're blessed in some way, aren't they?" Gina asked.

Lou allowed the hint of a smile. "You could say that." His eyes danced with a light of their own. "We didn't always have high-tech weapons."

Lou moved to the other swords, gathered them up, and folded them in his arms. "Now they're going home again."

After he moved away, Gina turned to Derek. He stared at the spot on the floor where his father had fallen.

"Derek."

He didn't answer her.

"Derek, are you all right?"

He finally looked her way and blinked. "I'm fine. You okay?"

"I'm more than okay." Breathing a sigh of relief, she started to reach out for him, but he turned away and headed toward the others. She dropped her chin to her chest and sighed, feeling strangely empty rather than victorious.

Something was still bothering Derek. Was it because she'd just killed his father?

No, that couldn't be it. He'd wanted Ben dead. So what was it? She had to find out.

She caught up with Derek and Lou as they were addressing the others.

"I think we're done here," Derek said. "We'll track the tunnels to their end, or see if they even have an end. We can set explosives, wire them to the remote, and blow them closed."

"I'll do a little investigating and see what I can learn about Ben's operation down here," Lou said. "I find it fascinating he had such an elaborate setup. Not at all what I expected."

Derek nodded and Lou walked away, the others following him.

"Are you sure you're okay?" she asked him.

Derek sighed. "I said I'm fine, Gina. Just need to get things wrapped up. Why don't you go help Lou? Need to get all of you topside."

"Okay." She started to turn away, then what he said sank in. She turned back to him. "Wait a minute. All of *us*?"

"Just go do what needs to be done."

"You're coming with us when we head back up, right?"

"I've got to blow this place. The portal, this cave, the entire tunnel."

He wasn't answering her question. And she didn't like the distant look in his eyes, as if he was already closing himself off from her. "What are you thinking? Tell me."

"You all need to get everything set, then get out. I'm going to set the charges down here and make sure they go off."

"Make sure they . . . You're planning to stay here while the explosion occurs, aren't you?"

When he didn't answer, her heart sank. He intended to die along with the demons because he thought himself one of them.

"Derek, don't do this."

When he looked at her, his gaze was cold. "You saw the change that went through me, Gina. You know what I am now. I could barely control it. I can't let what's inside me loose up there," he said, lifting his eyes to the ceiling. "I have to die with them."

A knifelike pain stabbed through her. Nausea rolled and pitched in her stomach and she placed her palm there, forcing a calm she didn't feel. "No. I won't let you do this."

"Babe, I have to. And you need to let me. You know what I've become."

"I don't need to let you. I'm not going to let you. This can't happen."

He brushed his fingers along her cheek, the sadness in his eyes tearing her apart. "There's no other choice. I won't run the risk of turning into a demon and hurting other people, especially you."

She squeezed her eyes shut for a second, forcing back the tears. How could he ask this of her? How could she leave him, knowing he was going to die? She refused to let him go. She was not going to lose another person she loved. He asked the impossible. "I can't."

He came to her then, pulling her into his arms and dragging his lips over hers, deepening the kiss until she couldn't hold back the tears. She grabbed onto his shirt, slipping her hands inside to touch the warmth of his skin. She'd opened her heart, finally allowed someone in. Would fate be so cruel to do this to her again? To rip away someone she loved?

She'd never survive it.

The kiss ended way too fast. Derek pulled away. Walked away, actually, turning his back on her.

"There's got to be another alternative," she whispered.

"There's no way to change what I am. Don't make this any harder than it already is."

Her mind, her heart, refused to accept this. But did either of them have a choice? She didn't want to lose him, didn't even want to think about him dying down here. But what if Derek was right? What if he *did* turn into one of those things and couldn't control it? God, he was right. He didn't want to die, either, and her whining about it wasn't going to make it easier on him. Emptiness surrounded her, yet she went through the motions. They didn't have much time.

"What do you need me to do?"

"Help the others search the rooms down here, then hightail that sweet ass of yours to the surface with the rest of them."

Casting him a lingering look of regret, she nodded and headed down the hallway. There was only one door at the end of the hall she was assigned to. Carefully pushing the door open with the butt of her gun, she was surprised to find some kind of mainframe computer and communication device. A fax machine whirred, spewing out a printed message, the entire room working like a normal business office. She half expected to see a bespectacled secretary or receptionist appear to ask if she needed assistance. The entire setup down here was just too odd.

Maybe Ben had some kind of alter ego on the surface. Mild-mannered businessman by day, vicious demon by night. Or something along those lines. Who knew? She refused to discount anything anymore, casting aside forever the words "impossible" and "unbelievable" from her vocabulary. Curious, she paused and waited for the message to finish printing, unable to resist taking a peek.

She pulled the paper from the tray and her stomach dropped to her feet. Dear God! Her hands shook and hope filled her as she pocketed the message, then set the charge and wire, anxious to hurry back to Derek.

He couldn't die now. He wouldn't want to. Not after he read what was on this page.

The message changed everything! She grinned and finished up the wiring, her pulse racing.

Derek twisted the wires together and waited at the entrance to the passageway back to the surface. Everyone else had gone up except Gina. He was counting on her to deliver the message to Lou. Once he sent her up, he'd cause a cave-in. They wouldn't have time to dig him out. Lou would save the others, knowing Derek would put a timer on the device.

Lou would have to take the launch and get to the ship in order to preserve the lives of the other hunters before the whole island went up.

It would be perfect. One button push of the remote, kaboom, end of demons.

End of him.

End of him and Gina.

Dammit. His insides churned. He missed her already, didn't want to let her go.

But he had to. He *had* to do this! His own wants didn't matter.

"Derek!" Gina whipped around the corner and threw her arms around him.

Shit, she was really making this a lot harder. "Gina, don't."

"You don't understand!" She pulled a piece of crumpled paper out of her pocket and shook it in front of his face. "Look at this!"

He opened the paper and scanned what looked like a fax. His blood heated as he read the words on the page.

Ben: Nic has returned to Sydney. Thought you'd want to

know your son finally made his way home. Will see you at the house as planned.

"Where did you get this?"

"In the room with all the office machines."

There was no name on the fax, no indication where it came from, and no originating fax number printed on the paper. But it was addressed to Ben. And though he read the words, it didn't seem real. Could this really be Nic? It had to be! His brother Dominic . . . Nic was alive. After all these years, what he'd hoped for was true. His mind swirled with the possibilities.

Ben had been so cryptic, but this was living proof that Nic was still around. In Australia. At some kind of house, which meant aboveground? It had to be.

"That's your brother, right?"

"Yeah." He rubbed his finger over his forehead and read the words again. They'd been so close when they were kids.

"You have to find him, Derek."

Derek tore his gaze away from the paper and stared at Gina, his mind a jumbled mess of contradicting thoughts. He had to blow these tunnels, had to eliminate the demons and himself in the process. But what about Nic? Could he die knowing his brother was still out there somewhere?

And in what condition? Was Nic human or demon? There was so much they still didn't know.

Goddamn, he needed answers.

"You can't die," Gina urged. "You have to find him. You have to go to Sydney."

"Nic's a demon." He had to be. No way could Nic have lived with Ben, with the rest of the demons all these years, and not be. That's why Ben had taken him. That's what his father had wanted, to turn both his sons and make them like him.

Gina squeezed his arm and shook her head. "But what if he's not? What if Nic never knew about his demon side, or managed to fight it off like you have?"

"You're grasping at straws, Gina." It pained him even to think about it. For all these years it had been so much easier to imagine the demons had killed his little brother, not that he had become one of them. "You and Lou and the rest of the hunters can find him and take care of him. I can't risk it."

But just saying the words hurt inside. Just to see Nic again brought him hope. And what if Gina was right? What if Nic had found a way? What if Nic wasn't a demon? What if he didn't even know about the Sons of Darkness? He hadn't been down here with Ben. He hadn't been part of all . . . this.

"You don't know that for certain, Derek. If Dominic is anything like you, he's tough and a fighter. What if he's resisted? What if there's hope for you, too? I won't let you give up yet."

He looked down at her and his heart squeezed. God, he wanted to believe. "And what if Nic is just like my father?"

"And what if he's not?" she argued, desperation hardening her voice. "You don't know, do you? Isn't it worth staying alive to find out?"

He swept the back of his hand along the softness of her

cheek. Her hope was like a beacon, and for the first time since Ben told him what he was, Derek allowed himself to feel a small drop of that optimism. Yes, there was darkness within him, but he'd lived all his life with demon blood running through him and somehow managed to fight its effects. Surely he could hang on long enough to find Nic and figure out whether he, too, had kept it at bay, or whether he'd accepted the Sons of Darkness.

Could he kill his brother? He'd have to if Nic had embraced the evil inside him. And then he'd take care of himself, too.

But in the meantime, Gina was right. Now wasn't the time.

"Let's go." He took Gina's arm.

"You're going with me, right?" she asked as they moved through the passageway.

He looked at her, at the light that seemed to glow from within her. She was his hope, his goodness. Her love would give him strength to fight the darkness. He paused for a second and realized what he'd just thought. God help him, he'd almost become poetic. Christ, that would have to stop.

He allowed his lips to quirk in a half smile. "Yeah, baby, I'm going with you."

Chapter Twenty-Four

Onboard ship, Derek closeted himself with Lou in one of the cabins. Lou listened while Derek revealed what he had thought about doing.

Lou leaned back in his chair and folded his arms across his chest. "Why would you want to die?"

"I'm a goddamned demon, Lou!" Jesus, didn't anything rattle the man?

"You are still the same man you were before, just with more knowledge. You didn't give in to the evil, you didn't join your father. Instead, you fought the beast inside yourself and came out stronger. I'd say you had a good day."

"For Christ's sake, Lou. It *wasn't* a good day. It was a shitty day. I could have killed Gina. Hell, I could have killed you or any of the other hunters. And frankly, I expected more from you."

"Like what? You want me to be afraid of you now? You want me to be shocked that you're a demon? Or perhaps you want me to kill you."

Maybe he expected just that. For Lou to take the decision out of his hands. "I don't know. Maybe."

Lou smiled. "Not today, son. Not tomorrow, either. I know you. Sometimes better than you know yourself. I know your strengths and your weaknesses. I've pushed you harder than you ever pushed yourself, and I know your limits. I also know what you are capable of doing . . . and not doing. You could no more kill Gina than you could kill me."

Derek looked at the floor, threading his fingers through his hair. "You have no idea how close I came. The urges inside me, they were so intense. The darkness, the hunger. I wanted to . . . God, Lou, it scares me how much I wanted to hurt her."

"But you didn't, did you? You battled it back, you controlled it. Have you taken the time to analyze your reactions, as I taught you?"

"Analyze? Hell, the last thing I want to do is think about it. I want to bury it and pretend it doesn't exist."

"And you know that's the wrong thing to do. Do what I trained you to do."

Sometimes he hated Lou. Especially when he was right. "I don't know. I was kind of too busy for any self-psychoanalyzing."

Lou's lips lifted. "Then do it now."

Derek straddled the chair across from Lou and scrubbed his hand over his face. How *did* he feel about it? "I was instrumental in the death of my own father, and yet that . . . thing wasn't my dad. I didn't feel a blood connection to Ben. Working with Gina to kill him felt like destroying a demon. Like any of the other demons I've killed. Should I feel so goddamned dispassionate about it?"

Lou shrugged. "Yes, I think you should. You never looked on Ben as a father figure. Why would you? Even as a child he never represented a parent to you. And meeting him down there and being told he was your father is no different from being introduced to a human male you had never met as a child and being told that man was your father. You had no emotional ties to Ben. Ben was a demon. Killing him should have no profound impact on you."

"Well, that's good to know."

"And what about the power inside you?"

"I can feel it surging through me. But I can control it now. It's almost as if I have the ability to summon it at will. It's manageable." At least for the moment, anyway. How long would that last?

"Good. Then quit worrying. You did what you had to do. You fought the demon side of yourself and came out on top. What happened to you down there has given you strength and power. Harness it and figure out how to use it to fight them. You've become a powerful enemy to the Sons of Darkness. That's a very good thing to the Realm of Light."

"But what if I can't control it at some point? What if I feel it slipping?"

"Then talk to me, and I'll help you. You forget you're not alone anymore, Derek. And you haven't been for a while now. You have always had me and the other hunters. Your brothers and sisters. Now you have Gina. Draw your strength from us and let us help you."

Derek felt the warmth and affection that he'd never allowed himself to feel before. He supposed he had Gina to thank for that. Now he recognized that Lou had been more of a father to him over the years than Ben had ever been. He nodded, grateful for the comfort he had needed more than he could ever express.

"Thanks. I need to go blow up the tunnels now."

Lou's lips quirked. "All in a day's work for a demon hunter, my boy."

Gina leaned against the railing of the ship and looked at the island, waiting for Derek to push the button that would obliterate the rest of the demons. The sun rose, a perfect pink backdrop against the emerald green hills and crystal blue waters. Such picturesque beauty above, such ugliness below.

They'd found no more demons in the tunnels, tracking them back for about a mile. Then they were blocked off. Had the demons cut them off? Or had they appeared right where the tunnels ended?

More mysteries they didn't have time to solve. Either way, Derek and Lou wanted the demon underground on the island destroyed.

"You ready?" Derek asked, looking down at her with a half smile.

He'd been quiet throughout all this. She wondered if part of him still felt like he should be down there in the tunnels. No matter how long it took, she'd make sure he never regretted his decision to stay alive.

"Hit it."

He pressed the button and she heard a low rumble, like thunder off in the distance. The treetops shook on the island, but other than that, nothing.

"That was it?" Shay asked.

"That was it," Derek answered.

"Pretty damned low-key if you ask me," Trace said.

Derek turned to Gina and winked before answering Trace. "It's supposed to work that way."

Gina grinned. All the hunters stood at the railing, watching. She felt so much peace as she looked around at the others. They were her family now. Only this time, she wasn't afraid to care. Derek had washed away her fears and taught her that loving didn't necessarily mean losing. He'd come after her when she was taken by the demons, showing her that depth of love meant risking everything. He'd have given up his life for her. And she'd risk everything for him, and for the rest of her newfound family.

The end of this part of the journey meant the beginning of a new adventure for her.

"I wish this was the end of it," Lou said, "but it's not. We may have closed the portal on this island, but there are others."

"So now what?" Trace asked.

"Now we hunt," Derek answered. He'd already filled them all in about his brother and about his half-demon blood. And what it could possibly mean. He wanted to be straight with them. They had shown no fear of him, accepted him completely. Gina knew how important it was to him, even if he acted as if he didn't care one way or another. As far as they were concerned, he was still the same Derek. Mandy even sniffed him and said as long as he didn't stink like a demon, he was okay to her. Gina laughed, grateful to all of them for their acceptance of the man she loved.

Ryder asked the question no doubt on everyone's mind. "Where?"

"We'll start in Sydney. If Nic is there, chances are there's a demon setup there, too," Lou said.

"Ah, going home," Trace said with a grin. "Any idea where in Sydney?"

"Not yet, but I've already got the Realm working on it. By the time we get there, we'll know where Nic is."

"Might as well relax for now," Punk said, beaming a smile.

"I could use a beer or two," Linc said.

"Game of cards sounds good to me," Ryder said.

"I'm in," Trace quipped.

Shay yawned. "I need a nap. A nice, long nap."

"Sounds like a good idea. Gina, I need to talk to you." Derek grabbed her hand and led her below to his room, shutting and locking the door behind him. He stared at her while she waited expectantly for him to come to her.

"Do you want to continue on with this?" he finally asked.

Gina tilted her head and frowned. "With what?"

"This whole demon thing. Because you don't have to."

"Huh?" What the hell was he talking about?

"You could go back to your life. To making movies, what you're good at."

"I'm not interested in making movies anymore."

"You're not?"

"No. When I started as a teen, it was a chance to get away from foster care, from any memories of my former life. I could be someone else. That was my escape from reality, from having to attach myself to anyone or any place. Hollywood and moviemaking is a fantasy land, a place where nothing real exists. For me, it was perfect. I could be anything and anyone I wanted to be. No one knew who I really was. I didn't have to care about anyone. I played a role and when it was over, I was gone."

"And you won't miss it?"

She smiled at him. "Not a bit."

He crossed to the porthole and stared out at the island.

She followed and placed her hand on his shoulder, turning him around to face her. "I don't understand. Don't you want me with you?"

"You know I do." His voice was almost a whisper.

"Tell me what's bothering you."

"We're going to Sydney, to hunt down Nic. It's going to be dangerous."

Oh. She was beginning to get an inkling here. "And?"

"There on the island, you did a great job taking care of yourself. We made a helluva team."

"Yes, we did."

"But that was before I found out . . . well, you know."

"Before you discovered you were part demon. So what's the difference?"

"I can help protect you against other demons. I can't protect you against me."

Now she understood. "I don't need protection against other demons and especially not against you. You're never going to hurt me." She laid her head on his chest and wrapped her arms around him. He threaded his fingers through her hair, kissing the top of her head. Then he stepped back and pulled her away, keeping an arm's-length distance between them. The hard evidence of his need for her was outlined against his jeans. She shuddered, her breasts heavy and warm, her nipples tightening at the thought of having him buried inside her.

God, she needed that joining with him. It had already been too long. She'd almost lost him.

So why was he pushing her away?

"What's wrong?" she asked.

"Are you okay with this?"

"With what?"

He looked down at himself. "With me. And you."

She frowned. "Huh?"

"You know what I am now."

She sat at the foot of the bed, knowing what he meant. "And what is that?"

"Part of me is demon."

"I realize that."

"Aren't you the least bit worried about what will happen?"

His gaze gravitated to the bed. Gina got hot just thinking about it, but she understood his concern. Funny, the thought had never occurred to her. Derek was still Derek. To her, nothing had changed. Now she had to convince him of that.

"So now that you're a demon, does that mean your dick will get bigger, too?" She batted her eyelashes at him.

He frowned at her, then laughed out loud. "You mean it wasn't enough for you as it was? Women. So hard to please."

She snorted. "Can I help it if I'm insatiable?"

He took a step forward, his smile dying on his face. "Seriously, Gina. You know what I mean. I talked to Lou. I don't know what's going to happen to me. What I'm capable of. I might—"

She held her hand up. "I trust you, Derek. You'll never hurt me. When you first realized your power, when the demon in you showed up, I saw what was in your eyes. If you were ever going to hurt me, you would have done it then. You didn't and you never will. Now come over here and make love to me. I need you." She opened her arms and he shuddered a sigh, then came to her, pulling her up and dragging her against him. When he planted his lips firmly over hers and took possession, sliding his tongue inside her mouth and licking against hers, she felt that familiar curling of her toes, a warmth in her stomach that told her she'd found what she was looking for.

Total and complete nirvana. She closed her eyes and drank in the feel and taste of him. He was no different now than he'd been before. His touch still possessed her completely and she wouldn't have it any other way.

She dragged her lips away from his and tilted her head back. "You're the same Derek. You feel the same, you taste the same."

"It feels strange to me. There's something different inside me."

"How?"

"I can't explain it. It's like a churning. Unsettled. Like a nervous energy."

Lifting a brow, she grinned. "Good. Use that. I like energetic sex."

He shook his head. "Dammit, Gina, I'm being serious here."

She reached up and palmed his cheeks, loving the feel of his dark stubble against her hand. "So am I. Don't be afraid to be a little rough with me, Derek. I'm not a china doll. I'm not fragile. I've felt you holding back."

"I did. I'm afraid of hurting you."

"You can't hurt me. Just love me, dammit."

He growled low in his throat, the sound wickedly sensual, then took her mouth in a kiss that could never be described as gentle or sweet. She welcomed his passion, needed it as much as she needed to breathe. He tore their clothes away, paying no attention to buttons, taking no care whether they ripped or not. Every tear of cloth excited her. Now that was a ravaging she could buy into. Moisture trickled down her thigh and she rode his leg, letting him feel her desire for him.

"You sure you want it this way?" he asked, his voice tight with barely leashed restraint.

"I want the real Derek," she replied, nearly out of breath from panting with need for him. She lifted against him, rubbing herself against him. "Show me what you've got."

She loved the animal side of him, fed off his hunger and need for her. Desperate to be closer to him, she backed up to the bed and fell on it, taking him down with her.

He cupped her sex, teasing her with soft movements that belied the taut tension in the corded muscles of his arms. The incongruity of his restraint and the passionate need she felt within him only served to prove her point. He could control the beast within himself.

"Oh, you're ready," he whispered, then dragged her legs apart and entered her with a savage thrust. She raised up and bit down on his shoulder, rewarded with his primal growl. He reached underneath her and grabbed her ass, raising her up to meet him, powering inside her with everything he had.

The beast had risen, and she met him eagerly, greeting him with moans and growls of her own. This was the Derek she wanted. The true Derek, holding nothing back, giving her all that was inside him.

Gentling now, he tormented her with slow thrusts, torturing her with every delicious inch of his cock until she lifted her hips and teased him back, undulating against him.

"Wild thing," he said, squeezing her buttocks to bury himself deeper inside her.

"Just like you," she murmured, wrapping her legs around him.

Then no words were spoken as he took her mouth again, his tongue plunging in and out, mimicking his movements as he brought her to the edge and back again.

She still felt the wildness within him, but he controlled it, as if he'd found a way to master it, use it to maximize her pleasure. When he nibbled her neck, his tongue rasping against the soft flesh of her throat, she cried out with ecstasy.

Yes, there was a monster within him, but she loved that

animal, clutching him closer to her, vowing she'd keep him safe no matter what.

With long, velvety hard strokes, he took her higher and higher, then crashed with her as she shuddered through a climax that rocked her senseless.

Afterward they held each other, not speaking for the longest time. Post-sex silence used to bother her, but not anymore. With Derek, she'd grown comfortable enough to hold him, run her hands over his muscled skin, and savor every second he held her in his arms, not knowing how long they'd have together. An hour, a day, an eternity—she'd take whatever she could get. It was all a gift.

And she knew why he was quiet. She knew what bothered him.

"Derek, look at me."

He met her gaze and she was lost in the storm of his eyes. What used to be unfathomable to her was now clear.

"I have faith in your strength. You can do anything you set your mind to do. You are one of the most stubborn men I know," she said, her lips curling in a teasing smile. "And I'll be right by your side to help you and kick your ass if the demon inside you tries to break free. I love you."

He pressed his lips to hers in a kiss so gentle it brought tears to her eyes. "I love you too, Gina. But I don't deserve to say that."

She touched his lips with her fingertips. "Yes, you do. We'll fight this battle together."

"What did I ever do to deserve you?"

"Something bad, probably," she teased. "I'm not the easiest person to live with."

"So I've noticed," he said as he licked her bottom lip.

"See? And now you're being punished."

His lips quirked. "So are you. Are you ready for what being with me entails?"

She grinned and teased his chest with the tips of her fingers, then lower, over the flat planes of his abdomen and lower still until she surrounded his rapidly hardening length. "Yes. Are you ready for me?"

"You tell me, baby." He laughed and dragged her on top of him, covering her lips with his.

As she melted against him, she didn't even think what tomorrow would bring. In a short span of time her entire life had changed. Maybe this wasn't what she'd planned for her future, but fate had a way of showing one the light in odd ways.

She'd used action and adventure as an escape her entire life. Hidden under the persona of Gina Bliss, never letting anyone see who she really was.

Turned out part of her really was Gina Bliss. Maybe the scared little girl from all those years ago was finally gone. She'd definitely proved she could fight creatures from the depths of hell and live through it, could face death and darkness and not cower or run in fear.

She'd even faced love, and the possibility of losing love, and come through it unscathed. She'd found someone to love her back despite all her faults.

If she could do that, she could do anything.

Bring on the demons..

About the Author

Jaci Burton is thrilled to be living her dream of writing romance, passion, and adventure. She enjoys immersing herself in the mystical world of the paranormal and believes that love really is the greatest magic of all. Jaci has published over thirty books in multiple genres and is a *Romantic Times* Reviewer's Choice Award winner. She lives in Oklahoma with her husband and five dogs.

Visit Jaci at *www.jaciburton.com.*

Read on

for a sneak peek

of

HUNTING THE DEMON

by Jaci Burton

Coming from Dell in fall 2007

Hunting the Demon

On Sale fall 2007

Prologue

Nic Diavolo stood in the dark place, hundreds of clawed hands reaching for him. They tore at his clothes, raking at his skin, the creatures' voices like a cacophony of humming bees. Now the buzzing grew louder, a chant of triumph as they surrounded him.

They'd finally won. All these years the monsters had chased him, and he had always run. Run as hard as he could, always slipping and falling, but he'd always stayed ahead of them. Always escaped.

This time, he had slowed down. Stopped. Turned and let them catch up, watched as five turned to ten. Then twenty-five. Then a hundred or more of the creatures. Horrifying in appearance, with their red eyes and long fangs, their dirty, claw-like fingernails reaching out to him.

When they reached him, he expected to scream.

This was it. The moment he had spent a lifetime fearing.

They touched him, their nails raking over his naked

skin. He shuddered at the first touch, revulsion and dread filling him.

But they didn't shred him to pieces, didn't sink their dripping talons into his flesh, didn't growl as if they wanted to tear him apart.

They stared at him in awe, touched him with reverence, bowed their heads.

He was their king.

At that moment, Nic realized something monumental.

He felt no fear.

And that was the most frightening thing of all.

Take your place.

He heard the voice, but didn't understand, couldn't see anyone around him.

You're home, son.

Recognition struck. It was his father. But Nic was confused, didn't understand the command.

These are your people, Dominic. You belong to them, and they to you.

Nic shook his head. Something wasn't right. He didn't belong here with these creatures.

"Dad?"

All he heard was soft laughter.

"Dad!"

The laughter faded, and he was once again alone with the beasts. They beseeched him wordlessly with their groping hands, their mumbled adoration. He began to suffocate as they closed in, unable to breathe as they pressed against him.

No! He didn't want this! He wanted answers, goddamit!

"Dad! Where are you?!"

The shrill alarm blasted Nic into an upright position. Covered with sweat, his heart hammering his ribs, he slammed his hands onto the mattress and blinked against the darkness, fighting for breath.

What. The. Fuck. Disoriented and shaking, he struggled for time and place.

His bedroom at the house in Sydney. No monsters. Not real.

Dreams.

Man, that was some weird shit.

Always the same. Okay, maybe this one wasn't exactly like the others. But still the same theme as the rest of them. Monsters and him and wandering around in the dark in search of . . . something. Seemed to be every night lately. Would they ever end?

He leaned over to the nightstand and punched a button, watching the slow crawl of the drapes as they opened, revealing a semicircle of floor-to-ceiling windows connecting him with the outside world again. With reality. It was still dark outside, but at least he had the comfort of the lights from the harbor, boats in the water.

Sydney was alive and breathing, even at five in the morning. And that was good enough for now. Sunrise would come soon, banishing away the last vestiges of the dream from the recesses of his mind.

He rubbed his temples, sucked in air, and shook it off. So he had dreams. So what? Too much partying is what he attributed it to. And not enough sleep. In every respect, Nic was normal. Healthy as can be for a thirty-three-year-old male.

Right.

"Fucking freak of nature, is what you are," he mumbled as he slid out of bed and grabbed his board shorts out of the suitcase he hadn't bothered to unpack yet..

The waves were supposed to be kickass right now. They were the only things that would have brought him home. Not that anyone was here anyway. His father wasn't, which was typical. And even if he had been here, he wouldn't have noticed Nic if he'd paraded naked into the kitchen with a girl under each arm.

He smirked at the shock value of that visual. He might have to try that sometime to see if it got a reaction from his dad or his uncle Bart.

Probably wouldn't.

With a loud yawn, he stretched, then slid into his shorts and shirt, went into the bathroom to brush his teeth, ran his fingers through his hair and splashed water on his face, hoping to shake off the nightmare.

One would think he'd downed enough booze on the plane from Singapore last night to sleep like he was in a coma. But oh, no. Sometimes he was lucky enough to remember the dreams.

Or cursed. He wished he couldn't recall them with such clarity.

The dreams terrified him. And he was too damned old to be scared of monsters in the dark.

As he came out of the bathroom the first line of dawn slipped above the horizon. He grinned, adrenaline pumping blood into his booze-soaked veins.

Time to catch a wave.

And forget about monsters.

Chapter One

He stepped out of the waves like the god Poseidon, at home in his element. Drenched, bronzed, his shorts riding low on his hips and showcasing lean six-pack abs, the sculpted body of a man who worked hard at his sport. There wasn't an ounce of fat on him.

His sun-tipped brown hair was cut short and spiked up in all directions as he shook the salt spray from it with a wild twist of his head. Shay held her breath, wondering if the shorts balancing precariously on his slim hips would drop to his ankles.

No such luck. She exhaled, reminding herself why she was here.

She was bait. Hard to believe the water god making his way to the beach, surfboard in his hands, was her quarry.

Dayum. She licked her lips and tipped her sunglasses down over the bridge of her nose, hoping her knees would stop knocking. She wasn't very good at this stealth thing.

Her heart was pounding, her palms sweating, and she hoped to God she remembered how to flirt.

Derek had informed her their intelligence on Nic indicated he went for blondes. Since she was the only blonde hunter, that put her front and center in their game of bait and snatch.

They didn't even know how much demon blood Nic had inside him, what he was capable of, if anything. Only that they had to grab him and get him out of Sydney in a hurry so they could figure it out.

So here she stood, on a secluded beach in Sydney, Australia, just past dawn, while the most gorgeous man she'd ever laid eyes on walked his way out of the ocean toward her.

And nearby the hunters were in place, ready to make the grab. As soon as she got him out of eyesight of the rest of the people hanging around the sandy beach. Surprisingly, they weren't alone, even though it was so early in the morning.

Which meant they had to lure him away. They had a plan, had discussed it, practiced it, worked it all out, knowing Nic had shown up here every morning to surf. Ever since he'd returned to Australia, he'd come to this location. At least in this he was predictable.

Shay hoped the rest of their intelligence about him was right—like the fact he really did like blondes, that he was one hell of a ladies' man, and that he was in the mood for a little action this early in the day.

When he cleared the waves he caught sight of her. She leaned against the shack where he'd stored his gear, struck the most seductively casual pose she could manage without looking obvious, and smiled as he approached.

"Mornin'," she said.

"G'day," he shot back, tilting his head to the side to size her up.

She suddenly felt naked in her all-too-tiny bikini, wishing she had a towel or a cover-up. But that would hide the lure, wouldn't it? Ugh. She much preferred killing demons to flirting with gorgeous men. Digging her toes into the sand, she said, "You looked great out there."

He grinned, showing off white, even teeth. "You surf?"

"A little. Not as good as you."

"You're not from around here."

"My southern drawl gave me away, didn't it? Not quite Aussie."

With a laugh, he said, "No, not quite." He laid his board against the shack and held out his hand. "Nic Diavolo."

"Shay Peterson." She slipped her hand in his and tried not to shudder. God, she had such a weakness for good-looking men. And damn, was Nic a prime example of perfection. Piercing blue eyes the same color as the ocean, a square jaw, straight nose, and a body she could spend days and nights exploring.

And he might just be a demon, Shay. Don't forget that.

Oh, yeah. She had forgotten. Just for a second she had simply enjoyed the company of a delectable hunk of beefcake. When was the last time that had happened?

Too long. Back before demons and an utter change in her lifestyle.

Back to work.

"So what are you doing in Sydney, Shay Peterson?"

"Right now? Watching you surf."

"On vacation?"

"Sort of. I'm definitely on vacation and enjoying this spectacular beach and ocean, but I'm also a freelance writer. So it's a working vacation. Hoping I can score a job while I'm here."

He nodded. "And why do I get the idea you being on this beach has something to do with your work . . . and with me?"

At least he hadn't told her to take a hike. "Because you're wickedly perceptive?"

"I'd be happy to talk surfing or anything else with you. And if you used your beautiful body as incentive, I'm not about to say no."

It worked. She almost sighed in relief. "I won't say no to an interview, either."

He arched a brow. "I like a woman who doesn't say no."

Oh, he was smooth. Too smooth. "I don't say yes to everything."

"Then you haven't spent enough time with the right man."

He was *really* good at this. Her body warmed considerably and the sun hadn't risen high enough yet to attribute it to the summer heat. "You think you're the right man?"

"Spend some time with me and decide."

This was working. She wasn't rusty at the flirting thing after all. Good to know. Now she had to finesse this just right and get him where she needed him. "How about I buy you breakfast and we can talk? Or . . . whatever?"

He had a lopsided grin that curled her toes. She melted into the sand.

Must remember he's a demon, Shay. You don't like demons. Derek as a half demon was just fine. That didn't mean Nic was fine. He could be a bad guy.

"Sounds good to me. Let me stow my board and we can grab a bite at the breakfast bar down the beach."

"Uh, I was thinking of someplace a little more . . . private?" Her body tensed as she waited for his reaction. *Please let this work.*

When one brow went up and his gorgeous eyes sparkled, she knew she had him.

"Sure, babe. You want me to follow you?"

She almost squealed in delight, but forced herself to keep her reaction low key, seductive even. "How about I drive? I know a great place, but it's off the beaten path a little."

"You familiar with out-of-the-way spots already? Thought you weren't from around here."

"I'm talking about the place I rented. It's secluded and I'd like to get you alone. For the interview, of course. I'll even cook. I make a killer omelet."

His eyes lit up with a sensuous gleam she couldn't mistake for anything other than what it was—sexual interest. Another time, another place, her pulse might be racing for another reason entirely. Right now she was just hoping against hope she could get him into position. Though her mind was conjuring up all kinds of positions she'd like to get Nic Diavolo in at the moment, and none of them had to do with what the hunters wanted him for.

"You've got a deal."

Once he stowed his board in his SUV, he followed her to her vehicle, one she had a damned hard time maneuvering since the steering wheel was on the wrong side. Everything in Australia was on the wrong side, including the roads. Fortunately, where she had to take him wasn't far.

Now that she had him, she was nervous. The car was small and he was big. And close, the tiny seats all too near each other. And she was trying to concentrate on the road and making it back to the house and remembering what she was supposed to do and say to him. And he smelled like salty ocean and she kept glancing over at his muscled legs and his arms, the fine hairs there bleached by the sun.

Maybe she should just kill him now. That would solve a lot of her issues, like how she could possibly be so damned attracted to a man who was probably a human-killing demon and son of Ben, one of the lords of the Sons of Darkness.

Then again, Derek was Ben's son and he was just fine. Normal. Human-looking and not a vicious demon at all. Well, he had turned vicious demon when he'd fought Ben on the island, but he hadn't turned on the hunters. He'd just fought the Sons of Darkness. The bad guys. And he hated the demon side of himself. Maybe Nic would be the same way.

And maybe not.

Shit. Sometimes she just thought too much.

"You doing okay over there?" he asked.

"Uh, yeah," she replied, shooting him a glance and a half-assed smile. "Trying to concentrate on your roads. They're on the wrong side."

He grinned. "I could have driven."

She shrugged. "I like a challenge."

"I like a woman with guts."

She turned into the long driveway leading up to the house on the cliff. Nice, private, still enshrouded in the morning fog that hadn't quite lifted this far out.

Oh, man. She could really like this guy. He was drop-dead gorgeous with a body to die for, charming and easy-going.

And in about five minutes he was going to hate her for all eternity.

Nic studied the curvy blonde as she exited the car and offered up another glimpse of her well-toned thighs as her shorts rode up her legs.

Damn. He'd caught a stellar wave this morning, adrenaline was pumping through his veins, his head was clear, and he'd been, if he was guessing right, propositioned by one hot woman.

What better way to start the day? And here he'd sworn off the opposite sex. So what was it about this one that made him jump back into the game again? He'd decided that women were after nothing but his money and he was tired of wasting his time. A year of solitude had done wonders. He hadn't missed them a bit. Until Miss Golden-Blonde-and-Gorgeous tossed him a little curve on the beach and he was drooling like he hadn't had any in a year.

Well, as a matter of fact, he *hadn't* had any in a year. Which probably explained his sudden interest. Though lots of women more beautiful than Shay Peterson had offered and he'd said no. Something about her hit him right away. Fresh faced and innocent, yet with a sensual allure his body refused to ignore. Whatever she was offering, he wanted it.

Why the hell not? It wasn't like he had anything better to do today.

"Nice place you've got here," he said, surveying the hill-top retreat while she fumbled for the door key.

"Huh?" She looked over at him, frowned, then nodded. "Oh. Yeah. Thanks."

She seemed distracted and a little ditzy. Then again, he didn't really care if they had brains or not. At least not for what they were planning to do. She was gorgeous, with her honey blonde hair, deep blue eyes, and full lips, and she smelled like a rain forest. Her body was nonstop curves and she was in great shape.

Who cared if she had a working brain cell? It wasn't like he was interested in a lifelong commitment. Though she did say she was a freelance reporter. And that took some smarts. He wondered if that was just a line to get him in the sack. It wouldn't be the first time a woman had used subterfuge to get him alone. He was pretty damn popular, mostly because he was rich and available. Women flocked to him thinking they might be the one to snag his heart and become Mrs. Diavolo.

Right. Like that was ever going to happen.

She was struggling with the lock. He slipped his hand in hers and took the key. "Let me do that."

She jerked her hand away as if he was on fire. Skittish much? Damn, she'd gotten nervous all of a sudden. He turned the key and unlocked the door, then pushed it open and let her go in first.

Besides, this way he could watch her ass. And a mighty fine one at that. He grinned.

"I hope you like eggs," she said as she led him down a long hallway. She seemed a lot more relaxed now.

"I love eggs."

The house was dark. All the shutters were closed.

"Don't you want to turn on some lights in here?" he asked.

"No, I like the mood. Come on in here."

She'd damn near run down the hall. Maybe she was really hungry. Or maybe they weren't going to have breakfast at all. She might be stripping and planning to offer herself up for breakfast. Who knew when it came to women? He never could figure out what they really wanted.

When he rounded the corner, his heart skipped a beat and he went cold.

There was Shay, chewing her bottom lip as she leaned against the kitchen counter.

But she wasn't naked and she damn sure wasn't alone. There were a half dozen beefy-looking guys flanking her. And a couple of women, too.

"What the hell's going on?" he asked.

"Welcome home, Nic."

He started to turn at a deep voice behind him, but then the prick of a needle sliding into his biceps made him jerk.

"Hey! What the . . ."

He couldn't even get the words out as he began to crumple to the floor. Strong arms circled him before he crashed in a heap. Nausea rolled in his stomach as he fought whatever drug they'd injected him with.

He heard them talking, but it was fuzzy, like an echo chamber.

"Derek, is that going to hurt him?"

Shay's voice. The only one he recognized. Then the guy's voice he heard behind him responding with "No. Just put him to sleep for a while so we can move him."

Shit, shit, shit. This wasn't good. Kidnapping . . . or something worse? He was losing it, couldn't stay conscious.

He'd been ambushed.

Ah, hell. He knew his dick would get him in trouble one day.